K

D0812565

Canyon Passage

Also available in Large Print
by Ernest Haycox:

Long Storm
Man in the Saddle
Sundown Jim
Trail Town
Trouble Shooter
The Wild Bunch
Alder Gulch
The Silver Desert

Canyon Passage

Ernest Haycox

G.K.HALL &CO.
Boston, Massachusetts
1985

Published in Large Print by arrangement with
Jill Marie Haycox

G. K. Hall Large Print Book Series

Set in 16 pt Times Roman

Library of Congress Cataloging in Publication Data

Haycox, Ernest, 1899–1950.
  Canyon passage.

  (G.K. Hall large print book series)
  1. Large type books. I. Title.
[PS3515.A9327C3 1985]   813'.52   85–825
ISBN 0–8161–3877–X (lg. print)

1

At the American Exchange

As soon as he entered Portland, Logan Stuart stabled his horse at the Fashion Livery on Oak and retraced his way along Front Street toward the express office. A violent southwest wind rolled ragged black clouds low over the town and the flatly swollen drops of an intemperate rain formed a slanting silver screen all around him, dimpling the street's watery mud and dancing a crystal dance on glistening rooftops. The plank walk-ways across the street intersections were half afloat and sank beneath his weight as he used them; at two o'clock of such a day the kerosene lights were sparkling through drenched panes and the smell of the saloons, when he moved by them, was a rich warm blend of tobacco, whisky and men's soaked woolen clothes.

Three or four sailing ships lay at the levee with their bare spars showing above the row of frame buildings on Front. Beyond Seventh, in the other direction, the great fir forest was a black semicircle crowding Portland's thousand people hard against the river. Tradesmen's shingles squealed on their iron brackets and a raw wild odor — of massive timbered hills and valleys turned sweet by rain — assailed Logan Stuart and as he turned into the express office he saw a stocky shape, vague in this agitated twilight, wheel abruptly through a saloon's doorway ahead of him. A four-horse dray came up Front at the moment, the great wheels of the dray plunged half to the hubs; the teamster's cursing, issued with vigor, was instantly lost in the steady tempest.

The express office was warm and quiet once the door had closed behind Logan Stuart. He dropped his saddlebags on the counter and watched a young man with a dry, cool visage rise and come forward. The young man, Cornelius van Houten, wore a pair of steel-rimmed glasses in whose lenses the room's yellow lamplight bloomed.

"Damp day," said van Houten. "How's Jacksonville?"

"Lively," replied Stuart and opened the saddlebags to lay upon the counter a dozen gold pokes crowded skintight with nuggets and dust. With the drawstring clinched at the end of each, they looked like fat summer sausages.

"Credit to account?" asked van Houten.

"I'll take back specie. We're shy on cash at the diggings. What time do you open in the morning?"

2

"Tomorrow's Sunday."

"Put the specie in the saddlebags. I'll get them before you close tonight and keep them in my hotel room."

"I'd guess you've got seven thousand there — and that's no trinket to be left loose in a hotel room."

"Cornelius," said Stuart with a smile that broke the rough reserve on his face, "gold is only yellow gravel."

"Ah," said van Houten, agreeably dissenting, "but the yellow color makes a difference."

"Butter's yellow, too, and you can spread it on bread. Ever try that with gold?"

"For a man of business," commented van Houten, "you have got odd notions. Were I a banker, as I someday shall be, I should conclude you unsound and lend you nothing."

"A man can choose his gods, Cornelius. What are your gods?"

"What?" asked van Houten.

Logan Stuart returned to the intemperate day. The rain had thickened until the buildings across the street squatted half vague in the sparkling downpour and ropy cascades splashed upon the sidewalk from gorged eaves. Out in the middle of the street a man stood on the surface of a stump with a set of muttonchop whiskers wetly plastered to his jowls and watched the yellow mud slowly flow around him. Stuart turned into a store at the corner of Alder, bought himself some dry clothes and made a couple of purchases for the Dance family away down the Oregon-California road, and thereafter walked a narrow plank across Front Street and entered a barber-shop near the American Exchange Hotel.

He had a bath, a shave and a haircut; and with a cigar fragrantly ignited between his lips, he went on to the American Exchange, got a room and ascended to it. He laid his wet clothes over a chair, walked a restless circle around the room and brought up at one of the two windows in the room to watch the storm-battered street below him. Above him, the peak of the hotel roof emitted a dull organ tone as the wind struck it.

With one shoulder tipped against the windowsill he achieved a moment's stillness not characteristic of him. He was a man of loose and rough and durable parts, like a machine intended for hard usage; there was no fineness or smoothness about him. His long mouth was expressive only when he smiled and his heavy nose swelled somewhat at the base to accommodate wide nostrils. He had the blackest of hair, lying in long chunks on his head; his eyes were sharp gray and well-bedded in their sockets — and all this made a face which in repose held the mixed elements of sadness and strong temper. Only when that face lightened did it show any sign of the rash streak which he possessed. He was a little under six feet, long of arms and meaty of legs, with a chest that had breadth rather than thickness. A scar shaped like a fish hook stood at the left corner of his mouth, the relic of some fist fight he had been rather eager to indulge in when younger. Now at twenty-eight he had better control of himself.

He could stand still only for a short while, and suddenly turned from the window, left the room and descended the stairs to the saloon which adjoined the American Exchange's lobby.

Henry McLane saw him at once and beckoned him over for a drink. "Just to keep the chills out," said Henry. "How's things at the mines?"

"Brisk," said Logan Stuart and heard the hoarse whistle of a steamboat in the river; that would be the *Belle* coming in from the Cascades run. He made room for himself at the crowded bar, beside Henry McLane, who removed his stovepipe hat and thumped it like a drum to catch the barman's attention. At five o'clock there was no natural light left in this drowned world.

"What are the Indians going to do this year?" asked Henry McLane.

"It is, so far, quiet and uncertain."

The barroom was at this hour of a bad day crowded, smoky and cheerful. Portland was a new and small town on the scarcely explored northwest coast, therefore Portland was still largely a town of bachelors arrived in search of the business chance; and the American Exchange bar served them both as a club and a commercial meeting point. Here were the plain types of a new land: the ship captain with his benign mutton chops and his frosty eyes; the farmer stained with the back country's mud roads; the emigrant whose manner was brisk and blunt and hearty and whose voice was pitched to Oregon's deep timbered reaches and long open plains; and the New Englander, so sharp and so cool, who had come here specifically for the mercantile advantages to be had in a fresh land and who meant to seize them and make his fortune. There was an Eastern twang in the room's talk, mixed with Iowa, mixed with Missouri, and mixed with Virginia's softness.

"Logan," said Henry McLane, "I have got a consignment of goods from the brig *Alice*, to be delivered to Clay and King at Jacksonville. I shall ship by the boat *Canemah* to Salem. Do you wish the business of packing it from there? General hardware, a few bolts of cloth, buckets, tin dishes, rope."

"How many mules will it make?"

"Twenty, I suppose. What's your freight?"

"Three dollars the mule per day."

McLane studied it a moment and nodded his head. "Agreeable. It will be at Salem on the twentieth of the month."

The deal having been made, Logan Stuart bought the second round of drinks, after which McLane excused himself. "I have got to see if George Miller can take a load of windows out toward Gale's creek."

"Windows — windows with glass?"

"We are becoming civilized," said McLane and moved away to intercept a man in muddy boots, round fur cap and a huge army overcoat. "George," he called through the steady confusion of the saloon. "George!"

The place was packed. Logan Stuart pressed his way through the crowd and circled a group who were deep in reminiscences concerning the emigrant trail. Five of Portland's leading businessmen sat at a poker table, closely engaged with some business speculation of their own; and a ship captain near by was in half an argument with another man. "Lumber's selling sky high in San Francisco and you'll make a handsome profit. You have got to let other men make a little. Don't haggle so damned much over the freight, my friend, or I'll pull out of here in ballast." When he left the saloon, Logan Stuart observed that Henry McLane was at the bar again, sealing another bargain.

He crossed to the clerk's desk. "Miss Lucy Overmire arrived?"

"In Ten," said the clerk, "just off the Cascades boat. She has been asking for George Camrose."

Stuart walked up a stairway whose red plush runner was stained with the day's fresh mud. He turned down the hall and he stood a moment in front of her door, visualizing her face with a keen start of interest; then he knocked and heard her voice murmur, "Come in, George."

She was in the center of the room when he

7

opened the door and she had a smile on her face. But it was a smile meant for Camrose and he now observed the smile change character. Something went out of it, he didn't know what; and something came into it, nor did he know what that quality was.

"George knew I was coming up, and asked me to bring you home. He had a sudden trip to make toward Crescent City."

"Will you mind having me on your hands, Logan?" Then quite unexpectedly she broke into a small, free laugh. "That was a foolish question. You don't mind women on your hands."

"Who has given me that reputation?" he asked.

"Rumor."

"Rumor borne by George Camrose," he said. "The man is building up his faithfulness at my expense. Have you got stout clothes? We leave before daylight and the weather is foul."

"I do not mind," she said and watched him with her lips retaining the smile in their corners. There was a speculative light in her eyes and the shape of judgment on her face — and this too was something familiar to him. They knew each other very well. She wore a brown and beautiful dress and her black hair was softly, shiningly plaited back of her head. She was a filled-out and mature woman within her clothes.

"Supper?" he said.

She moved to the bureau mirror to give herself

a swift glance; and, catching up a shawllike wrap, she moved down the stairs with him into the dining room. Talk made a great racket in the place; at the bachelors' table in the center of the room Logan Stuart saw Henry McLane, turned pink and dignified with his business trips to the bar.

She sat across from Stuart, pleasantly still; she was aware of her surroundings and occasionally her eyes showed curiosity and some vagrant thought stirred her face. Then he found her attention on him, once more with its deep and well-guarded interest. Sometimes warmth lay between them, strong and unsettling, and his own expression would sharpen; and at times like these the bare repose of his face would break, giving way to smiling restlessness. It was these times when she looked at him most observantly, trying to read him.

"How was your visit?" he asked. "How was The Dalles?"

"Quiet," she said. "But, Logan, there are a lot of cattle and horses up there which have been abandoned by the emigrants when they came down the river. They could be gotten for very little. Perhaps it would be profitable to buy and drive them to Southern Oregon."

"See any mules?"

She sat still, trying to remember, and for an instant he saw in this stillness a quality that struck roughly through him.

"No," she said. But she observed the change

9

of his expression and her guard lifted again. They ate a silent meal and moved back to the stairs. He walked up to her door with her and paused a moment.

"Five o'clock," he said. "And dress warm. We'll make Salem the first day and the head of the Long Tom the second. We ought to be in Jacksonville Friday afternoon. Is that traveling too fast for you?"

"No," she said. "I suppose you're going down to play a little poker now."

"I guess not. Good night."

Her answering "Good night" followed him. He went past the door of his own room and stopped at the stairs, looking back. She still stood by her door, the hall lamp showing the outline of her face.

"A woman, Logan?"

He laughed, and saw a sudden gust of anger come to her. She turned in and closed the door. He had been amused at her suspicion but, going down the stairs, he no longer found amusement in her judgment of him. He was restless, he was irritated and he thought: "George must have made me out a hell of a fellow. I shall have to speak to him." He heard the beat of the rain on the hotel wall and he went back up to his room for his coat and hat; afterwards he walked along the black gut of Front Street and crossed over to the express office. Van Houten had delayed closing time for him; and now brought the saddlebags out of the big

10

company safe.

"Sure you want to keep this in the hotel room?"

"It's all right," said Stuart and slung the bags over his shoulder. He waited while van Houten snuffed out the lamps and damped the cast-iron stove. Van Houten took up a dragoon pistol from behind the counter and locked the office door. He said something which was washed away by the tidal wind, and put himself between Stuart and the building walls as they walked back toward the American Exchange. He fell from the narrow crossing plank, up to his boot tops, and bitterly swore. At the hotel's doorway he stopped and said, "Luck." By the light glowing through the doorway Stuart saw that the young man had carried the dragoon pistol cocked and presented all the way from the express office.

"Keep your feet dry," said Stuart and watched van Houten vanish completely three steps onward; it was that black a night. He crossed the lobby and tramped up the stairs, at the upper landing he paused and then went on to Lucy Overmire's door. He knocked and heard her voice, still cool, call him in.

She stood by the window, now turning to look at him and show him the same reserved judgment he had seen before. "No," he said, "it wasn't a woman."

"Why didn't you say so, then?"

"You're marrying George, not me," he said.

11

"Why should I tell you where I'm going?"

Suddenly they were laughing at each other. She came across the room, the room's light richening her cheeks; she looked up at him, speaking with a blended sharpness and softness. "I'd never want a woman to make a fool of you, Logan."

"Do you question George like this?"

"Why," she said, "it has never occurred to me to doubt him."

"I am flattered by the distinction," he dryly said.

"George is less vulnerable than you, with women. He judges them more critically. You have too much compassion in you, Logan. You're fair game."

"Am I?" he said. "Yet he's engaged, and I am not."

"What have you got in the saddlebags?"

"Gold coin."

"I watched you from the hotel window. There was a man standing at the corner of Alder as you passed. He followed you across the mud."

"Good night, Lucy," he said and left the room. Noise came robustly up from the lobby and saloon. In his own room he put the saddlebags beneath the mattress at the head of the bead. He stripped to his woolen underwear and drank from the water pitcher, and then braced a chair under the door's knob. There were no catches on the two windows, but they were both fifteen feet or more above the street level and not to be worried about. He slid his revolver under the pillow, turned out the light and lay flat on his back, listening to the steady slash of the rain against the hotel; now and then a harsher gust of wind shook the whole structure. For a moment he thought of Lucy as she stood in her room, a fairer woman than any man had a right to expect; he remembered her face as it lightened with laughter, and the tones of that laughter, and he remembered how still her eyes could be, how deep in them were the strange things she felt. He fell asleep. . . .

He was a man who slept without dreaming, and who slept light. Thus when a gust of cold wind touched the back of his head his eyes came instantly open. He lay with his back to the side window and he had his arms beneath the bed covers so that he could not easily reach his revolver. There was a faint sliding sound in the room, and the sibilance of a man's heavy breathing. The breathing diminished for a little while, and then it grew greater and Stuart felt a hand move gingerly along the bed's edge. Stuart pictured the man's location — and swung and raised himself and seized the heavy shadow before him. His arms went around a thick body; he was carried off the bed by the man's rapid turn, and he was dropped to his feet. He hung on. He butted the top of his head against the prowler's chin and heard it crack; then the prowler's forearm came down on the back of his neck with all the power of a club. It stunned him and sent him falling backward upon the bed. He got his feet up and he plunged them full into the prowler's belly as the latter was about to fall upon him. His head ached in full violence, and flashes of light danced before his eyes. He heard the prowler stumble backward and curse under his breath; and then he reached under his pillow and seized up his gun. He righted himself on the bed for a shot. He fired at the man's moving shadow and in another moment the prowler, rushing low across the room, went out through the window, taking sash and glass with him.

He heard the man fall in the alley below. When he reached the window he saw nothing in the alley's black strip below him, but he caught the last swashing echoes of the man's steps as the latter ran through the pure mud toward the river.

Cold wind poured through the window and there was a racket in the hotel's hallway. The chair blocking the door capsized and the door wheeled open, letting in the sallow light of a hall lamp. A man peered through the doorway. "What the hell's going on —"

"Nothing," said Stuart. "Close the door and go away."

The door swung shut, blocking the violent gust of wind. Stuart stood still a little while, slowly turning his neck from side to side. "A funny one," he thought. "He must have had an arm like a chunk of oak. Damned near tore my neck apart." He settled down on the bed, he lay gingerly back, favoring the steady ache; he lay flat, staring up to the black ceiling. "It might have been Bragg," he said to himself. "It might have been."

The door opened again and Lucy's voice came across the room, gently disturbed. "Logan." The light was faintly on her and he saw her tall-shaped in her robe with her hair braided down behind. He saw the vague silhouette of her face as she walked toward him and stood over his bed. "Logan."

"Nothing at all," he said. "He got away. It was a bad try." His head quit aching; it ceased to pound as abruptly as it had begun, and presently he felt good. "Lucy, get out of here."

She stood wholly motionless, looking down at him. She said: "Did you get hurt?"

"No. You go on."

He watched her as she retreated; he saw her turn and look back a moment, and then close the door.

2

Lucy's Man

They left Portland at six o'clock of a rain-drowned morning, crossed the ferry and moved through the fir timber's dense twilight all the way to the Clackamas. Beyond Oregon City they came out upon the flat Willamette Valley, bordered eastward by the Cascades and on the west by the Coast Range. Ranch houses stood at lonely distance, low and dark in the rain fog, and now and then the pure mud road skirted the porch of a store or a rough frame cabin serving as a tavern for passers-by. At dusk of a weeping day they reached Salem, whose few houses were the outgrowth of a Methodist mission, and there slept.

The rain held on, turning the valley greener before their eyes as they pushed south. They ferried the Santiam at Syracuse City and spent the second night at the Harris Claim. The third day took them through Skinner's and on down to the valley's narrowing foot; and the fourth day saw them through the Calapooyia's rough

16

and timbered ridges — by way of the military road — and on to Jesse Applegate's house. The dark fir timber began to give way before oak and madrona and pine, and the rain ceased and the land grew warm and brown. They traveled fast, passing wagons loaded deep with settlers' household freight; they came upon mule trains and single travelers on horseback. On the fifth day they crossed the Umpqua at Aaron Roses's store and in the late afternoon they reached a little settlement built at the narrow mouth of a canyon whose sides rose up in increasing sharpness, heavy-clad with trees. All the country before them was massive and broken.

Cliff Anslem came out of his cabin while Stuart unsaddled.

"One miner killed on upper Graves Creek two nights ago," Anslem said. "It was Limpy's Indians, I think. There's a cavalry outfit somewhere in the canyon now, under that young fellow Bristow. Pack outfits have been going through doubled up for safety. Tomorrow mornin' you'll have plenty of company."

"Too slow," said Stuart. He turned to the girl. "We'll make a night ride of it and reach Dance's by daylight, if you can stand it."

Lucy nodded and walked into the cabin while Anslem drove the horses into his compound.

Four or five cabins lay scattered in the little meadow at the base of these rough hills and a steady current of wind came out of the canyon, cool and wild. A last sunlight streamed over the

17

meadow, strengthening the pungency of its natural hay. Stuart sat down on the edge of the dusty road; he leaned back and lighted his pipe and he heard the tinkling approach of a pack outfit's bell mare. Twilight began to flow off the mountain as the pack outfit, out of Scottsburg's settlement for the mines, arrived and halted to make camp. It was a Howison string, loaded with sugar, coffee and salt. A campfire blossomed in the shadows as Anslem called Stuart to supper.

The cabin was a single room with a bed, a table and a fireplace. Lucy lay on the bed, half awakened from her short sleep. She had her glance on the ceiling directly above her and the yellow lamplight of the room danced in her eyes. Stuart paused by the bed, his head dropped as he looked upon her. She lifted a hand to him; he took it, swinging her upright, and suddenly she laughed at him and made a quick turn away to the supper table. Mrs. Anslem gave these two a quick and slyly warm glance and afterwards served supper — venison and beans and biscuits. Horsemen fell out of the canyon at a whirling run and a sharp voice gave a command. Anslem rose and walked to the door.

"Supper's ready, Lieutenant."

The lieutenant, when he entered, was stained by a hard day's riding; he had a full beard to cover a youthful face and his eyes were dancing bright. He said: "Hello, Logan — Miss Overmire, how do?" and he took his place and made no ceremony about his meal.

"What's up there in the canyon?"

"A lot of tracks across the Cow Creek meadows."

Anslem said: "I'll saddle for you, Logan," and left the house.

"You're going now?" asked the lieutenant. "Limpy and his bucks are somewhere, but I don't know where. Maybe we'll have a quiet year."

Mrs. Anslem, standing before the fireplace's crane to watch the coffeepot, looked around at him. "There's never a quiet year."

Anslem had the horses waiting outside. Stuart rose with Lucy and as the two of them walked toward the door, Mrs. Anslem murmured: "Give my hello to the Dances and say I'm lonesome for talk."

Full dark was a cape loosely thrown over the mountains and upon the meadow and the baying of Anslem's dogs woke echoes far through the furrowed hills. Lucy's smile came down to Stuart as he handed her up to the saddle. He adjusted his saddlebags, he slid his rifle tentatively in and out of its boot and he passed a hand across the butt of his revolver. He said "So long" to Anslem and moved away with Lucy beside him. The canyon's breath was damp and cold upon them. The trail tilted up and the soft dust absorbed the sound of the horses' pacing. A creek ran hard beside the trail, musically brawling over its stones, and a night-prowling animal crossed fugitively before them and slipped into the timber. The sky was a steel-blue alley edged by the ragged shadow of timber. An hour from Anslem's they paused and rested and were still; and went on. A rising quarter moon painted dull silver patches on the canyon walls, and glinted against the creek and glowed dully on the bleached trunks of fire-killed firs. Another hour brought them to the head of the canyon and dropped them out upon a mountain meadow lying as a dark and half-hidden lake against the bulky shores of the mountains round about. A keener wind blew against them. Paused to rest, Stuart listened for whatever the wind might bring. He was sharp and he was wholly roused, but when he looked at Lucy he was smiling. Her voice came to him in careful smallness. "You are never happy except when in motion."

He said, "Hark," and thought he heard a running rumor in the night. Far over the meadow — a mile away — there seemed to be a party traveling. The horses were still, their heads alertly pointed; they were breathing deeper, they were scenting for something which interested them. Then the sound ceased.

They forded a shallow creek and turned into the meadow, crossing over. The creek's willows idly danced in the light wind and the creek was a pale and crooked streak. The massive black-ness of the mountains closed presently down upon them again and they began to climb steadily along a sightless lane between huge, still fir columns. Here he stopped once more to rest the horses.

She said: "A house, an office, or a woman you've known more than a week — these things grow old to you. You ride into Jacksonville, spend a night, and you are gone."

"My business needs a lot of riding."

"You ride for business — and you ride just to be riding."

"How is it you know that much about me?"

"No woman can look at a man two years without knowing something of him."

"You know more about me," he said, "than I know about you."

"Women are always more observant — and more interested."

He swung his horse around, caught the rein of Lucy's mount and moved off the trail. A sound grew greater above them and became the rush of a single rider flinging himself through this blind corridor without caution. He passed them at arm's length; he was making a small singing sound as he rode, as though breaking his loneliness. They heard him run downgrade and long afterward they made out the tattoo of his horse in the meadow below. Stuart and Lucy returned to the trail. He still remembered her question; he thought of it a long while as he rode.

"I want my business to grow," he said at last. "I want to see a Stuart & Company pack outfit stringing along every road. When stages come, I want them to be Stuart & Company stages. I guess I am ambitious."

"Even ambition would not push you so hard. You are not quite happy. Something bothers you. It may be something you look for, or something that dissatisfies you."

He rode on without comment, his mind half on her talk, half on the sounds and sensations around him. He heard her voice, so low and seriously soft, come through the blackness. "Is it a woman?"

"Damn George Camrose for giving me a bad reputation," he murmured. "Must it always be a woman who makes a man lie awake at night?"

"When the time comes, don't let it be an ordinary woman. Don't let it be a calm woman."

"Why not?" he said.

"You'd come to hate her," she said. They rode in silence, through midnight and the pit-black hours while the trail carried them higher into the mountains and a canyon deepened below them on the left, felt rather than seen. Once they caught a moment's view of a light burning far down at the canyon's bottom. "Ed Blackerby," he murmured. The air was thin and cold and the odor of the mountain was stronger and stronger; it was a wildness flowing from unknown reaches, out of places never seen since time began. Somewhere half between midnight and first dawn, he stopped for a longer rest and lifted Lucy from her saddle; her weight came

22

down against him and she stood passive in his arms for a moment, and her face tilted upward, so near to him that he saw the weariness on it. He dropped his arms and took a backward step to his saddle, unlashing an overcoat tied behind the cantle. He laid the coat on the trail and watched her sink down and curl upon it. He crouched near her and pulled the edges of the coat around her, meanwhile searching a coat pocket for his pipe. He held the pipe cold between his teeth while he listened to the forest, to the fugitive murmurings all about, the sibilance of disturbed brush, the faint abrasions of padded feet, the velvet whirring of wings, to all the undertones of this massive earth.

She was sound asleep when he bent down, half an hour later, and placed his hand on her cheek. He said, "Lucy," and heard her answer from her sleep. Her name was a pleasant echo, it was soft on his tongue and he said it again, "Lucy," and watched her sit up and turn her head in the darkness.

He helped her to the saddle and rolled his overcoat and lashed it fast. Resuming the march, they moved steadily through the low hours, through the world's ebb time, bending with the trail and dipping with it, into glen and up sharp slope and down sudden grades. The moon, pale and futile during the night, now vanished behind the massive western ridges and the blackness was greater than before. This was the time before dawn, when the vitality of all things burned fitful and uncertain. By degrees he began to feel the nearness of open country. The weight of the timber mass pressed less heavily against him and the color of the foreground grew paler, until finally the trail came out of the timber and descended in long, turning loops to a lower country. Just before daylight he saw a single light shining in the distance.

Morning twilight was breaking when he came before the cabin of Ben Dance and helped Lucy to the ground. Dance's dogs were shouting around him and the smell of woodsmoke and coffee laced the thin air. The cabin door opened and a flood of yellow light gushed out and a man took a quick step through the door and moved aside from it. He had a rifle across his arm, ready for use; when he identified these two people he let his robust voice fall upon them. "Come in — come in. Breakfast's waitin'. Asa, come out and get these horses."

Lucy went directly into the cabin. Stuart stood a moment with the saddlebags over a shoulder, watching morning spread over the eastern ridge tops; it moved in formless waves, spreading like mist, water-colored, trickling over the high summits and spreading downslope through the black hill creases. The sky began to grow blue, the stars slowly to fade. Young Asa took the horses away.

"The young lieutenant passed here yesterday," said Dance.

"One miner dead."

"Peaceful for this time of year," said Dance.

Stuart ducked through Dance's door and faced a bright fire on the open hearth. There was a table at which Lucy now sat; two more Dance boys sat by it, eating without lifting their heads. Mrs. Dance, scarcely forty, turned a pan of cornbread onto a platter and gave Logan a brisk smile. "How's Portland, Logan?"

"A thousand people, and raining."

"Ah," said Mrs. Dance and shook her head. Her skin was dark and her features were practical and pretty. "How can anyone live in such a crowd?"

Dance came in with a question. "You want me to change horses for you now?"

"We'll sleep till noon."

"Caroline," shouted Dance, "fix the beds."

A girl came out of the cabin's adjoining room and gave Lucy a nod and Stuart a longer glance. Her even "Hello" covered both people. She was near twenty with her mother's blue eyes and her mother's mass of light-brown hair. Her round arms were bare to her elbows, and her mouth was calm and full.

"I've got something for you," said Stuart.

"What?" said the girl.

"If you've got on your brown dress at noon I'll give it to you."

Caroline Dance tipped her head aside as she studied Stuart, and her lips showed a warming interest. "Perhaps," she said in a skeptical tone, and left the room.

Lucy rose from her breakfast and walked into the other room. Stuart loitered over his coffee and his pipe; the Dance boys rose and silently departed, like young hounds bound for a fresh scent. Dance sat at the table awhile to supply the week's gossip and then Stuart tapped out his pipe and stepped into the extra room. There were three beds in it and a rag rug on the dirt floor. Lucy lay already asleep, her hands doubled in front of her face. He watched her a moment, and then lay down on the adjoining bed.

At noon there were three horses waiting in the yard instead of two. Caroline Dance sat in the saddle of the third one when Stuart and Lucy came out of the cabin. Dance explained this in his vigorous voice: "Ma's sending Caroline down to Megarry's place. Missis Megarry's come to her time." Mrs. Dance stepped from the cabin with a plump package and handed it up to Caroline. "Now that's everything you need."

Stuart said: "You want me to send Dr. Balance back from Jacksonville?"

Caroline shook her head. She was in her brown dress and she had her hair done neatly up. "I can do everything necessary," she said.

"For sure," added Mrs. Dance, surprised there should be any question. "It's only a baby. You stay at Megarry's tonight, Caroline, and come home tomorrow."

The day was hot and still and the trail ran southward up and down a series of rounded knolls and ridges which were the ragged extension of the heavier mountains to the east. They slid into a short valley half surrounded by hills and passed a small settlement sitting beside Rogue River; they crossed the ferry and went briskly along the river. A few miles beyond the ferry, Caroline Dance drew in her horse before a cabin which was scarcely more than a lean-to. This was Megarry's. A woman came to the door and tipped her hand across her eyes against the sun. She said: "Caroline, you ain't much time."

Caroline sat still in the saddle, facing Stuart. She wasn't smiling but anticipation made her mouth quietly expressive. He had teased her with his delay, and she knew it, but it didn't trouble her.

He drew a small package from his pocket and he took his time unwrapping it. He held it concealed in his hand and rode his horse near her and bent to put his hands around her head. He swayed back on the saddle and watched her as she looked down to the cameo brooch hanging from its thin gold chain around her neck.

"Why," said Caroline with pleasure in her voice, "it's like my Missouri grandmother's heirloom brooch."

The woman at the Megarry cabin called in sharper tone: "There's no time, Caroline."

Excitement brightened Caroline's face and

although she was not an impulsive girl impulse nevertheless stirred her toward Stuart. Then she remembered Lucy's presence, gave her an oblique glance and swung down from her horse, at once going into the cabin.

Stuart and Lucy went on, pointing toward the opening bay of a valley ahead. The river was beside them but the ridges slowly receded to form a valley; the trail rose gradually from the valley and began to cut its way southwestward along the bench. Fort Lane showed in the distance, its log houses squatted under a full bright sun on the north side of the river.

"You would have had your kiss, if I'd not been present to interfere," Lucy commented.

"Yes," said Stuart, amiable.

"I'm sorry I caused you to miss it." She gave him a veiled inspection. "She's twenty — you're twenty-eight."

"What would you have me do?"

She met his eyes and she saw his smile; suddenly she began to laugh. "Oh, Logan."

The trail took them around the breast of a hill and, at sundown, brought them to a creek with its miners' brush lean-to shelters, its canvas tents and flimsy log structures. They crossed the creek and moved through a grove of pine and oak and at last came out into the irregular lane which was Jacksonville's main street.

It was a settlement of perhaps sixty houses built of logs and riven cedar shakes, all scattered along the creek and up the side of the surrounding hills. Supper time's smoke drifted out of tin chimneys and men strolled the street, stained by the yellow-green clay of the diggings. Riders drifted in and a pack train wound down the slope of the hills from the west.

Stuart and Lucy passed a pair of saloons and Howison's big hay shed; they skirted Stuart's own store and moved up toward a large log-and-shake cabin on the hill slope. Jonas Overmire stood waiting for them with his hands in his front pockets and his stovepipe tipped well forward to give his daughter a hand down and he raked back his beard before he kissed her. Mrs. Overmire came out to embrace her daughter, and then a shout reached them and they saw George Camrose leave his cabin and walk rapidly upgrade.

Stuart leaned his arms on the saddle horn to watch this scene. Lucy had turned about to meet Camrose as he approached. He was a high and handsome man, light of complexion and carefully dressed. There was no mining-camp roughness on him at all, none of the exaggerated mining-camp temper in him. He was cool and held himself on tight rein, so that even now, approaching Lucy, he carried himself with negligent restraint, as though he had seen her but an hour before.

Lucy, Stuart noticed, seemed to match that temper and that composure. She was unruffled and as certain of herself. She had a smile for Camrose and she looked at him directly; yet

Stuart saw no great fire of impatience in either of them, no impetuous wanting. He said to himself, "Is this the way a woman looks at a man she loves?" He pushed his hands heavily against the saddle and wondered what went on inside the girl. She murmured, "Hello, George. Are you glad to see me?" Camrose put his arms around her, smiling down. "You are always good to see," he murmured, and lowered his face to kiss her.

She did a strange thing. She turned her head and she looked at Stuart for a short moment with the gravest kind of an expression on her face and for that instant he saw some kind of shadow in her eyes. It was a thing quickly happening and soon passing, so that he was not certain of what he saw. She looked back to Camrose and took his kiss and stepped away.

Stuart said: "Is that the best you can do, George?"

Camrose stared at Stuart with a controlled grin. "Could you do better?"

"A hell of a lot better," answered Stuart and rode away. A gust of irritation unaccountably moved through him.

He cooked supper in the small room behind the store; he cleaned his dishes and strolled through the store's long main room, around the boxes and kegs and bales of merchandise stacked on the floor, past harness and lanterns hanging from the log beams. He gave a glance to the

30

well-stocked shelves and he stopped a moment to watch his head clerk, Henry Clenchfield, weigh out gold for a miner. A breeze came through the store to stir up the sweet and musty and pungent odors of all this merchandise.

He paused at the doorway and lighted a cigar. Voices softly traveled through the night's bland warm air and the lamps of Jacksonville winked tawny in the dark. A guitar somewhere sent forth its lively tune and men drifted in from the dark creases of the hills to break a long week's loneliness in the town's deadfalls; and families arrived from their donation claims along the Rogue.

He walked back into the store and sat down on a box. "Where's John Trent?"

"He'll be in from Crescent City day after tomorrow," said Clenchfield. "I sent forty mules on the trip. Burl McGiven left two days ago for Yreka. Twenty mules. Jack Card left this morning on the Applegate trip. Murrow and Vane Blazier will take the Scottsburg string in the morning."

"Put this on the book," said Stuart. "Thirty mules to be at Salem on the twentieth for Henry McLane's freight, off the boat *Canemah*."

"Where will you get the mules?" asked Clenchfield. "You have got too much business now."

"Maybe it is time to buy a few more."

Clenchfield was an old country man, stiffened by years of clerking. He was angular and bald and precise; and he had a good head clerk's feeling of owning his job. Steel-rimmed glasses rode low on a sharp nose and a high turkey neck rose through a collar considerably too large.

"It is time to take some money out of the business instead of putting it all back in. You have got a hundred thousand dollars of equipment."

"Why, Clenchfield, we must be rich."

"This firm," said Clenchfield, "is too big a boat for the water it floats in. If you had a bank to borrow on, it would not matter. Since there is no bank around here, you should be your own bank. You ought to have thirty thousand in gold coin laid by for trouble. You have not got it."

"What trouble?" said Stuart.

Clenchfield shook his head. "For the trouble that always comes. But you are a young man and trouble must beat you over the head before you understand. How did I get here, six thousand miles from Liverpool?"

"How did you get here, Clenchfield?"

"Once I was young and had a business, good as this. But I was like you and I went broke."

"Henry," said Stuart, "there is a difference. Liverpool was an old town, finished growing. This is a young town in a young country. It will never stop growing for a hundred years. We sail with the tide. It is a long tide. There will be no ebb in my time."

"All Americans think that," said Clenchfield. "They think the tide flows forever for them. But mark me: gold veins run out and crops fail and men starve and wars come and businesses fail, and towns die, and the hopes of men always run too fast and too far."

"If everything fails," said Stuart, "everything will start again."

"Well, you will buy the mules," said Clenchfield.

"So I will. The fun is in growing. Not in having thirty thousand in the safe."

"Wait till you're old."

"Never wait, Henry. Never wait for anything."

Young Vane Blazier, who was one of Stuart's packers, came slowly through the doorway, all legs and neck and wild black hair bushing down his head. He looked back of him into the night with an air of worry. He reached into his pocket for his tobacco plug; his long white teeth flashed as he bit into it. He replaced the plug in his pocket and tilted his frame against the doorsill, undecided.

"I'll take the Scottsburg ride with you, Vane," said Stuart. "We'd better be on the road by six."

"All right," said Blazier. Hard thoughts drew his eyelids half together and cut a notch in his forehead. Suddenly he seemed to resolve the problem, straightened his shoulders and returned into the night, passing Camrose and Lucy

Overmire as they stepped into the store.

Both of them smiled when they saw Stuart, as though the sight of him sitting inactive were a humorous thing. Lucy sat down on a drygoods box, facing him. "You were supposed to eat supper with us."

"It occurred to me you and George might like to eat without me," he said.

"A tender sentiment," said Camrose in a softly jeering voice.

"George," said Stuart, "when is this woman marrying you?"

"I doubt if she has decided," said Camrose and turned to Lucy, looking at her with his half-serious, half-smiling negligence. It was a kind of mask, this negligence, covering the man's real feelings. Whatever his real feelings were, they seldom broke through the screen he placed over him. "When are you taking me, Lucy?"

"Do you like poetry, George?" she asked.

"Must I like poetry to be your husband?"

"We shall be married when the leaves fall," she said. These people, Stuart observed, were again matching moods — her lightly indefinite manner against his smiling indifference.

"You string me up and let me swing," murmured George Camrose. "The leaves of the maple which fall early, or the pine needles which never fall?"

Stuart rose and jammed his hands in his front pockets; and the expression on his face drew Camrose's chuckle. "Our friend disapproves

34

of us, Lucy."

"I have known both of you a long while," said Stuart, "but these are times when you puzzle me. You are both acting like a pair of people at the edge of a river, afraid to cross."

"Why damn you," said Camrose, still smiling yet slightly stung. "You're a bit too blunt."

Lucy watched Stuart with closest attention, as though at this minute she had observed something new in him. Camrose was meanwhile embarrassed by the unfriendly strain of the scene and gave out a quick laugh to bring things back in better humor. "If you so highly approve of the state of matrimony, why not try it yourself?"

"The idea has occurred to me," said Stuart, and began to grin.

"Here, now," put in Lucy. "I should like to know about that beforehand."

"To help choose the girl? George, tell this woman she can't run both of us."

"Your judgment isn't very good," said Lucy. "You're impressionable. It would be like you to marry a widow with seven children, out of pity."

George Camrose found this extremely funny. He began to laugh and kept on laughing until tears got into his eyes. Out on the street a voice shouted and men began to run by the door toward Howison's hay barn; and a little miner paused at the door to say, "It is Honey Bragg and Vane Blazier." Logan Stuart walked to the doorway and had his look down the street; then he cut back, moving fast to the rear room. When he returned he had his revolver tucked in his waistband and, thus armed, he left the store. Camrose moved after him immediately; and Lucy Overmire said, "Wait," and caught Camrose's arm and walked with him.

3

Obscure Meetings

Jacksonville's idle men made a circle on the street, drawn by the sound of trouble, drawn by the hope of trouble; and lanterns hung high to make this drama visible to hungry eyes. Stuart heard someone softly begging with his voice: "Go at him Vane, he's offerin' you a fight — don't refuse it." He laid the edge of his shoulder against the ring of men and roughly shoved a way through until he was inside the circle. In the center of this circle stood Vane Blazier, his black hair streaming over a hatless head, his arms down and his body motionless as he faced Honey Bragg. Honey Bragg had already struck, for a single furrow of blood made a track on the boy's jaw. At the present moment Honey Bragg waited back, smiling.

"Boy," he said, "never crowd me."

"Nobody crowded you," said Blazier.

"You got in my way," said Honey Bragg. "You wanted a fight, I guess."

"The hell I did," said Blazier. "You walked

across the street at me."

"Well," said Honey, his words rising and falling, "now you call me a liar. I am going to bust you up proper, boy. I am goin' to scar you. I'm goin' to cripple you good. I'm goin' to gouge out your eyes and kick you in the belly till you walk straddle. I am goin' to smash your teeth to snags and bust your nose flat, so you'll whistle when you breathe."

More lanterns danced in the night, dipping and swaying in eager hands. Vane Blazier's eyes were bitter-black, his face gray and grown old. He stood fast because his pride would not let him move, but his legs trembled. He was afraid yet dared not show fear.

Honey Bragg saw all that too with his bright attention. Smiling, he pulled his lips flat against his heavy teeth; the smile was a crushed half-moon against an olive-dark skin faintly shining with sweat. He had short hair curled against a round head and an extremely short neck joined into huge shoulders and arms. He was pleased with himself and his nostrils were sprung open and he tilted his head back to study the boy in the way a man might measure an ox for a slaughter-house sledging; the feeling of it came out of him, the malign enjoyment was quite clear.

"Go on," said Vane Blazier, scarcely audible. "Let a man alone. I didn't pick this fight."

"He's calling me a liar again," said Bragg. "I don't like that, boys. You know me. You know I couldn't take that even from a kid that don't know better. I am going to drive him around a bit and break him up before I drop him. Give me room and I'll show you some fun."

The eager miners crowded nearer, shoved up by others lately arriving. The greasy lamplight flickered and flashed on all those eyes so narrowly watching for the promised brutality so that Stuart saw the lust for violence there, the greed for raw action, the fetid stirring of jungle wants. They were good men, with stamina and courage and kindness. Individually they were, but they were in a pack now, and the smell of the pack was on them as the uniform expression of the pack was on their faces, making all faces alike — the hollow-eyed expectation, the partly opened mouth, the tensed cheek muscles.

Honey Bragg had his fascinated and hostile audience in the palm of his hand. He had no friends here, for he was a man suspected of many things; in the heart of every onlooker was the hope that Vane Blazier would cripple him — a hope that had no foundation in view of his skill. Honey Bragg understood all this, and it pleased and amused him as he stood poised for the butchering. Vane Blazier knew it, too, and now cast a starved glance around him, where-upon Stuart moved across the open space, took place beside Blazier and faced Honey Bragg.

Honey Bragg had not been aware of Stuart's presence. This quick change of the scene set him physically back; he had been poised to attack, his heavy legs slightly spraddled, his round head tipped forward and his elbows crooked. His first reaction was to draw up his head and drop his arms; then he straightened and the smile went off his face while he watched Stuart with a moment's most profound attention. If it caught him off guard, it likewise startled the crowd. The murmuring, the advice, and the listless shifting ceased until there was no sound whatever around the circle.

"A little trouble here, Vane?" asked Stuart, casually. He dropped a hand on Blazier's shoulder and he glanced at Bragg with a face quite heavy, quite homely.

"Hello, Honey," he said.

Honey Bragg stirred from his preoccupied silence. His grin came back to him. "Why, Logan — how are you, my friend?"

"Hear you've been away."

Honey Bragg mentally picked the question apart through a moment's silence; he covered the silence with his continued cheerfulness. Presently he gave out a short laugh. "I'm here and there," he said. "I'm a restless man, always moving."

"How's the horse ranch, Honey?"

"Fine as silk. No horses now. Ain't seen you go by the place last few days."

"I've been away, too, Honey," said Stuart.

"Well, you're a restless man, like me," said Honey, repeating his brief laugh.

"I notice you favoring your right leg," said

40

Stuart.

"Horse bucked me off."

None of this talk made sense to the crowd which, hungering for a fight, now looked on with ill-curbed attention. All these roundabout men listened with closest interest, their glances darting from Logan to Bragg, and back to Logan. They waited for Logan to go on speaking, or for Honey Bragg to answer, but the moments dragged while Stuart stood idle and wordless. Bragg's narrow-placed eyes rolled from side to side as he cast a speculative glance around the circle. He stared a moment at Vane Blazier and brought his attention and its grinning brightness once more to Stuart.

He covered himself well, Stuart thought; there was a full anger in this man but, save for the fugitive shadows which chased themselves in and out of his mouth corners, he kept his mask of humor well in place. He would be calculating whether or not to push the issue, he would be balancing the fight and all that it might mean very cleverly in his head. Meanwhile Stuart said nothing; the burden was on Honey Bragg.

A small flurry of motion went through the crowd which now realized how things were going; Honey Bragg raked that circle with a glance which quickly suppressed the discontent. Then the smile came easily back to Honey Bragg. He said: "I'll see you sometime, Stuart," made a turn and broke a path through the ring with a violent use of his shoulders and arms.

He got to his horse and swung up, waited a moment for a pair of men to join him — and thus he ran out of town.

A muffled and exasperated grumbling ran around the circle. Somebody said, "Well, by God, it was a freeze-out." Then with a thoroughly unsatisfactory scene irritating them, the various miners drifted toward Jacksonville's deadfalls. Stuart said something very quietly to Vane Blazier who turned up the street.

He himself stood a short while longer on the street, listening to the three horses of Honey Bragg's party run eastward toward the valley, toward the ranch which Bragg operated some five miles away; and he was thinking: "He was afraid to bring it to a head. He's not ready."

"Well, Logan," said somebody, "you found out, didn't you?"

He turned to see Joe Harms and Jonas Overmire — Lucy's father — in the shadows hard by Howison's hay shed. Joe Harms sat, as he usually did, on a bench in front of the shed, a radical little man wearing a shabby suit, a head of thin white hair and a white goatee on a frail chin. This bench was Joe Harms's pulpit, on which he spent most of his day, and from which he dispensed his acid comments on the injustices of the rich and the ignorance of the poor. Overmire made a strange partner for him, being a lawyer, a man of some property and considerable education; yet the two were frequently together. Argument, amiable or heated, was a

42

bond between them.

It was Joe Harms who had spoken. Walking toward Howison's, Stuart saw the little man in his favored position, stooped over with his arms propped on his legs, his head thrown back to Stuart with his sharp and dissenting glance.

"What did I find out, Joe?"

"That he'll back down."

"No," said Stuart, "that wasn't what I found out."

Joe Harms inquisitively cocked his head and waited for an explanation that didn't come. Then he added: "You know somethin' about him. That's why he backed down. What do you know about him?"

Logan said, "You figure something out, Joe," and walked toward his store.

After he had gone on beyond earshot, Overmire murmured: "He put the weight on Honey Bragg, and Honey broke."

"Honey's nerve is good as any man's. Good as Stuart's. But you notice him stop and think, whilst he was watchin' Stuart? He added somethin' up — and it didn't add right. So he backed off."

"What would that be?"

"I'd like to know," said Harms. He brooded upon it awhile and presently added in a tone that was arbitrary and wholly beyond doubt: "Stuart's got to fight him."

"Why?"

"Because," said Harms with his continuing

certainty, "the town won't have it any other way. The boys were promised a fight and they didn't get it. Stuart's got to do it."

Camrose and Lucy were up the street and as Stuart went toward them he thought: "He disclosed his hand in backing away. It is well to remember." He stopped before the pair, and he observed Lucy's face to be stained with trouble.

"Playing a little poker tonight?" asked Camrose.

"No," said Stuart. "I'm going out to Scottsburg early in the morning. Good night." He started into the store, but Lucy reached out and took his arm and said, "Walk up the hill with us."

"You know," said Camrose, as they ascended the gentle grade, "I believe you would have enjoyed a rousing battle with Bragg."

"I was disappointed," admitted Logan. "But not for that reason."

"Ah," said Camrose. "The town's got it right, after all."

"What's that?"

"I heard the boys talking as they came back. They thought it was all very queer. Something under the woodpile."

"It will give the boys something to discuss on idle nights."

"You bet it will. They'll talk you two into a fight."

"Don't say that," said Lucy with some sharpness.

44

They had reached the Overmire house, and Camrose turned toward Lucy to say good night. Stuart stepped aside and made it a plain business to fish out his pipe and go through the motions of filling it. He had no wish to witness the intimacy between them; it was their affair, in which he had no proper part. But a renewed irritation went through him when he heard Camrose say so calmly to her: "I shall see you tomorrow. I have missed you."

"That's nice of you, Georoge," she answered, and once more Stuart caught that balanced and faintly formal thing between them. It was like a ceremony they had learned. He lifted his attention from the pipe and watched George bend forward to salute her with a brief kiss. George was smiling and his comment was faintly malicious.

"Logan disapproves. I see it all over him."

Logan said brusquely: "You ought to do your kissing in private, George. And you ought to do it better."

"Well, Logan, I shall ask you again: Can you do better?"

Stuart took the pipe from his mouth. An impulse rolled through him and made him reckless and then he was smiling down at Camrose and at Lucy. "George," he murmured, "you're making a mistake."

He waited for Lucy's voice to end this nonsense, to settle it at once by a rebuke that would send both of them away. He watched her,

45

expecting it, and saw that it would not come. She had not moved. She was looking at him with her face lifted, her lips motionless. He saw the quick rise and fall of her bosom, he saw the moonlight whiten her throat and he came hard upon her, drawing her toward him with one sharp gesture. Even then he waited for her protest and was astonished that it did not come; and he bent his head and kissed her, and despised George Camrose at the moment. Her mouth was firm when he touched it but the firmness dissolved before his rough handling and a warm wind whirled through him, and he felt the lightly clinging touch of her hands behind his shoulders. She steadied herself and did not pull away.

George Camrose's idle voice came from the outer distance: "You see, Lucy. Rough and clumsy in all that he does. There is no skill to the man at all."

Stuart stepped back. He had his pipe clenched in his hand and he had pressed it against her, and now he wondered if he had hurt her with it. She stared at him, saying nothing at all. Suddenly George Camrose turned down the hill with his laughter coming back in full echo, as though he had witnessed a great joke. He was still laughing when he reached the main street and turned east upon it.

"Logan," murmured Lucy, "I guess I don't like you."

"I should not blame you. Good night."

She reached out and caught his hand. He was sweating and his hand was damp and it embarrassed him that she should discover this. "Wait," she said. "I don't like you when I think of you kissing other women as you did me. Do you know what you'll lead them to believe? Do you know what they'll expect of you?"

"The truth is," he said, "that you and George are both wrong. I have had no affairs with women."

The information seemed to shock her. She looked keenly at him through the darkness, she put a hand on his coat and the sharp pressure of her fingers bit into his arm. "Logan," she whispered. "Oh, Logan." Then she wheeled quickly and went into the house.

Camrose moved through the street's lamp-stained shadows at a rather rapid pace, eager to have his feet under Jack Lestrade's poker table. The scene between Stuart and Lucy had passed out of his head as a thing which, while temporarily amusing, had no importance. He dropped a casual nod to Overmire and Joe Harms in front of Howison's barn, and he stopped a moment before the Bolden & Wilson Express Company's office — of which he was local manager — to try the door's lock and to test the solid wooden shutters which covered the windows. He had just stepped away from the door when a miner came out of Blacker's deadfall across the street's dusty surface, saw him, and came quickly over.

"Looking for you," said the miner. "Be all right if you open the safe and let me have the dust I stored with you?"

It was Johnny Steele who had prospected along the Applegate, had left a well-filled poke at the express office for safekeeping, and had announced he would be gone on a trip for a couple of months. Camrose thought, "What the hell brings him back so soon?" and his mind ran rapidly from one excuse to another. Steele saw his hesitation and was somewhat apologetic.

"I realize it is a nuisance at this hour. But I've got some poker to play tonight."

Camrose made a show of agreeableness. "That's all right," he said, and reached for his keys. When he got inside the dark office he lighted a lamp and turned back to Steele. "I'll have to ask you to stay outside while I open this thing. You understand it's a company rule."

"Sure, sure," said Steele and backed from the office.

Camrose locked the door and moved around the counter to the massive safe with its gilded eagles. He crouched down and rapidly twirled the knob, a tighter expression now on his face. When he got the doors open he glanced at the window shutters to reassure himself that they kept out curious eyes, and he rummaged through a heavy layer of buckskin gold pokes — each with its owner's name and the amount of dust it contained attached to it — until he found Steele's. He looked at the tag and rose to lay the poke on the gold scales. "Eight ounces," he said to himself in a toneless murmur.

He looked again into the safe, his mind spurred to extraordinary swiftness by a faint sense of desperation. He thought: "Jackson, no. Bellemyer, Stroud, McIver." McIver. Perhaps. McIver was away down at Kerbytown and probably wouldn't be back for a month. He took up McIver's pouch, opened it, and was careful to sift out upon the scales only the fine gold. This he transferred to Steele's poke until he was within two ounces of the required weight; then he found a small envelope of particular-shaped nuggets which, in originally borrowing from Steele's poke, he had taken care to remove and save. Now he replaced them at the top of the poke, weighed it again, spilled in a small quantity of additional dust to make the weight correspond with the tag, and cinched it.

Having returned McIver's poke to the safe, he went over to let in Steele. "There you are," he said, and pointed to the miner's poke still lying on the scales.

Steele gave the scales and the tag a casual glance. "Thanks for the trouble," he said, and opened the drawstrings to have a look at the top nuggets; he picked out one with thumb and forefinger. "See that? I remember where I found it. Damnedest thing. It was inside an old Indian skull. Well, I'm obliged. Owe you something?"

"No," said Camrose, "glad to do you the favor," and watched Steele replace the nugget. Steele's head was bowed over the poke for a moment, and Steele seemed thoughtful, and a smallest expression of puzzlement came to him. Then he cinched up the poke and left the office.

Camrose closed and locked the safe and stood for a moment with his arms on the counter, his face somewhat flushed and preoccupied. He thought: "What did he see that bothered him? What did I do wrong?" A slow fear moved small and distant somewhere within him. Presently he extinguished the light and left the office, locking the door behind him, and continued toward Lestrade's.

Lestrade's cabin was a few hundred yards beyond the settlement, built in a shallow canyon and surrounded by pine timber. When Camrose got to the place he found Neil Howison, Dr. Balance and Lestrade already seated at a poker game. Since they were all old acquaintances who met here almost nightly, there was nothing much to be said by way of greeting. Camrose simply sat down in a chair, received chips and cards, and began to play.

"Where's Logan?" asked Neil Howison.

"Probably asleep. He's going out tomorrow to Scottsburg."

"Always on the move," commented Howison. "I guess I haven't got the energy he's got."

There was a small fire on the fireplace hearth

and a pot of coffee suspended from the crane. Mrs. Lestrade sat by the blaze and from his place at the table Camrose watched the flame color her face and increase the mystery he always found upon it. She was, he thought, far too beautiful and polished a woman for these rough parts; she was meant for gentler places and she had come out of far pleasanter surroundings. Faithfully she had followed her husband in his search for health, silently enduring his strange tempers.

"Energy," said Lestrade in a half-mocking voice. "Well, I envy any man the possession of it."

He sat back, the room's heat lightly flushing normally colorless cheeks. He wore a jaded and disillusioned air, as though he understood the world pretty well and had little use for it. His face was of the brittle, narrow and handsome sort and he never failed to keep himself in the best of clothes. Apparently he had money and apparently excellent connections somewhere. His interest in life had pretty well narrowed itself down to a search for health.

"I understand," he said, "that Logan and Honey Bragg were pretty close to a fight."

"Bragg backed down," said Howison.

Lestrade showed a tinge of interest. "Never heard of him doing that before."

"I don't understand Logan's interference," said Howison. "He's been around here long enough not to step into another man's quarrel."

51

Dr. Balance, older than the rest of them, reached for the whisky bottle and poured himself a comfortable jot. Always a busy man, he came here to relax his middle-aged bones, to hide out for a short while from the incessant calls upon him; he had white hair, a well-larded figure and a pair of eyes which had a good deal of power. "It may be," said he in a dry manner, "that he disliked seeing young Blazier slaughtered. The rest of you, being intent on a Roman holiday, perhaps did not consider that point of view."

Howison made his frank admission. "I don't know of anyone around here who cares to meet Bragg. It would be a grisly business."

"A comment on this town," said Balance, "that Stuart should be the only one."

Howison shook his head. "It was an odd approach. I don't recall Logan made any challenge. It was softly done, by George it was. Then it was entirely up to Bragg. I got the distinct feeling there was considerably more to it than what we saw."

Lestrade lifted his head, now definitely interested. "What would that be?"

"I don't know," said Howison.

They played on in this manner, sometimes talking, sometimes silent. Later Lestrade came back to the subject, speaking to Camrose. "Better tell Logan to walk softly with Honey Bragg."

Camrose said: "Let Honey Bragg walk softly."

"Bragg's a sort of friend of mine. You can't

52

fight white man's style against a damned beast. I shouldn't like to see Logan crippled."

"You've got some queer friends," suggested Dr. Balance.

Lestrade said amiably: "I did not say I liked him, or trusted him, or would defend him. I only said he was a friend."

"Good God," said Camrose, "what's your definition of a friend?"

"Any man, I suppose, whose character lends support to my belief that the human race is a great mistake." He was seized with a fit of coughing and bent forward in the chair, his face coloring from the effort. Dr. Balance observed him professionally, but said nothing. Lestrade murmured: "It is always cold and damp. Is there no heat anywhere in the world?"

"You ought to live in the Southwest," said Camrose. He watched Marta Lestrade rise from her chair, turn around the room and pause in a corner. Her hair was silk-fine and as black as the blackest thing in nature; her features in repose were clear and settled and sad. The sadness, he had observed, was a constant thing, tinging every other expression her face revealed. Her eyes touched him and he thought — as he had thought before — that beneath her faithfulness a great fire burned.

"Why run from pillar to post?" said Lestrade. "The day of ending comes soon enough. It might as well come here as elsewhere."

Boots trotted through the night and a fist

struck the door, and the door opened to show a miner. "Balance," he said. "There was a cave-in up at Happy Camp. We brought a man in. He's got a crushed chest."

"I'll be there. Go back and get his shirt off."

The miner went away at the same time gait while Balance cashed in his chips. "Marta," he said, "could I have some coffee?"

"You're cool about it," observed Lestrade. "And in no hurry."

The doctor stood up and accepted the coffee. He made a bow to Mrs. Lestrade and sipped at the drink gingerly. "No, I'm not in a hurry. I work long, but I keep a pace. Otherwise I would die. As for the man, if his chest is really crushed there is no need to hurry. I can do little for him. And of course I am cool. Only a fool would get excited." He put the cup down, smiling away the rebuke he now proceeded to give Lestrade. "But although I may be cool, Jack, I am not cynical. If I were an amateur philosopher with time idle on my hands, as you have, I might afford that luxury."

"Why, damn you," said Lestrade with good-natured venom. "Do you mean to say, after all your experience with the sweaty, dirty carcasses of people, their dumb brute follies, their superstitions and ignorances and crooked cheap passions, that you still regard them with any degree of pity or sympathy?"

The doctor's tongue could be sharp when he chose to make it; he made it so now. "You're no realist. You're a dabbler. I know more about people in a minute than you do all year. I know what they're made of and I know what they can do when their resources are strained. I do more than pity them. I respect them." Having said it, he calmly continued sipping his coffee.

"Ah," said Lestrade, with an impatient wave of his hand.

Camrose said: "Death comes sooner if a man gives up. I think you've already made your surrender."

Lestrade stared at him. "You're no better than I am for sympathy. Mostly you are out for George Camrose. You do not waste energy in any other direction."

Camrose smiled. "You may be right. I presume it is fortune we are all after. So then it becomes a matter of how it shall be soonest reached."

Marta Lestrade watched him as he talked. He was conscious of the force of her dark, wary eyes. Lestrade likewise studied him with considerable calculation. "It is a series of figures nicely lined up in your ledger. I wish you luck. It is a brutal world. A world meant for fighting and survival. The Christian virtues are for the meek and mild — to console them in their failures."

"There is a tide," said Camrose, "and the thing is to go with the tide."

"Do not float on this tide too long," warned Lestrade. "The first two years of any mining camp are always the best. After that the slack sets in." He put his arms negligently over the back of his chair. "You are the complete opposite of your friend Stuart."

"He requires different things of this world."

"What does he require?" asked Lestrade.

"A good fight, a good laugh, a good run. He has the common touch. Most people will love him where they will care little for the likes of you or me. Perhaps it is his vitality."

"A pretty sermon," commented Lestrade and rose from his chair. "Pretty enough to put me to bed. But, remember, fortunes are not made on sentiment. Fortunes are made by rude and rough ways. Fortunes are seized, and when you close your hands upon them, you must necessarily smash something else, and somebody else."

"I have dwelt even upon that somewhat," murmured Camrose, still smiling.

Lestrade stood at the doorway of the cabin's second room, seemingly frail in the lamplight, yet humorously contemptuous of frailty. "You have dwelt on many things, apparently."

Howison got up from the table. "It is a dull conversation. The both of you are worrying a dead rabbit around the floor."

"Certainly they are," said Dr. Balance and laid down his empty cup.

"I'll walk to the camp with you, Doc," said Howison. "I'm of poor sorts tonight."

"What's your trouble?" asked Balance.

"I sent Bill Brown as express to Yreka tonight, carrying considerable gold. I'll feel better when I know he has gotten safely through."

Balance stood a moment, watching Lestrade and Camrose with his dissecting attention; it was as if he had seen symptoms of a sort about these men and now took the time to hunt down causes. Presently his lips folded together and with a nod at the room he turned out of the place with Howison.

Lestrade, posed at the edge of the cabin's adjoining room, smiled faintly at Camrose. "The doctor does not like us tonight," he observed. He made a graceful flourish of his hand toward his wife, said, "Entertain our guest, Marta," and closed the door behind him.

Mrs. Lestrade placed her back to the fire and drew both hands behind her, the effect of which was to pull her body straight and slim within her dress. She looked across to him and he thought he observed once more the suppressed rebellion within her. "Do you believe all the strange things you've been saying?" she said.

"As between men I do," he said. He rose and walked toward her, excited by her. "As for a man and a woman . . ."

He was not certain of himself, or of her. He paused, on the edge of daring, on the verge of adventure. She seemed to be waiting for him to continue; her silence pushed him forward as much as anything else. He turned back and got his hat and said, "I shall be going." Then he came before her again and struggled with the notion of seizing her and kissing her. It occurred to him she must be seeing that impulse in him, but if she saw it she made no attempt to restrain him. He held himself tightly together, his voice dropped low. "Who knows what happens between a man and a woman? It can't be explained. Good night."

He swung and left the house. Mrs. Lestrade moved around the room, picking up the dishes on the table. The inner door opened and Lestrade appeared there, watching his wife with an odd critical glance. "Gone already?"

"Had you expected him to stay?"

He had become a harder man, merely by his passage in and out of the other room. There was a sharpness on him now to replace his former weary invalid's manner. He took his hat from its wall nail and moved to the door, Marta's glance following him. She said: "To Bragg's?"

"Yes," he said. "Marta — be nice to Camrose."

"Why?" she asked. "So that he will keep coming here to lose more money?"

He searched her face and weighed her darkly reserved manner. It amused him to say: "When I am dead he might make you an excellent marriage."

"At least," she answered, "it would be a marriage."

Balance and Howison walked in complete silence all the way to the middle of town, at which point the doctor turned toward his office. Howison called after him: "See you tomorrow night for another game."

Balance paused and turned about and shook his head. It occurred to Howison that the doctor carried something in his head which he had not meant to speak of, and it was clear that he overcame some doubts in order to say what he at last did say. "No, Neil. Not tomorrow night. Nor the night after — or any other night."

"Quitting poker?"

"At that place, yes. I would advise you to do the same."

"The conversation bored me, too, Doc. But it was a passing thing."

"Neil," said Balance, "I should like to tell you something. Our friend does not have consumption."

"What is it, then?" asked Howison.

"That is the point. He by no means is an invalid."

Howison had the extreme desire to question the doctor further, but before he could do so Balance swung and moved on to his office.

4

The Second Woman

The least variable habit of Logan Stuart's life was his hour of rising — which was at four-thirty. For a man who was scarcely methodical in any particular, this set rule was more or less a way of demonstrating to himself that he could follow discipline if he chose. In only one other particular did he deliberately test his own will: during one month of the year, and always in February, he quit smoking.

On this morning he shaved and cooked his breakfast while the town still slept, and afterwards walked through the store's pungent shadows to open the front door. A thin night-chilled air came against him with its dry and sweet and winey odors, and day moved in broadening bands out of the east and the first echoes of the waking town were magnified by the hour's intense stillness, the hollow impact of an axe on its chopping block, a metal stove door slamming, a man's spongy coughing. Smoke rose straight from chimney tops; the tarnished silver dust of the street showed a thousand agitated prints of the previous night's liveliness, and a man lay asleep in this dust with no protection at all save for the furry hide of a dog who lay against him. Looking at him for a curious moment, Stuart identified the sleeper as John Steele.

Under the roofs of this town men slept with their common dreams and wakened and walked abroad with a common hunger and a common crankiness, and felt the same morning hopes stir through them and were lifted by some kind of ambition. Some were brave and some were scoundrels and some were smart and some were fools, and all of them reached a level largely of their own making. They were equal only in that they came of the same clay and would dissolve to the same dust; yet at this hour he felt his closeness to them, knowing that he was whatever they were.

He turned back into the store and sat up to Henry Clenchfield's desk, and he lighted his pipe and began his chore of going through the bills, the accounts and the ledgers of his freighting and mercantile business which was a thing scattered throughout Oregon's southern half — the money owed and the money due, the pack outfits scattered along one trail or another, the goods oversupplied and the goods needed, the hay and oats in the barn, repair bills, the gold dust received for shipment and the credits therefor made. He bowed his shoulders and went through all of this. He had the sharpest kind of memory for details; he knew the characteristics of each mule in his service and the load it could carry, he knew all the roundabout trails, the fordable river crossings and the kind of bottom each ford possessed; he always knew where grass and water were best for a camp.

Stuart & Company had begun from two mules carrying a stove up the Applegate; now as Clenchfield had mentioned, it had a hundred thousand dollars in stock and equipment. It was a personal venture, and everything was in the venturing, and very little in the having. The town now was fully awake and the sun arisen. Down the street he heard Vane Blazier swearing the Scottsburg pack outfit together. Clenchfield came in, shaved and neat and sour.

"I expect," said Stuart, "it will be the *William Tell* arrived and unloading at Scottsburg. What can we use?"

"No hardware. Get gingham, soap, wool cloth if they've got any. Woman's stuff. But don't overbuy. You always overbuy."

"We always oversell."

"There's an end to that, soon or late."

This was the old argument which never had a conclusion. It was ended this morning by John Steele who had risen from the dust with his torn and gritty clothes. Steele was of Stuart's age, a normally cheerful and sensible young man; but he had come into Jacksonville with a month of lonely prospecting behind him — and he had

had his fun. He stood in low spirits before Stuart, his face scratched from fighting and his eyes bloodshot. He managed a small and wan smile.

"I must have had a hell of a good time. Don't remember a thing about it, though. Shouldn't a man have a few memories for a thousand-dollar bust?"

"You were honey bait for the bears," commented Stuart. "I'm a little surprised. You know these deadfalls, Johnny."

"Sure I do," agreed Johnny. "Still, when a man works like a horse for a year and then one day asks himself why he's working, and gets no answer, it is a disturbing thing. So I thought I'd loosen up, and maybe I'd find out why I was working."

"Did you find out?"

"Yes," said Johnny, "I did. But I wish I hadn't. Now, I'm going to buy out Billy Clayford's claim on the creek. I'd like a stake for it, Logan. Five hundred dollars. Think I can pay it back ounce a day."

"Henry," said Stuart, "put Johnny Steele down for five hundred."

Clenchfield said, "Ah," and managed to put into the single expression his complete disgust; he moved on out of the building.

"You got a Scotchman there," said Steele. "Thanks, Logan." He plunged his hands into his trouser pockets and suddenly brought one hand out with a small nugget. "Well," he murmured with mild surprise, "not clean busted," and stared at the nugget. It seemed to remind him of the previous night and gradually his lids crept across his eyes until they were half covered. "Logan," he said, "how long does it take to open a safe?"

"Half a minute — mine at least."

"Ten minutes would be pretty long wouldn't it?" commented Steele, and left the office.

Stuart took up his pipe after Steele left and thoughtfully repacked it and lighted it. He thought, "What safe? Camrose's?" and slowly shook his head. He rose and moved around the counter and went into his quarters to catch up his saddlebags and his rifle; when he came back into the big room he found Clenchfield returned.

"Five hundred dollars," said Henry. "At no interest. If you have got to loan, make it at a profit."

"Henry," said Stuart, "we're making money, are we not?"

"It is no argument. You've not got a hard head."

"Always let the other man make some money, too. Never try to get it all for yourself. I'll be back in ten days."

He went out in a fine frame of mind; the day was good and the prospect of being in the saddle pleased him greatly. Vane Blazier and Zack Murrow were even then lining the pack mules through town, the bell mare plodding wisely at the head of the procession. He moved on to his barn and saddled the red gelding; he was ready to lead it out when Neil Howison came in and looked carefully around the barn, obviously wanting privacy. Howison looked extraordinarily depressed.

"Logan," he said, "Bill Brown was held up last night near the Mountain House."

"How much are you out?"

"He was carrying twenty-five hundred dust."

"You want help, Neil?"

"No, I can stand the loss. But listen. Either the road agents are simply waiting for whoever came along, or they found out what Bill was carrying and were waiting for him in particular."

"How could they know? You tell anybody?"

"I mentioned it in only one place — last night at the poker game. There were just four people. Balance, Lestrade and his wife, and Camrose. If I cannot trust them, who shall I trust?"

The light of the barn was quite dull and Logan Stuart had lowered his head against the gelding to give the latigo a last pull. He finished the chore and turned to meet Howison's searching glance. Howison wanted an opinion from him; when he failed to speak, Howison's face slightly hardened. "Who can I trust then?"

"I don't know," said Stuart.

"Balance told me last night he proposed not to play cards at Lestrade's in the future and suggested I follow suit. What's up, Logan?"

Stuart freshened the light of his pipe and for a moment Howison caught the expression on the man's face; it was something like the look he had showed Honey Bragg the night before, watchful but deliberately bare. "For twenty-five hundred dollars, Neil, I guess you're entitled to suspect anybody you choose."

"Balance also said Lestrade did not have consumption — and was scarcely an invalid."

"So?" said Logan.

Observing this lack of surprise, Howison suddenly grumbled: "Am I the only blind one around here?" He saw that he would get no additional information from Stuart, and added: "I propose to send Bill Brown out again, as a decoy, with no great quantity of dust on him. I propose to tell one less person in that group each time, until I narrow the thing down to one man."

"A good idea."

"Suppose it turns out to be the wrong man?"

Stuart walked the gelding from the barn and stepped into the saddle. He settled his hatbrim against the sharp sun streaming low from the east and he stared at the distant rim of the mountains. "If you find the wrong man, Neil, that man is nevertheless a thief."

"Disagreeable business."

"Yes," said Stuart. "For your information, I gave up poker at Lestrade's last week." He turned after the pack outfit which, having crossed the flat part of town, now rose along the side of a ridge and curled gradually around it to the northeast.

Leaving Jacksonville, the trail cut over the point of the foothills which bordered the valley's flatness. Out on that flatness stood Table Rock with its spectacular level top and, in the foreground, the rectangle of Fort Lane. From the fort the valley broke into lesser fingerlike valleys which in turn were at last absorbed by the heavy mass of the Cascades. Here and there in the visible distance the log hut of a settler sat lonely and small.

They crossed the Rogue ferry and followed the trail through willow, pine and oak as it ran smooth and ran rough and all along this way the three men — Stuart, Blazier and Murrow — kept sharp lookout; for this was on the reservation which, empty as it seemed, contained the mercurial Rogues, whose motives were never known. In the middle of the afternoon the pack outfit paused at Dance's, where Caroline poured buttermilk out of an old Wedgwood jug and looked on at Stuart with her thoughtful smile, while he drank.

"Scottsburg?" she said. "You travel a lot, Logan."

"Caroline," he said, "when will you be twenty?"

She looked at him with an attempt to read the reason for his asking. Behind her calm manner a liveliness had its sudden way and her lips mirrored the change. "I am already twenty," she said.

He said, "Mighty old," and stepped up to his saddle while Blazier and Murrow lined out the mules.

She was accustomed to his mild teasing; she had usually a steady sort of smile for it, and sometimes a distant gaiety of her own to match his manner. But she was essentially a sober girl and this was a sober subject with her. "Why yes," she said, "I have been old for three years almost. It is a pity. I shall be late starting my family."

He folded his hands on the saddle horn. "Why, Caroline, you have got plenty of choice in the valley. I can think of twelve men, offhand."

"So can I," she agreed, "but it isn't a thing where you count eeny-meeny-miny-mo, is it?" Her eyes were a powdery gray; they regarded him with a firm attention, to see if he was laughing at her, and once again some inner excitement showed its brisk motion in them. "You go on, Logan," she murmured. "The day's wasting and I've got butter to make."

She stood before the house with her hands across her apron and watched him depart; and when he turned, just before entering that belt of dark timber which marked the beginning of the trail's laborious passage of the Umpqua Mountains, he turned and waved back to her and her own hand lifted in answer — not rapidly but with a certain hesitation, as though she were not sure she ought to do it. Her father saw this from another part of the yard and now moved over to her.

"Caroline," he said, "you like him?"

"I guess I do," she said, most calmly.

Dance scrubbed a hand across his whiskered cheeks and studied his daughter with a desire to give her proper advice; it was a hard thing to do with a girl who had grown into a woman too young, who was as mature as his own wife.

"Well, then," he said, "if you want to catch a man you have got to work at it."

She still watched the trees into which the pack outfit had gone, and from which the bell of the lead mare sent its musical and diminishing sound. "I'd want no man I had to catch," she said.

"Why, sure," he agreed. "You catch him and he catches you. But you got to do your share. A man always figures he does the catchin', but the truth of the matter is it is the woman who brings him up on the rope, him not quite knowin' it."

She looked at him with a solemn interest. "Is that the way you got Mother?"

"I fought for your mother," he said at once. Then he saw the contradiction and gave out a cheerful laugh. "But your mother give me sign enough to go ahead and fight. You got to give a man the sign."

"Maybe it's so," she said. Behind the composed expression, a little-girl eagerness vaguely stirred and vaguely displayed itself.

Four and a half days out of Jacksonville, Stuart's pack train reached the Umpqua's head of navigation. The river, searching for the sea, had here cut a notch through the Coast Range and had left only a narrow strip of meadow between mountain and water. On this cramped flat spot was Scottsburg, its cluster of houses sprung up on the strength of the pack-train trade. The ship *William Tell* lay by the bank with a gangplank thrown over to the back doorway of Poole & Hutchinson's store.

Stuart made his purchase from the ship's stock, loaded his pack mules and started on the return trip. All the way from Jacksonville Johnny Steele's remark concerning the Camrose safe had been on his mind; and now, homeward bound, he came to grips with an issue he had long refused to meet.

In this country most men were rough and plain and direct since they could be little else. George, alone of his friends, held to his polish, his light cynicism, his complexity of character. George always walked Jacksonville's streets with the manner of a man strolling along the city park on a pleasant Sunday afternoon. It seemed necessary to him to be a little gay, a little sardonic, yet never to reveal his full emotions; and in fact he never presented himself fully to anybody. Still, under it all, there was a charm to the man which laid its bonds upon those he chose to like.

Friendship was an entire thing, or else it was nothing; therefore it made Stuart uneasy to be looking into George Camrose as critically as he now was. What lay behind that charm — substance or weakness? Was the man's laughter something human and generous, or a shallow echo out of a mind that had no strong faith? And what was that indifference which always guided George Camrose's words and manner — even in those scenes, as before Lucy, when the sight of her and of all that she meant should have swept aside the conventional mannerisms of his life? If he could not be roused then, what was there in him to be roused?

These were the questions he asked as the pack train steadily footed its way down the trail, made camp, and went on again. Silent in the saddle, he added up the little stories which had singly come to him concerning Camrose, the stray suspicion which Johnny Steele had dropped, the losses at poker which he knew Camrose had sustained, his friendship for Lestrade who was, as Balance had said, not the sick man he pretended to be. By night, squatted before the campfire, he nursed his pipe and pried away at Camrose with his questions; wrapped in his blanket, he watched the starshine and came slowly to his conclusion. It was not possible to judge a man completely, it was never certain what lay real and unchangeable at the farthest corner of a human heart; as for George Camrose, there was some weakness in him but since Lucy loved him, there must be worth in him other eyes could not wholly see. In any event Lucy had taken him and that was the end of the story.

He grew more and more silent until at last he scarcely heard the few words Vane Blazier spoke to him during the day. If a man had the picture of a woman in his mind, and heard through all the hours of the day the tone of her voice, and caught the fragrance of her at any odd time in any odd place, why shouldn't he fight for her? What was George Camrose's indifference before his own never still desire for Lucy? He remembered Camrose's idle amusement as he, Stuart, had kissed Lucy and had stepped back to hate George for that foolish humor and now he wondered what Camrose's depth could be, to remain unmoved at such a sight.

All the way to Canyonville he was thus wrapped around. Suddenly, as they started through the mountains, he was through with speculation and he knew what his part was; it was what it had been before. Now he began to talk, and to be cheerful. Zack Murrow and Vane Blazier both looked at him with considerable surprise. "What's been eatin' you?" asked Blazier.

"The next forty years," said Stuart.

"Why," said Blazier, "a man can't look that far ahead."

"Not as far off as you think."

The canyon passage was quiet, with young Lieutenant Bristow and his twenty dragoons camped in boredom at Wolf Creek. "Peaceful," he said. "You who knows about these people? I feel them somewhere in the timber, watching. They are a brooding race." By twilight of the fourth night the pack train halted at Dance's and Stuart and Blazier and Murrow took their ease at the supper table. The three Dance boys, wild and shy, ate without speech and rose and silently departed into the shadows. Dance sat back to enjoy himself with his pipe. Mrs. Dance and Caroline were at the supper dishes.

"The lieutenant," said Stuart, "doesn't know what to make of the quiet spell."

"He's just ridin' back and forth, makin' the trail broader," said Dance. "The Rogues can hear him for miles. It's a way of passin' the time, I suppose, but if trouble starts he'll get himself bushwacked first off. He don't know Indian style."

"Why don't you tell him?"

"He's got a little brown book. If it don't come out of the book, it ain't true."

Murrow rose and departed to his blankets outside the house. Van Blazier, following suit, stopped at the doorway to look in Caroline's direction. Interest held him there even though shyness kept him silent. He watched her as she moved around the room and presently, when she became aware of his interest and looked to him, he flushed and left the room. Dance, observing it, gave his daughter a sly grin; she returned to her chores.

"Ben," said Stuart, "you're ten miles from a neighbor, and right in the track of trouble if it breaks."

"Why," said Dance, "I have got a stout house if they strike, and I have got three sons who will know by morning if an Indian has been within two miles of this place. Mark me, I put no trust in the peace treaty with 'em. It was their land we're on and they don't forget it. When they come here and talk easy, I know what's behind their eyes — it's ordinary hate. But we got strength and they can't beat us unless they do it by plain surprise. They know that and they'll remain still — unless a medicine man stirs 'em up, or unless some white man commits a murder that starts them off."

"Both possible."

"We are sitting on a powder keg," said Dance, and found nothing in the foreboding statement to disturb his comfort. "If they struck quick they could wipe out every settler between Evans Creek and Anslem's."

"You'll know it beforehand," said Stuart. "They'll start moving around. They'll get bolder when they ask for food. They'll get insolent. That's the time for you to fort up."

Mrs. Dance, having finished her work, now quietly moved into the bedroom. The curtains sang sharply on the wire when she closed them, drawing Dance's attention. He said, "This is my fort and damned if I budge," and then he sat still a moment, fingers pulling at his beard. Presently he rose with a great yawn and moved over the puncheon floor in his moccasins, dropped a covert grin to his daughter, and vanished behind the curtains. There was always a little deviltry in this man and it now made him say loudly to his wife: "Anna, even the chickens ain't gone to roost yet."

His wife's calm voice had a good enough retort. "You've got more mind than chicken, I do trust."

Caroline swept the floor and stood a moment in the center of the room, considering what had been done and what was to be done. She laid out that next day in her mind so that when it came she would rise early and be at her work without the need of stopping to plan. Presently she removed her apron, with a lighter humor replacing the fixed graveness of her cheeks. She took a round reed basket from a shelf, it containing torn stockings and darning thread, and sat down in the rocker. When she had gotten well at this chore she paused a moment and lifted her head to look at Stuart with a glance that he was wholly unable to make out.

He knew her to be the calmest of girls, always disposed to take the practical view of things; he knew her to have her own will, and a great deal of self-confidence. Beyond this, he was not certain. She was mature in so many ways; yet now and again when he saw the graveness leave her face, and the sparkle of little-girl excitement come to her eyes, he wondered where youngness ended and maturity began. Sometimes it seemed to him her quietness contained the sharpest kind of wisdom, but at other times he thought the quietness might hide a great deal of wonder and a great deal of soft, warm dreaming. She was to him a frequent contradiction.

"Logan," she said, "do you really think the Indians will break out?"

"Always possible. They've caused trouble each year so far."

"It will be nice, someday, when we don't have to worry about that any more."

"Someday there'll be town all along the valley."

"Now that," she said, "I'm certain I'd not like. This is best, the way it is."

She usually liked things to be as they had been. It was a strong, conservative streak in her. She suspected change and was made uncomfortable by it. He let the silence continue while he pulled at his pipe and kept her close in his mind. If she married him, she would follow him, for that was in her nature; yet would she like the kind of life he gave her? Would she ever discover that though he might bring her much, one thing would be missing?

She had meanwhile gone on with her darning, the heat of the room coloring her cheeks. She was prettier, he thought, than he had before noticed her to be; she was sweeter, her features warmer and more expressive. Suddenly she stopped her knitting and looked up to him and he saw once again that trace of fugitive excitement play across her face.

"No, I wouldn't like it. This is a nice place. My father built it and I want to live in it. I'd like all my children to grow up here. When they get old enough I want them — if they are boys — to take land near by. If they are girls I want them to marry neighbors and not move off. It isn't good for people to always move and be torn up. I like to get up early and watch the sun come over the mountain. I like to watch the mist lie on the meadow at night. I like to hear people, away off — their voices coming ahead of them when it is quiet. When I am dead, I'd like to know my children stand where I stood and see the same things."

"The man you get," he said, "might not want to stay here."

She lowered her head to the darning. "I know," she murmured. "But at least it is good to think of, if it is never anything more than that."

"Make you unhappy to move away?"

She went on darning for a short while, thinking carefully of it. Then she said, quietly, "No, not unhappy. My grandmother moved and my mother moved. I can make a new home as well as they. Only, I would hate to move too much.

It would be hard to be always fixing a new cabin or starting a new garden."

Her mind went at once to these things, solid and permanent and useful. He knew as much about her then as he thought he would ever know, the next moment he knew less, for she said something that puzzled him.

"I miss my grandmother. She was such a smiling woman. I always liked to watch her sit and rest. Her hands were pretty and her face was so smooth. She had twelve children and they all grew up and they all went away and now she's alone in Kentucky. I feel so sad for her being alone. People ought to be close. Families should stay together. It would be a delight to sit down to Christmas dinner with everybody there. I remember Mother saying the Boyd family, back East, once had eighty-three to Thanksgiving. It must have made all of them feel good."

The little things, he thought, were close to her; the little things were big to her and she made her world out of them. He rose and tapped the ashes of his pipe into the stove and refilled it and sat down again. She had ceased to work. She sat still, directly watching him, and he thought she wanted to say something to him. It was a clear and bright urge in her eyes; it made all her face hopeful. This was Caroline, as much of her as she cared to let anybody see.

"What, Caroline?"

She said, "Do you like Jacksonville?" It was

not the thing she had meant to say, he realized.

"It is a place to do business in," he said.

She resumed her knitting, and spoke again. "You're not a religious man."

"I don't get to church much, maybe I should."

"When it's handy," she said, "you should. Not that I'd care for an extra-religious man. They all look so dry and hungry."

He sat back in the chair and quietly laughed. Her glance came up to him, pleased that he was pleased. Afterwards, in the still idle voice, she went on: "Are you very thrifty? Folks say you make money but don't keep it."

"I don't pay much attention," he said.

"Men are not much in that habit," she said, as though meaning to excuse him. "But you are restless. Everybody says so."

"Yes," he said, "I guess I must be."

"I suppose it is easy to be that way if you have nothing much to do at home but bach." Now, still with her head lowered, she added an irrelevant question. "When is Lucy to marry George Camrose?"

"I don't know."

"I don't think I'd want him," she said and looked up at him with a rather quick swing of her head. It was then that he felt his uncertainty rise again. He smiled at her, saying, "Everybody's got a taste of some sort," and at the same time he wondered what things stirred behind her simplicity. Forty years lay right here at this moment. How was anybody to know what the wise thing was, or the good thing, or the honest thing? There was only one thing certain — which was that the forty years would not wait.

He got up, knowing he had the decision here and could not delay it. So he said, "I understand everybody's going down the Applegate tomorrow night to raise a house and see Gray Bartlett and Liza Stone married."

"Yes."

He moved once more to the stove and knocked out his ashes. He said, "I'll be there," and turned around to watch her.

She sat with her hands still on her lap, looking across the room to the wall. Her face was as clearly expressive at this moment as he had ever seen it — nor did he ever again see it so graphically register the light and the shadow of her feelings — the pleasure his words had brought, the wonder and the fullness of heart which followed, and the strange, small stirring of sadness which came after. She lifted her shoulders and looked around to him, smiling at him and smiling for him. "Yes," she said, "I'll be there, too."

"Good night," he said, and moved out of the house toward his blankets. He heard the soft bell-like echo of her voice come after him. "Good night, Logan."

5

Doubt Begins

After the sun dropped behind the hills west of town, there was by summer a long and beautiful hour in which both shadow and light seemed to stand still. Sauntering up the gentle grade to the Overmire house, George Camrose now and then looked back to see supper fires burning along the creek and the smoke rising into the pearl-colored air. The town's streets were empty during this hour and a feeling of loose ease came over it as though all men, paused from sober work, now waited for evening and the excitement of evening. "Shedding righteousness and embracing revelry," he thought with his usual sardonic twist of mind. The two had two characters: by day it was sweaty and impatient and grimly at labor; by night it turned bawdy. Often he had thought of this, and often had decided that men who toiled so long for their riches and spent those riches with such swift abandon were fools scarcely to be pitied.

Lucy was at the door to meet him with her

calm pleasantness. He ate with the family and for a little interval sat in the room while the lamps were lighted and the conversation moved casually from one thing to another. In a little while Lucy rose and looked at him, and the two passed into the darkness and strolled along the edges of the town, the hot day's odors quite strong around them.

"Well," he said, "it's been just another dull day. Nobody killed, nobody robbed, no ten-pound nuggets."

"We always live on the edge of expectancy, waiting for big things to happen."

"Typical mining-camp feeling. Always expecting a big tomorrow that never comes."

"Yet I do love this country. I am quite happy here."

"Ah, Lucy," he said, "there's so much of this world we're missing. This is only one lonely little spot of it. We're three thousand miles off the main road."

"You sound rather jaded," she said thoughtfully.

"I'm partial to mansions with plush furniture and God knows what I'd give to step into a restaurant and have music with my dinner. I'm anxious for the next move"

"What will that be?"

"Either to be transferred to the company's office in San Francisco — and I'm sure you'd like that — or else to get into another kind of work. I know mining and mining towns and I

82

fancy I might someday go East and place myself with some of these big houses which handle mining interests." Then he added something else, without changing the expression of his voice. "When are we to be married?"

They were arm in arm as they walked silently forward. Her lack of instant answer caused him to look at her; and then she said: "I had not known you were very impatient about it."

He kept his lightness, his faint air of amusement at himself. "I am not the rough and overwhelming kind, like Logan."

She spoke quickly. "Let's not grow too serious."

"I'm trying to tell you something, Lucy. I'm not the kind of a man Logan is. He is not responsible for his character and neither am I for mine. We happen to be what we are, nothing more or less."

"Have I ever questioned it?"

"Sometimes I feel you make a comparison which leaves me at a disadvantage. But, Lucy, I do love you very much."

"Why, George."

He saw that he had succeeded in profoundly stirring her, and he drew her forward and kissed her. It was a soft kiss, soon done with; immediately afterwards he stepped back to observe her face in these velvet shadows. "Should I be rough and violent? I think you expected it. Should it be fury and thunder to be real?"

Her voice had a sudden energy in it. "Why

do you always pick things apart?"

"It is a streak in me, I guess. Or a fear that I may not be rough and bruising enough."

"Are you trying to tell me you resented the way Logan kissed me? After all, you brought that on rather deliberately. Why did you do it?"

He shrugged his shoulders and only said, "It irritated Logan to have me do it."

"You didn't show it."

"I never show myself." He laughed a little and took her arm, the two of them retracing their route toward the Overmire house. "You two are much alike," he said. But he was rather gay, his little gust of emotion having passed, and at the doorway of the house he removed his hat. "Let's not wait too long. I'm very lonely."

"George," she said, as serious as he had seen her at any time, "don't make things complicated between us. Don't be so filled with wonder and doubt. Let everything be simple and straight."

"My thoughts seldom ever travel a straight line," he said.

"Doesn't your affection travel in a straight line?"

"Yes," he said. "Yes, I believe it does."

"Then let it be straight. You must not confuse me."

He bowed to her with his outward cheerfulness; he searched her face with a moment's care, seeking some fugitive expression which might betray other emotions she might be hiding from him. Then he walked down the hill, turned at Stuart's store and passed from sight, eventually to appear again on the pathway to Lestrade's.

She knew where he was going and she thought: "He would rather play poker than stay here." It was a thing that should have made her both resentful and jealous, but it did not. She folded her hands across her breasts, remembering that once tonight he had greatly moved her for the first time in many days. It took her back to the beginning when she had been so sure of him and so sure of herself, when everything had been wonderful between them, when she waited for marriage with a terrible impatience.

She was shocked by the realism of her present thinking. She was angry at him for taking this clear thing which had been between them and muddying it with his questions, his indifference, his odd inflections. She recalled the guarded remarks people had made about his poker-playing habits — said in jest and quickly dropped, yet deliberately intended as warnings. She saw his face, its charming handsomeness and its gay changeability — and then she saw the little things she had not noticed before, the narrowness of that face and the sharp edges of it. She checked herself at once. "I must stop this." If he was what she had thought him to be a year before, he must still be the same man now. And this was the thing that unsteadied her the most — this doubt of her own judgment; she had been made changeable and fickle and cheap in her own mind.

And it hurt her to think how great and powerful a sensation Logan Stuart's kiss had shot through her — how vivid and how lasting it had been, how unsettling it was even now. "I should be ashamed of that," she thought. "I should be ashamed to realize another man could create that feeling in me." Sometimes she was a stranger to herself, astonished at the things she had not known were in her, and as she faced the night she had a very real fear of the future. Some unlovely thing was happening to her. She hated it and resisted it, but could not stop it.

On his way down the street, Camrose passed Joe Harms who, as usual, sat on the bench in front of Howison's hay barn. He had no greeting for Harms and Harms had none for him; the truth was that Camrose had always distrusted the frail little man's manner of sitting spiderlike in the shadows, spying upon the town. At the express office he turned in, locked the door behind him, and lighted a lamp. Then, casting a glance at the window shutters to be sure they were tight-closed, he worked the safe's dial and swung open the heavy door.

The gold dust bought by the company lay on the upper shelf, waiting convenient shipment, and the gold coins used in daily business were all carefully stacked there; on the lower shelf stood the fat pokes of the miners, held for them as a matter of safekeeping only and returnable to them on their demand. McIver's poke was the one from which he had been currently borrowing and now he lifted it and set it on the scales to refresh his mind as to the quantity he had already borrowed.

A slight grimace stirred his face as he watched the scales dip; and he stood in considerable thought, his elbows on the counter. McIver was supposed to be on a prospect somewhere down the Rogue and therefore not due back for some time. Yet suppose he came suddenly in, as Steele had done? The truth was, the game got increasingly risky; one could not go on forever juggling dust, and forever hoping for a night's luck at poker to balance the account.

He restored McIver's poke to the safe and stood in thoughtful debate. A good night's winnings would change all this, and sooner or later that was bound to come. There was also another possibility, which was that one of these miners who had left gold here for safekeeping might die in some sudden accident or brawl, leaving the gold unpossessed. He had thought of it steadily for the past two weeks, turning the prospect over and over in his head. McIver's death, for example, would be for him a stroke of luck. He shrugged his shoulders and, with some slight qualms, slipped a hundred dollars of the company's gold coin into his pocket and locked the safe. Presently, with the office closed behind him, he continued toward Lestrade's.

A few moments later Joe Harms walked from the narrow space between the express office and Howison's barn; all during the recent minutes he had stood in a crouched position against the express-office wall with his eye pushed against a knothole in the building's rough walls; it was a very small knothole, yet it had given him an excellent view of Camrose's actions.

The Lestrades and Howison were comfortably gathered around the fire when Camrose arrived; and Mrs. Lestrade rose to mix him a hot whisky punch. "Really," said Lestrade, "we've not got enough customers for a game. Logan's out of town and Balance is off somewhere on mercy's errand. Drink your punch, George, and call it a day."

He was never a genial man whose sense of hospitality reached out to warm others; and this night he seemed more indrawn than usual, almost to the point of waspishness. He sat close to the fire as though unable to get warmth enough into his bones, and his face was tired. Mrs. Lestrade was, Camrose thought, definitely oppressed by her husband's temper; she was very quiet, very sober. Howison, seeming also to sense this lack of pleasantness, suddenly finished his punch and got up to depart. "Tomorrow's tomorrow."

"There'll be an end to tomorrows soon enough," said Lestrade.

"Very cheerful thought," said Howison dryly. "You're full of self-pity."

Lestrade lifted his head to rake Howison with an embittered glance, whereupon Camrose observed for the first time that Lestrade's eyes were considerably bloodshot, as though the man had been heavily drinking.

"Now, now," said Camrose. "This is scarcely the way to begin or end an evening."

"End it any way you please," retorted Lestrade, and fell into a spell of coughing.

Howison had gone to the door. Following him, Camrose turned to observe that Marta Lestrade watched her husband quite closely and with almost a complete absence of expression. She lifted her eyes and met Camrose's glance and held it over a long moment. After he left the house, joining Howison, he tried to fathom that glance, and a small excitement ran through him as he played with the notion that she was silently speaking to him.

Howison went glumly along the path, still obviously out of sorts. Camrose said: "We have got to make allowances for a sick man, Neil. He's dying."

"Is he?" said Howison briefly, and swung toward his own cabin.

Camrose called after him. "Tomorrow night, Neil?"

"No, think not."

Camrose strolled on alone with his evening at loose ends. He had gone to Lestrade's eager for poker and he had come away with the eagerness unabated. It was an appetite he could not control and suddenly he turned into Hobart's deadfall, found a blooded game in progress there and made a place for himself at the table. This night, he thought, would be better; this night his luck would change.

Lestrade rose up from his chair with a changed manner and reached for his hat. He grinned at his wife. "Do you think I play the part of a petulant invalid well, Marta?"

"Too well. They left here disliking you."

"They don't come here out of affection for me at any event," he said. "Balance comes to escape the pains and aches of his customers, Howison comes because he is a bachelor with no better place to go, and Camrose is drawn by the hope he'll make a killing at cards. Or perhaps —" and he gave his wife a cool appraisal — "to watch you for a sign of approval. Do you give him a sign of approval, Marta?"

"You are nasty tonight."

"I am a realist, and all realists are nasty when they jar the romantic myths people like to wrap around themselves to cover their shabby sins."

"Are your sins any less shabby, Jack?"

"I am honest about them. I do not pretend."

"You are always pretending. You think that by admitting your sins you are being a very strong character."

He was at the door. He paused there to look back with his sharp and antagonistic glance.

"You are pretty blunt."

"I thought you admired honesty."

He showed a slight color and confusion, which was rare to him. "There is such a thing as faithfulness."

"I suppose," she said, "you are going to Bragg's to tell him what Howison told you about Bill Brown tonight."

He wheeled through the door and slammed it behind him; and presently she heard him ride away to the northeast. She stood before the fire, the blaze throwing its light on the frozen calmness of her face; but as time went on the heat seemed to thaw that expression until her lips and her eyes were loose with despair. Turning, she left the house and walked on through the scattered timber; she was scarcely conscious of her direction and when she reached the creek and found it barring her way, she stopped — and something broke within her and she began to cry.

Johnny Steele, walking abroad in the night, heard the sound of this crying and came on until he was near enough to recognize her. He said: "Anything I can do, Mrs. Lestrade?"

She seemed unaware of his nearness; she remained erect, both hands cupped to her face, racked by the increasing violence of her crying. She had started and she could not stop; the spasms grew greater and greater and her breath lifted and fell in swifter, sharper gasps. Johnny Steele was appalled by it. A woman's tears were foreign to him and a woman's grief was a terrible thing to witness. It came to the point where he could no longer be a spectator, and so he stepped forward and put his arms around her.

Then he knew how bad it was with her. He was a stranger, touching her, and she was so blind and heartbroken that she wasn't aware of it. She turned in his arms and laid her forehead against his chest and continued to weep; he tried to hold her tight enough to stop her shuddering but he could not, and that was a thing that got into him and shook his nerves. He thought to himself: "Goddamn whoever did it," and an extraordinary pity went through him and he became this woman's fiery partisan.

He had no idea of how long he stood in that position. Time ran on considerably and at last he noticed the lessening of her body's shaking. It was, he thought, like a violent southwester blowing itself out; and afterwards her weight rested more heavily against him, as though she had been exhausted. Presently she drew back and became aware of him.

He was embarrassed at what she might think of him. He said, "I'm Johnny Steele," and regretted the rough appearance he must be making. "I heard you, and came up. Anything I can do?"

She shook her head. He had of course often seen her in camp and often had observed her prettiness, now it was more than prettiness to him and he felt somehow obligated and bound to her. Meanwhile, she had taken her time to study him and had reached some sort of conclusion about him. She turned away but in a moment she swung back. "It was good of you. You'll say nothing about it?"

"I'll say nothing. But if it's any kind of trouble I can fix —"

"No," she answered in her soft and depressed voice, and disappeared in the trees.

He turned toward the street with the keenest memory of his arms holding her. He paused before Corson's deadfall, then swung away from it with no appetite for a drink. "Probably that damned husband of hers," he thought and was considerably enraged at the man. He reached a small shack on the town's western side and stepped in, lighting a lamp; and his immediate move was to have a look at himself in the mirror. What had she seen? One more miner's sunburnt and ragged face, marked by its occasional scars? He thought: "I have been a big fool. What the hell is there to be proud of in a thousand-dollar drunk? It's time to settle down." Then he thought: "I ought to shave every morning."

Honey Bragg's cabin lay beside a wandering, half-dry creek four miles from Jacksonville, largely hidden in a thicket of willow and scrub oak. Coming through this thicket Lestrade picked up the glitter of Bragg's light and took care to send a call ahead of him. A pack of dogs rushed

93

out of the shadows, all baying, and Lestrade began to curse at them as he got down from his horse; then Bragg's voice moved up from the deeper shadows, calling off the hounds. Lestrade stepped into the house, with Bragg coming behind him.

Lestrade irritably said: "If those curs ever dig a fang into me, Honey, I'll slaughter the whole damned pack." There were three other men in the small, earth-floored cabin. Lestrade gave them a quick glance and a nod and wheeled to face Bragg, whose fleshy lips and brightly dancing eyes had an easy smile. Honey was affable when he chose to be. Honey was a schemer who could meet a man with any temper he chose, and now he chose to be pleasant.

"They're to keep strangers from slippin' up on me." He gave the three men a signal with his hand, whereupon they moved out of the cabin. When they were beyond earshot, Bragg said: "What's it now?"

"Howison is sending Bill out again as messenger. Same road."

Bragg turned to the doorway at once and called, "Boys, get up the horses."

Lestrade said: "What's between you and Stuart?"

Honey Bragg came about, smiling but alert. "Nothing at all."

"He had something on his mind the other night when he faced you."

"He stepped in to protect the kid. He didn't

94

want to see Blazier busted up, because Blazier works for him."

"You backed away from a fight. That's not your usual style."

Bragg ceased to smile and his temper, always a treacherous thing, grew unstable. "Don't ask questions."

"So, then," said Lestrade coolly, "he's got it on you. You were all set for a scrap, and when you're set for a scrap it is something you've got to have right away. But he came along and you dropped it entirely."

Bragg's nostrils swelled wider and his face, in line and shadow, began to distill the basic cruelty within. "Never mind," he said in the briefest of tones.

"If he drives you out of the country, it would spoil the good thing we have now. Better leave him alone entirely."

"If I fight him I'll do the driving," said Bragg.

Lestrade shook his head. "You can't drive him anywhere. You ought to be able to whip him, but you can't drive him. In a brawl you might kill him. If you did, you couldn't stay here a minute. The whole camp would be after you. Maybe that's why you avoided the fight."

Bragg showed his irritation. "He made a fine play of it. He's got the camp thinkin' him the best rooster on the street." He stood still, unsettled and vindictive, as he reviewed the event. It was a thorn in him which gouged and festered. "I should have done it. Got to be done sometime."

"Why?" pressed Lestrade.

"Because. That's answer enough for you." Bragg pointed a finger at Lestrade. "You find out when Stuart is going to ship gold."

"I told you about the Portland trip. You had no luck at it. You never have luck when it's Stuart."

Bragg stared at Lestrade so steadily that the latter presently shrugged his shoulders and departed. He was always glad to have these meetings done with.

At the end of an hour Camrose was considerably ahead of the poker game; whereas before he had made up his mind to play only until he had recouped his losses and afterwards to abstain from gambling, he now forgot his fears and his self-lectures and once again planned on running his luck to the farthest point. Talk went on endlessly around him as men came in, drank, and departed. A quarrel sprang up and blew over. The smoke got thicker in the deadfall and the temperature rose until sweat shone like oil on all the surrounding faces. There was discussion to be heard concerning pockets and lodes and drifts, of Sterling's richness as against Coyote Creek, of a little nameless gulch west of the Applegate wherein somebody had discovered and lost gravel so rich it had a yellow cast in the sunlight. There was talk of women, of memorable drunken sprees, of food, of Indians, of fights and fighters. On that subject an argument presently rose concerning Stuart's skill as against Honey Bragg's brute power.

Camrose's luck had once more taken a turn downgrade and he was irritably intent on the game; even so, he listened to this talk.

"He backed off from the scrap, didn't he? He was afraid of Stuart."

"Ever see his arms when he ain't got a coat on? I seen him once when he put a sack around his fist and busted a piece of lumber six inches wide. I seen him break four of George Dyer's ribs. He ain't afraid. He don't need to be."

"Then why didn't he fight?"

It had begun as a private argument, but it soon became a subject of general argument, to be analyzed and guessed at, to be enlarged, to be magnified with stray suspicions. Bragg's fights were cited and his strength was recounted. Logan Stuart's height and weight were added to the record, and surmises made as to his quickness.

"No long-necked man can beat a short-necked man his size. Stuart would get his head torn off."

"I saw Stuart step around a balky horse once," said another. "He's fast. Bragg would rush him, but Stuart wouldn't be there. He'd weave and whirl."

One more man put in his contribution. "All you fellows are talkin' about Bragg bein' afraid. Maybe it's Stuart who's afraid. He didn't offer a fight."

Several voices came down on him at once. It sat ill with the men in the saloon to hear Stuart's courage questioned. "By God, what you think he stepped up to Bragg for? He opened the door and he left it open. Bragg never walked through it. You a friend of Bragg's?"

"I never said I was. I only asked a question."

"It was a damned-fool question."

"Makes no difference. He can't lick Bragg. Nobody can."

"You think so? About how much money you want to put up on it?"

"Well now, brother, if you're so proud of your money, you name the amount."

"A hundred will suit me."

"That's fine."

The two stepped to the bar with the crowd and called on Hobart to hold stakes. Hobart said: "All right. Let me get this. Johnny Ball bets Ira Mullins one hundred, even, that Stuart can't whip Bragg. Any time limit on this?"

"Let it ride. The fight's not far off."

"Suppose it comes out a draw?"

"A draw?" said the Bragg man. "Not a chance. If Stuart's on his feet when Bragg walks away I'll consider I lost."

There was, even in this crowd so partial to Stuart, considerable murmured assent to that conviction; the brutal record made by Bragg impressed all of them. Camrose, now steadily losing, got up from the table in bad temper and walked to the crowd.

"Just what makes you gentlemen so damned sure of a fight?" he demanded.

The saloonkeeper, Hobart, answered for the crowd. "Why, George, everybody knows there's got to be a fight."

"How do you know it?"

"Well, good God," said Hobart, "one's best man and one's second best — and it's got to be settled, ain't it?"

"Does it occur to any of you that you're pushing Stuart to a hell of a beating just to satisfy your curiosities?"

"Then he shouldn't of set himself up before Bragg in the first place," said Hobart.

"If you fellows are so dead set for a fight, why don't some of you have a go at Bragg? I'll lay an open bet there isn't a man in the house who can whip Bragg. Five hundred dollars on it. Let's see your sporting blood."

There were no takers and Hobart passed off the offer with a wave of his arm. "You're just standing on your sore corn, George. Stuart can handle himself."

"A very easy thing for you to say since it is not your skin. Want to bet five hundred Stuart will whip Bragg?"

Hobert looked momentarily thoughtful. "No," he said, "I wouldn't go that far. But you wouldn't bet against your friend, anyhow, George."

Camrose looked around the crowd, hating everybody in the room. He said with deliberate intent to throw a scare into them: "I think Bragg ought to know who is doing all this betting and talking. It might interest him."

He had not realized, until then, how oppressive a threat Bragg's name was. The two betters at once swung away, and the rest of the group immediately lost interest in the subject. He had some hard looks from the group, and Hobart said: "If you don't like this camp, why do you stay here?"

Camrose returned to the game, but it went no better. At midnight he placed an I.O.U. for five hundred dollars in the hands of Gordon Thackeray and left the deadfall. The wind, brushing his sweaty face, brought a sharp reaction of coldness and he walked toward the express office in blackest spirits. "I should have quit when I was ahead," he told himself.

6

New Cabin on the Rogue

Stuart reached Jacksonville with the pack train around noon of Saturday; at two o'clock he was once again riding the trail this time bound for the cabin raising down the Rogue. With him were Lucy and Camrose, both in the lightest of moods; and also with him were Vane Blazier and Mrs. Lestrade.

"Where's Jack?" asked Stuart.

"He's not been feeling well," said Mrs. Lestrade.

"Sorry to hear it," commented Stuart. Mrs. Lestrade looked at him with a moment's close interest. She was in a most attractive dress, its color brightening and heightening the charm of her face. She was a woman soft of manner, speech and gesture; in her own way she was as striking as Lucy Overmire, yet in every respect those inward qualities which reflected themselves through her features were more pliable than those of the other girl. She had not the definiteness of expression, the sense of robust emotions under discipline, the feeling of strong will. It was as though, loving warmth, she was numbed by coldness.

It was late in the afternoon when they reached the pile of rough lumber and logs which marked the future house of young Gray Bartlett and Liza Stone. Bartlett had picked a long narrow meadow which lay against the river and the river's willows; and being practical, he had also located himself beside the California trail, to combine farming with chance profits from accommodating travelers.

The settlers — there were a hundred of them — had come from thirty miles around, drawn not so much by the fact of a marriage as by the need they felt for an occasional cheerful gathering. Saddle horses and wagons stood idle in the meadow and men were already notching and setting up the log walls of the cabin while others, with saw and wedge and froe, were riving out the cedar shakes to be used on the roof. There was a lively argument going on between two men, concerning the advisability of slanting the window frames for better protection against Indian attack. Another crew had set about erecting the fireplace which, being a matter of some delicacy, had been put in the charge of the man who seemed to know most about the depth and width necessary to assure a proper "draw." "You got no draw," he said, "and you got no cabin. I wish I had some animal blood to mix with this clay." Slightly down the meadow, a separate group was throwing together a temporary lean-to to serve as a barn.

This was in effect a holiday effort of the neighbors, over which young Bartlett had no control. He had indeed put in a request that the cabin have only one door, but was overruled by older heads. "You want two doors, in case trouble comes." Young Bartlett said, "Well, all right," and offered no more suggestions. It was much the same with Liza Stone who sat prettily on the brown meadow grass while the neighbor ladies, walking around the interior of the cabin, much to the irritation of the builders, made plans as to the disposition of the furniture. Liza smilingly agreed to all their proposals; and to herself said: "I'll move it the way I want it when they're gone."

In the meadow a fine fire cheerfully burned while women bustled about making a community supper, and other ladies came up with their own particular specialties — pickled peaches, huckleberry pie, blackberry pie, cider, fresh butter molded in pretty patterns, homemade cheese, summer sausage, Indian relish, and cucumbers in cream and vinegar, and jellies and jams and fruit butters, all of these compounded out of old recipes brought from Vermont and New York, from Missouri and Kentucky.

Shortly before sunset the house was done and perspiring men came out with the heavy log ends with which they had beaten down the earth floor, which Liza Stone's mother had insisted on in preference to puncheons "because the earth is more healthy." The wedding gifts began to move in: a four-posted cherrywood bed which had traveled two thousand miles overland, homemade chairs and table, dishes and cooking utensils, a feather mattress and pillows and a patchwork spread, a barrel of sugar and a barrel of flour and sides of cured meat; and all the trinkets and objects of a home. The ladies made the last touches. A fire was lighted — the superintendent of the fireplace construction narrowly watching the smoke lift from the chimney — and the bed was made. A rug was laid down and a lamp placed on the table beside a Bible opened at the Psalms. The dishes were put in the cupboard and a brush broom tipped against the wall. A man drove up with a wagon and a team; in the wagon were a plow and a harrow. He got down and tied the team to the house door.

"Now," said Liza Stone's father, "let's have the wedding."

The minister stood bareheaded in the meadow, the two people came before him, and the crowd made a circle around. The sun dropped west and the hour of water-clear light was upon the land, with its fragrance and its stillness so complete that the minister's voice moved round and resonant all down the meadow. He married them and he pronounced his benediction, and then he put his Bible in his rear trouser pocket

and stood back while young Bartlett, considerably unstrung by his audience, accepted his wife
with a vigorous kiss. The new Mrs. Bartlett was
smilingly composed; she bent forward and kissed
the minister.

"Supper," called Liza Stone's father. "My
God, we got aplenty."

Stuart got his supper and walked over to
where the Dances had gathered on the grass.
Vane Blazier had previously joined this group,
and had taken his place beside Caroline. He had
been talking, but now he fell silent and seemed
ill at ease. Lucy and Camrose and Mrs. Lestrade
presently arrived. Johnny Steele walked past the
group and said "Hello, Logan," and went
quickly on. He was shaved and wore a white
shirt and a good black suit — and he looked
pretty substantial.

"I ain't had such a good time since I don't
know when," said Mrs. Dance. "Folks do get
awful alone-feelin'."

"It occurs to me," said Camrose, "that the
Bartlett couple are pretty much by themselves.
No neighbor closer than three miles, and the
reservation right across the river."

"There'll be too many neighbors inside of a
year," said Dance.

The fall day had been warm. Now coolness
flowed from the river as the shadows came; the
big fire was replenished and the flames grew
yellow against the forming darkness. With supper done, people sat lazy around the meadow,

their talk and their laughter freely running, and youngsters raced through the willows, all crying out.

"I must get that chow-chow recipe from Mrs. Bartlett," said Mrs. Dance in a dreaming voice.

Stuart stretched back on the grass, so turned that he saw Caroline's face, its youngness intermixed with its unplumbed maturity. She felt his glance and met it; she held his attention with as much deliberate intention as he had ever seen in her. It was as though she felt something deeply, and wished him to feel it as well; she was speaking to him in this way, saying those things she would never bring herself to say openly.

Camrose spoke in his idle, detached fashion. "The illusion of peace is upon us."

It was not the kind of talk, nor was he the kind of man, these people understood. His manner was not quite frank and plain enough for these direct settlers. Only Mrs. Lestrade seemed to be affected by his remark, her dark eyes turning on him and remaining a moment. Lucy's only answer to Camrose was a half smile; afterwards her attention traveled to Caroline and became thoughtful. Suddenly Dance let out a whoop and rose from the ground to shout: "Buck, where's your fiddle? Where's Simon to call for us? Come on now — come on! We got to dance off these provisions before we go home!"

The stars were brightly glinting in a sharp-black sky. Dance, still shouting, disappeared in the river's direction; he was gone a little while and then came laughing back toward the fire with a keg under his arm. He got a bucket and he poured the contents of the keg into the bucket, and walked into the house for a dipper. He came back with a second bucket and, with both buckets and the dippers, he made his rounds.

"Whisky or water? Can't dance without sweatin'. Whisky or water?"

The fiddler found himself a seat on the wagon standing near the house and tuned his instrument; the caller took his station and slapped both hands sharply together. "Partners form your sets! We got room for two sets at a time."

"Caroline," said Stuart and rose. He took her hands and brought her up. "It is time to be foolish."

She studied his face and weighed his words; her answering smile was uncertain and gently stirred by excitement. "I guess it is not so foolish, is it?"

All the group looked on, Mrs. Dance with her quietly anxious interest, Vane Blazier in dark resentment, Mrs. Lestrade whose mouth sweetened at what she saw, Camrose with his sudden knowing grin — and Lucy Overmire. Lucy's attention was closely on these two and her expresison was one which seemed to be half startled by what she saw here. Camrose turned to her: "Let's join them," and got to his feet.

Couples moved toward the fire as the caller sang out, "Form and balance all! Let 'er go Jed!" The fiddler sank his bow on the fiddle's strings and swung into a reel. The two sets formed — four couples to a set — near the fire. The caller's voice whipped them around; they stepped over the summer's slick grass, out and back. "Oh take your girls, your pretty little girls," suggested the caller while the onlooking spectators brought their palms together to beat out the music's rhythm. "Virginia is a grand old state. Come on boys, don't be late."

Somebody threw fresh wood on the fire and sparks flashed with white brilliance against the night; the sets turned and wheeled and the steady hand-claps made a hard pulse all through the night. The fiddler on the wagon seat drew out his bow upon the last note, and laughter boiled and new couples ran into the light to take their turn. The fiddler cried, "Where's that bucket, Dance?"

Suddenly a man spoke one sharp word which arrested all of them, which turned them around to see the six Rogue bucks standing beyond the fire, their naked upper bodies shining like dull copper.

A man trotted toward the wagons, clearly with the intent of getting his gun. Dance brusquely called at him. "No, Pete. No." Dance put down his buckets and faced the Indians, calling to them in their own blunt language; the motion of his arm drew them forward until they were well within the circle of light, all lean men with their ribs making rippled patterns against their skin, all with lank hair hanging down about their heads as a frame for their coarse and unsymmetrical faces. Light touched their eyes, vaguely flashing on those muddy surfaces, and their lips formed sharp downward curves. One of them pointed at the whisky bucket.

"No," said Dance.

That same one pointed to the new house and talked quickly, bitterly. When the Indian was done speaking, Dance stood still and a heavily strained silence fell, the settlers looking upon the six Rogues with their memories of past disasters and treacheries, of families lying butchered in remote cabins, and the sudden crack of guns out of ambush, and the wild whoop of attack. These were memories luridly alive; the six savages standing here personified the uncertainty and the never quite extinguished fear which hung over them.

Dance began to talk, using his hands to make smooth motions through the air; he was calm and easy about it and almost smiling, but positiveness went with his words. Meanwhile Logan Stuart had picked up a muslin sack from somebody's supper basket and now went around the grass, filling the sack with leftover food. He handed the sack to Dance and watched the wary eyes of the Rogues drop to it and steadily stay upon it. Dance said a last word and tossed the sack to the spokesman who, casting a last brightly intolerant glance around the crowd, stalked off with his people.

The fiddler said: "Let's go — let's go."

"We were careless," said Dance. "Where's my boys?"

His oldest son came trotting in from the dark like a lean hound. "We been watchin' 'em for half an hour," said the boy. "It's all right. They got no guns. There ain't any more around. We're watchin'."

"That's better," said Dance and was broadly pleased as he watched his son wheel away. Dance picked up his bucket and banged the dipper against it. "Water's all gone, but whisky's just as good for sweatin'!" The fiddler swung into a tune.

Caroline Dance, during this scene, had stood alone with unruffled interest. Coming back to her, Logan saw once more on her face the reflection of an inner hardihood, stronger than any other quality she possessed. The appearance of the Rogues had made her grave, but she had not known fear. Her glance came to him and her smile woke at his smile; and suddenly he took her arm and moved away with her into the shadows.

"Caroline," he said, "what were you thinking about?"

"It is such a nice house Liza and Gray have got. If it were my house, I'd have a storeroom added. A kitchen ought to be big."

It was the practical things which captured her mind; her thoughts were direct and simple ones. The fire was a bright cone in blackness and the music came out to them brisk and lifting, with the steady shouting of the settlers and the clapped-out rhythm of their hands moving through the dark. Fall's smell was a thick fragrance around them, rising from the lush earth, from the hills so darkly ridged beyond them, from the river — all this stirring Stuart's wonder. Around him was the timelessness of this universe — these wild odors which had been here since the beginning, this slight wind and those blackly suggested hills farther away; and the arch of the sky above. There was something in it for a man to understand; there were hints in it, and now and then a feeling came out of it to touch him and to set his mind alive. Something waited for him somewhere, but what it was he never could know; for when his thoughts moved close to the mystery, the mystery retreated and left him puzzled. Was a man for walking and riding, or was he for thinking? Was he meant to hope for what he could not have or was he meant quietly to work out his day?

"Logan," said Caroline, "you're not always so quiet."

It occurred to him then that he knew little about her, and that she knew little about him. Would he hurt her for not bringing more to her than he could, or would she know? It was not a question ever likely to be answered. "At this moment," he said, "I'm wondering if you like me well enough to make a marriage out of it."

Her answer had long been in her mind, ready for him if he ever asked for it. It came promptly to him now in a voice small enough, and yet cool enough — and quite certain. "Yes."

He kissed her, healthily and hard, and he felt her arms grow tight against his back. Afterwards she pulled her head down until her cheek was against his chest; she stayed that way a long moment, not speaking. The pressure of her arms remained until, made curious by her silence, he drew away. She lifted her face to him, with all its tremendous seriousness visible to him even in the darkness.

"I wish," she said, "nothing would ever change, that it would always stay the same — no more people or houses or new things. Everything just as now."

"Why?"

"Everything's good now. It could never be better."

"Don't you want a good road over the mountain, a nice town near by —"

She looked at him, smiling at her opinions. "I know it will change," she said. "But I can wish for it not to, can't I?"

The music began again and the figures of the dancers moved against the dull red cast of the dying fire. Caroline and Stuart walked slowly back to the little group lounging on the grass.

Mrs. Dance said, "Caroline, it is about time to pick up and go." But this wasn't on her mind as she eagerly read her daughter's face. Caroline saw the question. She said, "Yes," and quietly laughed.

Mrs. Dance got up with an excited gesture and gave Stuart an impulsive kiss. "You're a good man, Stuart. You've got a good girl."

Camrose, half asleep on the grass, rolled around and sat up. He said, curiously, "What is this?" Then he saw what it was and got to his feet and seized Stuart's hand. "Damned glad to hear of it." Mrs. Lestrade had risen, her face soft and stirred. People began to come up, catching the scent of news. Dance, made brashly cheerful by his bucket and dipper, sent a long halloo to the black sky.

Stuart watched people come to Caroline, watched Caroline meet them with her composure. She would already be thinking of the house and what the house should contain; she would be making her plans, quietly and with sureness, and placing the little objects about her which she treasured so much. He had not looked toward Lucy. He had kept his eyes from her. But he saw her now, standing before Caroline and speaking her words with care, with that grace upon her which she always possessed. "Caroline," she said, "I am so happy for you."

He saw Caroline's face grow firmer, he observed a shadowed wisdom come to it. Caroline was a woman at this moment, closely staring at another woman, and Caroline's words had reserve in them. "That's nice," she said. Lucy turned away, never looking at him.

People stirred around, catching up their possessions, and began to move out of the meadow. Stuart gave Caroline a hand to the seat of her father's wagon and stood with his hat removed while the wagon rolled into the night. Then he went to his own horse, and joined the Jacksonville party waiting for him. A small group of relatives tarried in front of the new cabin, and voices of the departing settlers came back through the night as they called out their last farewells.

Stuart joined Mrs. Lestrade and Lucy and Camrose, and found that Johnny Steele was returning with them. These five moved south without talk, until Stuart remembered Blazier.

"Where'd the youngster go?"

"He pulled out alone," said Camrose. "Don't you know why?" Camrose's voice was easy and laughing. "Lucy, tell our friend why."

Lucy was riding beside Camrose, with Stuart back of them. He saw Lucy's face turn toward Camrose and he saw its silhouette. He could not see more and he could make nothing of her tone, which was plain and colorless. "Don't be unkind, George."

"What's unkind?" asked Camrose jovially. "You broke Blazier's heart, Logan. He thought Caroline was his girl."

Lucy's voice sharpened: "Let it be," and

114

when Camrose, still enjoying his own cleverness, started to speak again, she cut him off with a still more abrupt manner. "Let it be."

"What have I said?" asked Camrose with some surprise. Then Mrs. Lestrade, sensing what Camrose did not, began to speak softly of other things.

Stuart rode without talk and was alone with himself. A thin moon lay askew in the low south and the river's surface near by was a dull silver ribbon freckled with the shadows of its willows. A coyote sounded in the hills and a quiet wind blew. He thought of many unrelated things, without much interest, without buoyancy.

Nor did Lucy speak again during the trip. She was asking herself — in so insistent a way that she even feared Camrose might catch the current of her thoughts, "Why — why?" This night had done what Stuart's kiss had not done; it had revealed something within her which she had suspected and had not wanted to know. But it was too late an answer. Her own original error could have been mended, had she been sure it was an error; now it could not, for it was no longer her error to mend. And again she asked herself: "Why — why did he? Why should he? It isn't what he thinks it is. We are both fools, and we are both wrong."

7

Blood Lust

Finished with his morning inspection of the ledgers, Stuart got to thinking of the coming winter, and of the spring to follow, and of the years beyond. Each new cabin — such as young Gray Bartlett's — was a dot on the land's former emptiness. Wherever those dots began to cluster, a settlement was taking shape; some would grow and some would die, and it was never clear which would survive. Rich little valleys lay untouched until a venturesome family, risking the Rogues, moved in. Then another equally venturesome man erected a gristmill and a community was born. It was a guessing game and this was the fun of it — the guessing and the planning and the riding; afterward it was Clenchfield's job to count the shelves and add up the bills. But Clenchfield was in one particular completely right. Stuart & Company had grown so fast that it had no fat on its bones; if it were to grow farther it would need some kind of money in addition to that which it had

116

in the till.

Clenchfield had steadily argued against venturing; all his words were colored by the conviction that a man who dared too much inevitably met disaster. But Clenchfield was from the Old World — and the Old World had trained its children not to dare beyond their proper place. Clenchfield did not understand that America was all motion and change, that failure was never permanent unless a man deliberately made it so, that disaster was something to meet and forget and walk away from. America had no limits except those a man placed upon himself. The yesterdays Clenchfield loved did not exist here at all. The todays Clenchfield labored so hard to keep balanced and exact would soon be dead tomorrows. When a man tied himself to a piece of time, that piece of time, always moving backward into the mists, took him with it until both the man and the piece of time were dead and forgotten.

But Clenchfield was right in saying that Stuart & Company needed more money. Its growth perpetually starved it; what it needed was a substantial line of credit from a banking house, and there was none nearer than San Francisco. It was, Stuart thought, about time to go south and secure some kind of commitment from a financial institution like Crawford & Company.

Neil Howison, stepping into the store, found him thus plunged in contemplation, with a cold pipe clenched between his heavy teeth. "What's up?" said Howison.

Stuart leaned back and lighted his pipe. "Just figuring."

"You're always figuring. Ever get anything settled for good?"

"Never try."

"Logan, I have made a disagreeable discovery. I laid my trap and caught something. Bill Brown was held up again in the mountains."

"You've got it pinned down? No mistake?"

"Only one man knew about it," said Howison. "I hate to think of him as a crook. I've played a lot of poker at his table. I've drunk a lot of his liquor. Whom can I depend on? Doesn't friendship mean anything? Is everything rotten in this world?"

"You have made a painful discovery," said Stuart. "You will make more."

"A common road agent. A thief. A night rider. Giving me a smile and meaning nothing by it. It makes me sick."

"The gentleman does not do his own dirty work," said Stuart. "Bragg's in it, too."

"If you knew all this, why have you been playing poker in Lestrade's house?"

"So that I could draw my conclusions about him."

It rather nettled Howison to think that he had been walking through situations without being aware of them. "How much do you know? What do you know about Bragg?"

"We all know about Bragg."

"Not enough to make him back down from a fight as you did," pointed out Howison. "You know something else that's got him worried." He waited for Stuart to shed light on the subject. When it did not come he spoke again. "Bragg will not be satisfied to have you running around with information that might cause him trouble."

"Maybe you have noticed," said Stuart, "I usually have a gun when I meet him."

"If he wants to kill you badly enough he can always find ways of doing it. You're in a poor situation."

"Say nothing about it," said Stuart.

"We'd better tell Camrose to quit playing cards at Lestrade's."

"Let him find out for himself. He wouldn't believe us."

Stuart started to speak further, and forbore. Howison noticed this and his thoughts briskly rummaged the relationships between the various members of this group. Then he thought of Marta Lestrade and he recalled the way George Camrose occasionally watched her. Here was something else he had in his innocence over-looked. He was about to mention it when he checked himself with a definite feeling of em-barrassment. The ground got thinner and thinner under him as he recalled the friendship of Stuart and Camrose, and Camrose's engagement to Lucy — and here another possibility began to uncover itself — Stuart's friendship for Lucy. Stuart's eyes were closely scanning him so that

Howison had the feeling that Stuart followed his reasoning. The big man's face was barren, and that in itself was a warning. Howison thought, "I've got to back out of this before we get worse ground." Then he said aloud: "Better tell George to quit playing poker. He lost a hell of a lot of money the other night at Hobart's. Thackeray's got his note for five hundred dollars."

"I didn't know that," said Stuart.

"For a man whose business is handling money, he's too careless."

Henry Clenchfield came in and Stuart surrendered the high stool to him. "No grubstakes so far this morning," said Stuart, and turned to the doorway. Sunlight ran fresh and fine through the town, flashing against window panes, cutting long, sharp shadows against the dust, and brightening the dust's velvet-gray carpet. Stuart tilted his hat against this sun, cast a glance down the street and presently wheeled back into the store. He lifted his revolver from the holster — kept on a peg near the doorway — snugged it in his waistband beneath his coat, and walked out again.

The scene arrested the attention of both Clenchfield and Howison. The latter immediately stepped through the doorway to have a look.

"What is it?" asked Clenchfield.

"Bragg," said Howison and stood watching the street.

Stuart moved east on the street, passing Ling Corson who was at the moment sweeping out his saloon; the outcoming air of the deadfall made a stagnant pool in the fresh smell of the day. Bragg was near the foot of the street and now walked forward at a rolling gait, his whole body made grotesquely formidable by the great breadth of his shoulders. His shirt collar lay open, exposing the dense hair which matted his chest. He kept his eyes on Stuart and he had pulled his lips away from his teeth in a kind of smile. He stopped at a distance of ten feet. He said, "Hello," and his eyes ran up and down Stuart's shape with a close attention. "You're up early."

"What's on your mind, Honey?"

Honey Bragg gave out his short half laugh and wrinkles sprang around his temple corners as his eyes grew narrow. He was sly and unpredictable and his impulses might carry him in any direction, and these impulses were working on him now, behind the spurious humor. Stuart saw them shuttle back and forth on the man's face and make faint changes on the fleshy lips. Then Bragg lowered his cropped bullet head and momentarily stared at the ground. Wind ran strongly in and out of him and the muscles of his arms stirred beneath the flimsy shirt. Stuart noticed the black tufts of hair growing above the man's wrist bones. Then Bragg's head lifted swiftly to show the heat running through him, urging him, making him restless. Brutality throbbed in the man — and that too was a sign on his face. Almost anything would make him jump into a fight, Stuart guessed.

"Let's have a drink," suggested Bragg.

"Too early," said Stuart.

"Well," said Bragg, "I'm thirsty, early or not." But he remained still, half inclined to fight, half inclined to be cautious. Stuart reached into his pocket and got out his pipe and tobacco. He filled the pipe and lighted it, and felt the steady, strong beat of his heart; it was a sound back of his ears and a steady drumming in the middle of his belly. Honey Bragg's stare was a continuing thing, the laughter abating, the pressure increasing. Only a small thread of caution restrained the man, and now he beat at Stuart with his eyes, watching for weakness that would set him into motion.

Logan took a long drag on his pipe and removed it. He tapped out the ashes and put the pipe in his pocket. He had never liked pressure from any man; the push of a man's hand, the sound of an ill-meant word, the sight of hostile eyes — these things were quick to rake him. He drew his teeth hard against his lips and let Bragg see how things stood with him. Yet it occurred to him that he was holding himself in more carefully than of an earlier day. When he had been younger he would have spoken out at once. He said, "Am I getting old, or am I afraid of this man?"

Bragg let go with his brief laugh. He said, "Well, a drink's a drink," and moved around Stuart.

Stuart continued to the foot of the street, observing that men had appeared from the town's houses to witness this scene. Trouble was an odor that passed through any kind of wall and shook men alive, swaying the educated and the ignorant alike — for all men worshipped strength, even the gentle minister who thought of righteousness as a sword to slay evil.

He came to the long shed which was his mule barn and storehouse and found Vane Blazier mending harness. The boy heard him but held his head down as he worked. "Vane," said Stuart, "you'll pull out for Salem in the morning with thirty packs. Henry McLane has got a consignment there waiting for us."

"All right," said Blazier.

Stuart walked through the shed, appraising the piled-up goods; some of this stuff would be all right when rain and snow came, but the rest of it needed to be put into the store for protection. He said, "Hitch up the wagon," and he thought to himself, "I'll have to keep Vane under sight today. Bragg may try to break him up."

Presently Blazier backed the wagon into the shed and the two of them fell to work loading and carting merchandise to the store, and unloading. The town came alive and disturbed dust trembled in the full sunlight. On the second trip to the shed Stuart peeled off his coat and laid his revolver aside, drawing Blazier's first direct glance. Blazier asked: "Bragg in town?"

"Yes," said Stuart.

"Don't buy any trouble on my account," said Blazier. He spoke it in a voice which contained a small quality of offended pride. Stuart straightened from his work.

"This is a matter which started before you came into it at all."

"I can fight my own battles," insisted Blazier. He had a chip on his shoulder; he was a young man thrown off his balance by ideas that wouldn't let him alone.

"Vane," Stuart said, "if you've got something to talk out, let it rip. You've been making a speech to yourself all morning."

Blazier threw Stuart a tough stare. "I can tell you this. She don't like towns. She don't like big things. She don't like movin' around or changin'. You'll run her from pillar to post. I don't like it."

"It was her choice," pointed out Stuart, gently.

"It ain't right," said Blazier. "You're not the man for her. You'll make her miserable. You don't look at her the way I do." He stopped himself quite suddenly and walked from the shed.

Stuart sat silent on a box of goods. "That boy," he thought, "loves her. Yet that's not the answer, for if she had felt the same way toward

124

him she would have taken him, not me." It was a queer business — this confused wandering of people towards things they wanted and could not have, this waste of hope, this silent resignation to less than they wished. Nobody truly knew anybody else. It was a world wherein people walked with their desires and seldom attained them. But it was all in silence, held away; and men walked soberly by other men, concealing themselves; or laughed together, and held away their real thoughts.

Vane Blazier returned to the shed, and made a brief apology. "I had no right to mix in your personal affairs."

Stuart said, "I am sorry the way it turned out for you." He stood up and laid a hand on the boy's shoulder.

"I'll have to swallow my medicine with less fuss," said Blazier.

"Well, let's load boxes."

Joe Harms crouched on his heels at the base of Stuart's store wall, half asleep under the sun, when Stuart came up with the next load. Out of this motionless posture his warning softly emerged: —

"Bragg's up at Stutchell's deadfall."

The town had begun to fill up; the word was out, the word was traveling. Making his back-and-forth trips, Stuart watched the audience grow and discreetly station itself at doorway, in deadfall, and along the shaded building walls. Joe Harms, never changing his position, issued his reports as Stuart came by.

"He went toward the creek, back of Howison's."

Stuart cooked his noon meal and afterwards lay on a row of boxes in the store's main room with a cigar, making the most of the hour. Clenchfield said: "The lads are bettin'."

"Where are the odds?"

"Against you," said Clenchfield. "Don't let him bruise you. He'll get your eyes if he can. You remember Paul Gerritse, with nothin' in his sockets but tears? Kill him and be done with it."

Clenchfield was old and mild, yet here he was with first instincts growling through him. Stuart watched his clerk and marveled at that rejuvenation of a dry husk. Some things were deeper than learning, some things broke the flimsy bindings of civilized conduct. This was one of those things, and love of a woman was another. What did it prove? A man was a mysterious thing, knowing himself no better than he knew others; a fugitive, a shadow, a being that knew greatness but made itself little out of fear; man was a seed caressed by the sun and rain. Man was anything he wanted to be. The winds at night whispered his destiny to him and the sky beckoned him and all things in nature conspired to make him big; but he would not be big. Stuart lay quietly back, the taste of the cigar and the smell of the cigar good to him.

George Camrose came hurriedly into the store, troubled and with a thin sweat on his light face. "If Bragg had taken a drink and gone back to his ranch, it would have been all right. But he knows the crowd is watching him. He knows he can't back down the second time."

"Henry," said Stuart, "go hunt up Blazier. I want him out of Bragg's way."

Camrose said: "You'll have to stop him with a gun. You can't match him with your fists."

"He knows that, too," said Stuart. "I can't use my gun if he has none. And he'll not have one."

"Here's the town pushing it on. By God, I'm ashamed of the human race!"

"It's better than that," said Stuart, carefully putting his words together. "They've seen Bragg win his fights too long. It's made them doubt there is such a thing as justice. They've got to know if there is such a thing."

"So they're willing to see you cut to ribbons. Is that justice?"

"They'd rather see me cut up than see the idea lost," said Stuart. He rose, watching Clenchfield pass out through the door to the street. "George," he said, "how can you afford to lose five hundred dollars?"

Camrose stared at him with a moment's embarrassment. Then it passed away, leaving him watchful. "If I couldn't afford to lose it, I wouldn't be playing, would I?"

"You can't afford it if you give out I.O.U.'s."

Camrose displayed a touchy temper. "I wish this town would keep out of my business. It is a damned whispering gallery."

"Exactly so," said Stuart. "A lot of whispers can feed on five hundred dollars. Jacksonville is wondering about a man in your position losing at poker. You've got to watch yourself."

"Who spoke to you about it?" demanded Camrose, obviously touched on a tender spot. Stuart, watching Camrose, saw him throw up his guard; he saw a faint pulse of apprehension. George, he thought to himself, had the thing on his mind, for he added: "I've got a right to know."

"There are too many men thinking it's queer," said Stuart bluntly.

"Do you think it?"

"Yes," said Stuart.

He saw Camrose balance between anger and injured feeling; then he watched this old friend inwardly shrink, and at that instant Stuart knew more than he cared to know.

"Did it ever occur to you," said Camrose, "that I've played a lot of poker, and may have built up a stake?"

"Your luck around this camp," said Stuart, "has been bad. Everybody knows it."

A slack and sallow expression showed on Camrose's light features, as though he had been struck in the stomach. "Is it being said I've borrowed the money from the safe?"

Stuart said with a deliberate severity: "You

128

had no other place to get it. How much are you shy on your books?"

"If you think that about me —"

Lucy Overmire came into the store. She said "Gentlemen," in a light voice and smiled at them. She was quick to observe the preoccupation on Camrose's face. "Am I interrupting something?" she asked.

"No," said Stuart.

"This isn't Saturday is it? The town seems full of men."

"I guess they all got lazy at once."

Johnny Steele stepped into the store. He said, "Logan, he's —" Then, seeing Lucy, he ceased to talk. The girl was now definitely aware of the unusual atmosphere; she ceased to smile. "Is it Honey Bragg?"

"Where is he now, Johnny?" asked Camrose.

"At the foot of the street, leaning against the corner of your place." Johnny Steele looked long and questioningly at Stuart. "Everybody's expectin' you out there." He waited a moment and added in a sharper voice: "You're goin' out there ain't you?"

"You got a bet on this, Johnny?" asked Stuart.

"Well, yes, a small one."

"Which way?"

"Why damn you, Logan, which way you think I'd bet?"

"Then I suppose I'd better go win it for you," said Stuart. Camrose grumbled under his breath and walked from the room, with Johnny Steele following. Stuart rose from the packing box. His cigar had burned down to a stub and now he gave it a regretful glance and dropped it on the floor; he put his shoe on it and looked over to Lucy. He smiled slightly at her.

"Why can't they let you alone?" she demanded. "It's cruel."

"Temporary cruelty. It will pass. That's better than things which stick on and never quit hurting."

"Are you trying to tell me something?"

"It was just words," he said.

"You don't just talk words." It was the first time since the night of the cabin raising she had looked at him with the old familiar interest. That night had done away with an expression in her eyes and it had taken a warmth out of her voice, as he had wished. Even so, this moment brought some of that back and revived in him the same sudden physical shock. He had never been ashamed of that before; now, engaged to another woman, he was.

"I wish you'd tell me what you have in your mind," she said.

He saw Johnny Steele at the doorway, anxiously looking in. Johnny expected something of him — as all this town did — and his slowness disturbed Johnny and the town. "Lucy," he said, "stay in here," and walked to the door.

Johnny Steele said, "He went back to

Stutchell's."

The sun was on the western side, throwing Stuart's shadow before him as he walked toward the foot of the street; heat warmed the back of his neck and the rich odor of dust was in his nostrils. He passed Joe Harms and the dry little man stared at him and the man's lips moved, saying something without force enough to make it heard. Behind Stuart, at some distance, a man's words were quite audible in the stillness. "He's goin' into Stutchell's." Swinging into the place, it occurred to him the town would be disappointed if this fight would finish and end where it could not be seen.

The deadfall was a single-story log building thirty feet long by fifteen wide — the roughest kind of place, cluttered by chairs along the walls, a table in the center of the room and a bar across one end. Stutchell was behind the bar and Honey Bragg stood against it. He was half turned and therefore saw Stuart at once; his fleshy mouth stirred slightly and a muscular reaction rippled along his body, stiffening his shoulder. There was a bottle and glass in front of Honey Bragg but it didn't appear to Stuart that the man had been drinking very heavily during his six hours in town.

Stuart spoke to Stutchell. "Put out a bottle for me, Harry — a full one." Stutchell's breath ran short and fast and fear made him pallid as he placed the bottle on the bar. Stuart was sorry for the man and he said: "You want to stay in

131

here and watch this, Harry?" Stutchell said nothing.

During this short time Bragg had kept his round head half lowered and his glance on Stuart. A half smile remained, lips drawn back from his massive yellowed teeth; there seemed to be some kind of amusement in the smile, Stuart thought. But something else was in the smile as well — a saturnine pleasure, a savage stain of expectancy. He spoke briefly to Stuart.

"I've got no gun. Put yours away."

"I'll keep it where it is."

Honey Bragg dropped his arm from the bar and made the slightest turn. The strange, dancing smile was a bright screen covering the lightless evil in him. He said, "Let's keep this thing a fair fight. I've got nothing against you. It's the boys that want the fun. Let's give 'em a good fight, no hard feelings about it."

"What the hell are you lying for, Honey?"

"What have you got against me?" asked Honey Bragg, smooth and inquisitive. "I blow off steam. I'm handy with my fists. But what have you got against me?"

"You'd like to know exactly how much I know, wouldn't you? It's been on your mind a long while. You'd feel a lot easier if you could find out."

Honey Bragg's laugh ran short through the room. "Ah, you're talking riddles to me, Logan." Then his head dropped until his glance was half screened by his eyebrows, and all the good nature left him. "What's in your mind?"

"The picture of a tree, you swinging from it."

It seemed enough to verify the man's suspicions. He drew a gusty breath and let it fall; he stood dark and brutal before Stuart. "You're making a mistake keepin' that gun on you. I've got to figure you're going to use it. So I guess I have got to break your neck before you get the chance. Stutchell, remember I warned him. You hear, Stutchell?"

Stutchell murmured with a wholly frightened voice: "I hear."

"Look at Stutchell," said Honey Bragg. "Look at him, Logan."

Stuart's hands rested on the bar idly, close by the bottle he had ordered. He turned his head half toward Stutchell, and then swung it back in time to see Honey Bragg gather his thick body together and jump forward. It was what Stuart had guessed the man would do — and what he had ordered the bottle for. His hand swept up the bottle by the neck. He stepped back to avoid Honey Bragg's outstretching arms; he aimed the bottle at Bragg's round head and brought it down, lifting on his toes to get force into the blow. Launched in full attack, Bragg could do no better than jerk his head slightly aside. The bottle struck him slantingly above the ear and broke, and the ragged remnant scraped down the side of his face, leaving its deep red track.

The steam went out of Bragg. He wheeled and seized the bar to support himself; his mouth opened from the shock and he clung to the bar, his face dull and his hand dropped. Stuart saw the man's ear half torn away, hanging loosely down. Suddenly Stutchell was yelling at the top of his voice: —

"You got him — you got him! Kill him now!" Jacksonville's citizens were crowded at the door, staring in, and boots stumbled around the deadfall as men sought to station themselves at the windows for a fair view.

Stuart wheeled about and seized a chair. He raised it over his head, watching Honey Bragg who should have been unconscious on the floor but was not. This man was a burly brute with bones like those of a grizzly, with an oxlike vitality. All his victories came from this thick-shield of bone and muscle, this insensitivity to injury. Bragg cursed as he came around; he was alive and stung and dangerous as he pushed his legs apart. He saw the chair come at him and raised his hands against it. The legs of the chair struck him first and broke away; he went backward, he swayed and brought his arms against his head. Stuart had the remains of the chair in his hands — back and seat — and he swung once more and caught Bragg on the head with the edge of the seat. The sound of that blow went out from the deadfall, clear enough to make men yell at it.

"You got him!" cried Stutchell. "Beat his

134

brains out! Poke his eyes out!"

Bragg said in a growling voice, "The hell I'm out. Stutchell, I'll kill you." He turned his back to Stuart deliberately and pulled his head down, making a shield of his back; he put pressure on the bar with his arms and side-stepped to the corner and he came around with a hard, grunting sound, propped against the wall and waiting for his legs to hold him. Blood ran rich-red down his cheek and his curly hair was wet with it; he shook his head steadily to clear wool out of his brain, and through this wool he peered patiently and blackly at Stuart. He was murmuring in a coarse voice, in a voice made terrible by its conviction, by its unchangeable intent. "That's all right, Logan. That's all right. I'll get you in a minute. I'll put my arms around you and I'll break your back. That's all right."

Stuart struck him again with the chair seat. Bragg took the blow on a raised arm but the force of it sank him to the floor. The chair fell apart in Stuart's hands and he walked away and got another and came back, watching Bragg turn and seize the edge of the bar with his hands and crawl erect. Suddenly Bragg whirled and made an impetuous rush at Stuart. Stuart took a rapid step aside and plunged one leg of the chair into Bragg's mouth, crushing the man's lips and flinging him back upon the bar. Bragg's vitality was a frightening thing; he had suffered badly, he had taken blows which would have killed a frailer man, and yet he remained erect, largely past the power of deliberate thought but sustained by a sheer animal force. He held his odd grinding tone: "That's all right, Logan. I'll get you in a minute. I am goin' to get you on the floor and step on your guts and break 'em. That's all right, Logan." He seemed to be fighting off a drowsiness. Logan lifted the chair and measured Bragg with the coolest kind of attention; he feinted with the chair and he saw Bragg's arm swing up in defense, and then he brought the chair swinging down on that arm. He heard the bone snap and he saw the chair break; he threw the chair aside. "Now we can close in, Honey."

Bragg stared at his crippled arm. He moved his arm at shoulder and elbow; he brought it up and saw the bend it made below the elbow. He let it fall again and studied it as though he were a distant spectator to something that puzzled him. He brought his good hand slowly across the wreckage of his face. "You think I won't do it, Logan?" he asked, and pushed himself away from the bar, his good arm lifted.

This man was a bull, primitive and unchanging; his mind was nothing but a pulpy core surrounding a single hunger — to attack, to destroy. The fear of pain was not in him or, if it was, the need to smash was so great that it destroyed pain. He struck out with his good arm, strange sounds clogging his throat. Stuart met his attack directly parrying the blow and stepping in for a hard punch to Bragg's stomach.

Dull a man as he was, Bragg had a fighting slyness; he had not put all his weight into the attack and now he wheeled and struck again, catching Stuart flush on the mouth with his fist.

It was a disaster running down Stuart's spine. It seemed to crack his neck and it sent a roar through his head. His eyes lost focus, so that for a little while he could not see Bragg and therefore he moved slowly away, with the smell of blood strong in his nostrils. Bragg sensed his chance and rushed forward, striking again. He missed a direct blow, came hard against Stuart and rammed his knee into Stuart's belly. At this close distance, Stuart flung an upward punch at Bragg's solid chin; he lifted himself to get weight into the blow and he felt the shock register on the nerves of his arm. Bragg's head tilted back; he began moving away, weaving as he moved, waving his heavy arm before him like a stick. Stuart went at him, driving the arm down. He hit Bragg in the flank, he struck under the burly man's heart, he drove a blow hard into the pit of Bragg's stomach and saw the man's face grow loose. Bragg, in retreating, at last got his back to the bar and once more his slyness came to his rescue. Sliding aside along the bar, he raised a foot and plunged it into the lower part of Stuart's belly.

It sent Stuart backward off balance. He struck the small table in the center of the room, and fell with the table dropping on him. He rolled again, knowing himself in great danger, and he saw Bragg rush to the nearest wall and seize up a chair with his one good arm. Bragg yelled, "By God, I got you!" Bragg stumbled forward and tried to kick the obstructing table aside. He failed and, yelling again, he threw the chair with all the strength left in him.

Stuart rolled, hearing the chair smash beside him. He kept rolling and sprang up, and wheeled away as Bragg charged him. Bragg struck the saloon's end wall and slowly came around. Stuart was in the middle of the room waiting for him.

"Time to put out the lights, Honey," he said, and lifted another chair.

Stutchell stood pale and numb in a corner, cringing against the logs. Honey Bragg suddenly became aware of his presence and turned and struck him to the floor with one blow. Bragg kicked at him and drew Stutchell's scream; at this moment Stuart brought the chair fairly down on Bragg's head and shoulders and stunned him. With the chair jammed over his head, Bragg dropped and slowly tried to free himself. His breathing had grown hoarse and heavy and he kept murmuring to himself as he worked. Finally he got the chair away from him and he sat on the floor, staring out of eyes that were filmed with blood; he tried to clear them with his hand. His vision remained bad and then he began to groan and to talk to himself as he turned to the wall and rose. He faced the wall, scarcely knowing it; he cocked his fist and struck the wall.

"Not there," said Logan.

"Come up to me," said Bragg, turning about. "Come up and make it even. Come on."

Stuart walked over the room, watching Bragg's arm draw back. He feinted at Bragg and drew a last blow from the man; then he stepped in and beat Bragg on the side of the face, swinging this bloody, indestructible hulk slowly around. Bragg touched the wall again and bent his head against it, wholly exhausted and wholly helpless.

"Come around, Honey," said Stuart. "I haven't started working on your eyes yet."

Bragg wheeled to the door and found it blocked by Jacksonville's men. He said in a heavy voice, "Get out of my way." The crowd backed off from it to give Bragg all the clearance he wanted. "Damn dogs," he said. "Damn yellow dogs." He had his head down and so saw the prone Stutchell. He kicked Stutchell again and left the deadfall.

Stuart followed him down the narrow lane of miners as the latter moved at a drunken, ambling pace toward his horse near Howison's hay barn. Once Bragg turned about and for a moment it appeared that he intended making another stand, but he shook his head and swung off when Stuart closed on him; and continued to his horse. He untied the reins and put a foot in the saddle; he gripped the pommel with his good arm and made two false tries before he reached the saddle; and here he sat, drenched in his own blood, with his ear flapping against his cheek and the broken aperture of his mouth revealed as he sucked hungrily at the warm afternoon air. He looked down at Stuart with his hurts beginning to show on him, with his agony starting; even so, the primitive cunning still pulsed in his mind and treachery still lived in him. Stuart drew his gun and pointed it at Bragg.

"Don't try to run me down."

Bragg let the half-lifted reins go loose. "You know what I'm going to do?"

"I know what you'll try, soon as you're able."

"I'll close your mouth for good," said Bragg in a dead soft voice. "I'll catch you. There's a thousand places to catch you. I'll catch you."

"By the bend of the river, Honey?"

Bragg gave him a steady stare. "That might be a good place," he said, and turned the horse, walking it slowly from town with his broken arm swinging at his side.

Weariness deadened Stuart as he walked up the street. The nerves of his arms began to ache violently and his mouth hurt him. Part of the crowd began to move with him toward the store and voices came at him with hearty approval. A man slapped him on the back and he looked up to see Johnny Steele talking. "It was good — it was good," said Johnny. "Nothing like it

140

ever was or ever will be."

"That's fine, Johnny," said Stuart. "Now you can collect your bet."

Steele understood him; he felt the force of the remark and he went silently along a little distance thinking about it. At last he lifted his head and made his defense, which in a way was a defense for the camp as well. "Maybe it seems hard to you," said Steele, "but we've seen the day when Bragg was licked. It wasn't a day we thought we'd ever see. That's something, isn't it?"

"I guess that's something, Johnny," agreed Stuart and passed into the store. Lucy was at the doorway, turned stiff by her watching; her face was harsh and the harshness was slow to dissolve as she looked at him. He went by her, to the rear room; he sat down on the edge of his bed and reached for his pipe. He filled and lighted it and took a drag of smoke and pulled it away with a sudden distaste. The smoke burned in the cuts of his lips. He bent over and propped his head on his hands and stared at the floor, bracing himself against the waves of pain which came in a steady tide. He found himself tensing up as they arrived, and relaxing momentarily when they went away. He had taken more blows than he thought — and all of them were harsh ones; he would have been a mass of beaten pulp had he not crippled Bragg at the beginning. He felt low and dispirited: he felt disgusted at himself, he felt dirty. "I'm old enough not to roll in the dust like a mongrel," he thought.

Lucy came quietly into the room. She put her hand under his chin and drew it up until she had a full view of his face and he saw her eyes travel over his face carefully. She still had that frozen, repressed expression. "You'll have to go to Dr. Balance." Suddenly she sat down beside him on the bed and put an arm around him, drawing his head against her shoulder. "Logan," she said, "Oh, Logan!"

"Never mind," he said. "It will pass."

"He'll be at you again. Why didn't you kill him?"

Camrose shouted across the length of the store and came rapidly on. He stopped at the room's doorway and observed the scene. He said quickly: "How bad is it?"

"Not bad enough to die," said Stuart.

"Bad enough," said Lucy, and held her arm in its place. She looked up at Camrose. "Is the town happy? Are you all pleased?"

"Why, Lucy," said Camrose, "I never pushed this thing."

Lucy rose and moved to the door. "You ought to heat up a tub of good hot water and sit in for an hour. It will take the soreness from your body. George, start up a fire. Bring him up to the house when he's through."

Camrose said, "All right," and then thought of something else. "What was that you said to Bragg about the bend of the Rogue? If you

142

know something, you'd better turn it over to somebody before you're shot off your horse."

Lucy left them. Stuart listened to her steps cross the floor, and then he raised his head and said, "Shut the door, George." Camrose turned and gave the door a push.

"Now," said Stuart, "how much have you borrowed from the safe?"

The question caught Camrose off guard. He met Stuart's dark stare with a sudden irritation. "That's my business."

"No, it is not. It is the business of the company whose money you've borrowed. It is also the business of the girl you propose to marry. You have got a habit of fooling yourself."

"Nothing's out of the way," said Camrose stubbornly. "Everything's all right."

Stuart rose and felt the fresh leap of pain in his body; it shortened his temper. "Nothing's all right. The money in that safe is trust money. You had no right to touch it. The moment you touch it, even if it is only for fifteen minutes, you've got yourself on the wrong track."

"Are you suggesting I'm crooked?" asked Camrose with growing antagonism.

"I'm saying it, not suggesting it. You have got to quit poker cold and you have got to quit wishing for easy money. If you do not, you'll wind up with an empty safe and a charge of embezzlement against you. Either you'll be in jail or you'll be a fugitive."

"Here, here," said Camrose, "I can't let that stand —"

Stuart brought the flat of his hand hard against Camrose's chest, knocking his friend against the closed door. "By God, you laugh at too many things, you take too many things easy. There's an end to that. You've got yourself half argued into stealing. That's plain enough, isn't it? Stop trying to excuse yourself."

"Is that all?" said Camrose in a cool, furious tone.

"You're always sliding away. You've always got an excuse, you've always got a smile or a shrug of your shoulder. You think you can tell this to Lucy and smile it away? You think she'll smile it away?"

Camrose moved to a window and put his back to Stuart. He kept his back stiff, making it express his outrage. "Logan," he said at last, over his shoulder, "how long have you known this about me?"

"Six months or better."

"You haven't got a high opinion of me, have you?"

"How much are you short?" said Stuart.

"Two thousand."

Stuart opened the door and walked into the storeroom. Clenchfield sat bowed over the high desk, making it quite obvious that he was busy with his own chores. Stuart said, "Give me two thousand, Henry," and he waited at the counter while Clenchfield counted it out. Stuart looked straight at Clenchfield and said, "A grub-stake, Henry."

"So it is," said Clenchfield and added nothing to that.

Stuart went back to the rear room with the gold in his pockets. He dumped the coins on the table. "That's my opinion of you, George."

He saw pride form its refusal in George Camrose's eyes; then he saw something get at that pride and bend it. He stood there, bound by friendship to this man, yet a spectator to the easy and plaint and half-cynical workings of Camrose's nature. He knew the smile so well when at last it came, charming and smooth in the way it washed everything away.

"All right, Stuart. You were always the Puritan. You don't understand the Cavalier."

"Speeches are no good. Stand up and do the right thing. You know what it is."

A few moments before it would have invoked George Camrose's anger; but now Camrose was in the full swing of his new mood. "I know," he said cheerfully. "I shall set it straight. There never was any evil in it, but I shall clear it up."

He put the money into his pockets, achieving a kind of disinterested air and thus making the gift less important than it was. "Now," he said, "you are going to tell me to play no more poker."

"That's right."

"I shall do it," said Camrose. "Though it will be a damned dull world."

145

"What's wrong with this world? It's big enough for you isn't it?"

"The voice of the Puritan again. Coming to the house for supper?"

"No."

"Lucy will give me hell," said Camrose and went away. He passed Clenchfield without giving the clerk a glance; he was acutely aware of the man's possible knowledge of him, but he walked straight on, got to the street and turned toward Hobart's deadfall, finding George Thackeray idle at a table.

"I'll take up that I.O.U. now," he said to Thackeray.

Thackeray thrust a hand into his pocket. "Flush tonight?"

"Flush enough."

"How about a little game?"

Camrose considered the matter, negligently accepting the note and tearing it across. "George," he said, "I like poker. I'd rather play a game of poker than eat. Yet in my job I'm supposed to be like Caesar's wife."

"What was that?"

"Above reproach — above suspicion."

"It's a free country," said Thackeray. "Man can do what he damned pleases."

"When a man handles money as a business, he's got to be careful."

"Suppose we play at my cabin — nothing said and everything quiet."

"That's better," said Camrose, and turned

from the deadfall. The weight was off his mind, and he felt entirely cheerful. Thackeray was disposed of and Stuart's loan would permit him to replace his borrowings from the safe. Then he thought: "If I get in that game tonight and a good hand comes up I ought to have enough cash in my pocket to push my luck. Six good hands in the course of an evening would set me up." So, with that decision made, he walked toward the Overmire house.

8

At the Creek

At ten o'clock that night George Camrose walked from Thackeray's cabin and felt the warm night's air to be quite cold against his face. He ran a hand along his forehead, squeezing away the oil-sweat, and he spoke to himself with a dull bitterness: "I'll never learn to let well enough alone." He had lost his cash, and Thackeray held his note for another thousand. All of them at the poker table had looked at him in a rather odd way when he rose to leave. They would be wondering how he could stand those losses, and they wouldn't keep it a matter of confidence forever. The camp would presently know the story; in due time Stuart would know it.

He walked into Hobart's deadfall and downed two substantial drinks of whisky; he heard a man call his name and turned to discover Mack McIver grinning at him — that same McIver who was supposed to be down the Applegate prospecting. He said, "Hello, Mack," and gave the man a smile, but a loose sensation rushed through him and he grew confused as he thought of McIver's gold poke lying half empty in the office safe.

"No luck," said McIver. "I just wore out my shoe leather. Let's have a drink."

"Thanks," said Camrose, "but I've got to go see Stuart."

McIver said, "Well, I'm going to get drunk. See you tomorrow."

Camrose walked into the soft night, remembering McIver's last phrase. He got out a handkerchief and scrubbed his forehead. He thought: "Does guilt show on a man's face, or is it something he always imagines? God damn Thackeray! How did the bets get so high so fast?" He saw Joe Harms seated in his cramped position before Howison's shed and passed the man without speaking and unlocked his office door. He barred the door behind him and cast a glance at the shutters. It had never been like this before — never this trapped sensation, this incoherent back-and-forth shuttling of his thoughts, this morbid self-condemnation, this physical sickness in his stomach.

He knew to an ounce how much he had taken from McIver's poke; yet he opened the safe and got out the poke and weighed it. Then he counted the company's gold coins stacked on the upper shelf. He closed the safe and stood back with both elbows hooked on the counter. "He'll be here first thing tomorrow for his poke. As for the gold coin, I've got a week or two before anything could happen." Then he was struck by the coincidence of two miners within the last few days coming to reclaim their gold dust. Was a grapevine rumor going through the camp about him?

He left the office, locking the door behind him, and turned toward the Lestrade cabin. He thought he heard some kind of noise to the rear and turned sharply about, but he discovered nothing in the black shadows. "I'm in a hell of a position," he told himself, and with all this on his mind he knocked at the Lestrade door and heard Marta's subdued voice invite him in.

She was in the rocking chair by the fire; she looked up at him with the usual engraved darkness on her face, the usual shadows in her eyes. Camrose closed the door and put his back to it. He said: "Where's Jack?"

"Riding," she said.

"Always riding," he commented. "Balance or Howison show up tonight?"

"No," she said. "How is Logan?"

"Battered."

"Somebody ought to shoot Bragg," she said with a lift of resentment in her voice.

He gave her a closer glance. "You like Logan pretty well. Wonderful thing to have people like you."

"Natural people are always liked," she said.

"We're all natural are we not? I'm natural, am I not?"

She turned the subject. "You look pale. Don't

you feel well?"

"Well enough," he said. But he thought to himself: "It shows on me," and the chill sensation went through him again.

She rose from the rocker and stood gracefully against the wall, and continued to observe him. He was aware of the blend of softness and hot desires in this woman, the emotions capable of so much violence and yet held under such rigid control.

"You seldom smile, Marta. Why not?"

"George, could I say something to you?"

He thought quickly, and with elation, "She's making the first advance," and he moved toward her. She shook her head at him. "Stay there. You've tried to read things in the way I've looked at you. The things you think you see," she said quietly, "are not there. You have got Lucy. What more could you want? Why should you try to be adventurous?"

"I need your friendship," he said quickly.

"That's not what you have been thinking," she said.

He showed color. "Have I been that crude?"

"You're greedy and you're unfaithful. Don't come here any more."

He said: "Are you afraid to have me near you?" He closed the distance and he got his arms around her. He felt her suddenly resist him, but he dropped his head and kissed her — and stepped back. Her expression hadn't changed, but her voice was hard.

"You're a fool."

"I think," he said resentfully, "you have used your eyes on me at times." Then he felt cold and desperate and trapped. "Marta, we've been friends a long while. Why should it change?"

"Balance and Neil and Logan have been friends also. But have you noted they don't come any more?"

Now he was alert and suspicious. "Why not?"

"Good night," she said, "and don't come again."

"Here," he began. "I'd like —"

He was stopped by the cold repulsion on her face. It astonished him that so much force of character could come from this softly-tempered woman. He had the feeling as he opened the door and looked back to her that he was involved in a mystery of which he knew little; and in this frame of mind he closed the door and walked quite slowly toward the center of the town.

She listened to his steps die away. Afterwards she turned to the fire and sat in the rocker, crouched forward in a strained and tense attitude and staring at the heart of the flame. "The story will be the same here as it has been elsewhere," she thought. "But at least Lucy won't be hurt."

Lestrade sat in the smoky light of Bragg's cabin and watched the bearlike man with an interest that had no sympathy in it. The other

152

three riders, all stray figures out of nowhere, stood by, likewise silent and curious and unmoved. Somewhere distant in Lestrade's mind was a keen side-thought concerning this. "Hell of a thing for a man to be so much of a savage that nobody gives a damn."

Bragg lay on the bed, full of pain. Balance had been here earlier, before Lestrade's arrival, to set the broken arm and to perform rude surgery on the cut ear; but there was nothing much to be done about the splintered front teeth or the torn lips. These had swollen, making his face incredibly ugly. He had taken a terrible beating but, after the manner of his kind of man, he was fortified now by a pride at his own endurance. "Can't kill a fellow like me," he murmured. Pain caused him to move his feet along the bed; it made him slow and thick-headed.

"I told you to keep away from him," said Lestrade. "Now you're laid up for God knows how long. It plays hell with our business." He had been cautious on previous occasions before Bragg's three followers; he seemed unconcerned now. "What was the remark he made about the river? He's got it on you, hasn't he?"

"What?" said Honey, his eyelids creeping together.

"Would it be that pair of fellows bound for California last winter? The two found dead in the creek willows?"

He watched Honey's face closely and witnessed the little changes of expression. He grinned at Bragg. "Once in a while you let your foot slip. You're smart enough up to a certain point. After that you're a damned bear running wild without brains. You'll be lucky if you don't get chased out of Jacksonville. Or hung."

Bragg softly and cautiously framed a single word on his lips. "Wait."

"You're thinking of Stuart," said Lestrade. "If you killed him, you'd have to run for it. This town likes him. They'd string you up in a hell of a hurry."

Honey shook his head. "It won't do. He knows more than I like."

Lestrade said: "What else does he know?"

Honey made a pointing motion to himself and then to Lestrade. The latter said with challenging tone: "About us? How would he know? And how do you know he does?"

"That draws you, don't it?" said Bragg. He was sharp enough to witness the changed manner it produced in Lestrade and he enjoyed what he saw. "Different now, ain't it?"

"You'd like to get me in deeper, wouldn't you Honey?"

"Oh, you're deep enough. High-tones like you make me laugh. I can take care of myself in trouble. Can you?"

"We'll both take care of ourselves," said Lestrade smoothly. "Let Stuart have his fun. We'll be doing business here for quite a while yet."

154

Bragg said: "Find out when he's going to take another load of dust to Portland."

Lestrade left the cabin, got on his horse and wound through the willows. Reaching the trail, he paused a moment to look back at Bragg's cabin lights, and then he moved on. But he had stopped long enough for a lone-watching man, crouched not ten feet way, to identify him. Johnny Steele, slowly grown suspicious of George Camrose, had come here to see if Camrose had secret connections with Bragg; and now he had discovered this other thing. He sat still, listening to Lestrade's horse drum away. "Why," he thought, "the man's a plain crook. That's why his wife was crying. She knows it." He turned it over and over in his mind. "Bragg and Lestrade. And maybe Camrose, too. Well, I'll find out."

Lestrade put up his horse and went into the cabin to find his wife before the fire.

"Anybody been here?"

"Camrose. I sent him away."

"You should be kind to our customers, Marta. He's been a good meal ticket." He grinned at her and moved to the wall cupboard for the whisky bottle. "Bragg took the worst beating I ever saw. He's badly cut up."

"Good," she said. "Good."

He gave her a side glance and drank the whisky in one long gulp. "It's odd that none of the other boys have been here for a week."

"Is it so odd?"

155

He straightened and gave her a penetrating glance; he stood still, with a thoughtfulness coming to him. "Where have I revealed myself, Marta?"

"People sense things like that. We'd better leave before they really know. I'd like to leave a few decent memories behind me."

"I thought it was my safety you were worrying about." He moved into the adjoining room, presently calling to her in his lightly skeptical way. "At times I have thought you might be fond of Camrose."

"He is a weak man," she said.

"Marta, is there any man in this town you look upon with desire?"

"Why do you ask me that?"

He came rapidly out of the other room and caught her arm and pulled her from the rocker. His face was rough with temper. "You didn't answer my question." He drew her forward and kissed her; then he stepped back to look upon the unyielding calm of her face.

"Even when you loved me," he said, "you also hated me. You can hurt a man merely by not speaking to him. I feel your judgment now. It is disillusioned, it is condemning. Would it be possible to change it — to start over again?"

"You could not change," she said.

"Am I as weak as Camrose — is that what you mean?"

"Let's not talk about it."

His one revealing moment passed on and he

156

pulled himself behind his covering skepticism. "I presume it is too late," he said quietly, and stood silent a long while, watching her and wondering about her. "Did you ever stop to think how close heaven is for all of us — and yet how far it is when we lift our hands to touch it?"

Camrose strolled up the street, noting that Joe Harms had at last abandoned the seat in front of Howison's stable. This was now near midnight, with the deadfalls still active; otherwise the lamps of the town had begun to wink out one by one, and miners were slowly walking toward their cabins and tents and brush shacks along the creek. There was a light in the rear of Logan Stuart's place, and Camrose stopped at the front of the store, with his problem going around and around in his head. The thing seemed to be turning him unreasonable; he kept jumping at the same blind barriers, running up the same alleys of hope and finding the same futile endings. How was he to make up his losses? How was he to take care of McIver's half-emptied gold poke? What was he to say to Logan Stuart when the latter discovered what had become of the loaned money?

He looked toward the Overmire house and observed a light still shining from the window. "If I had only played it safe when I had the chance." Now it was that he realized how dangerous a game he played — and the fatal consequences of that game; he passed a hand across his forehead and gave out a small, soft groan. "God, if I could just turn the page back!"

A party of miners came from Hobart's all drunk, and stood noisy and contentious in the street until at last one man pulled away and walked east toward Howison's. One of the others called after him. "Where you goin', Mack?"

It was McIver, ragged and round-shouldered against Hobart's lights. McIver barely was able to keep on his feet. He yelled: "I am goin' to hide in the brush before the Injuns jump this camp."

George Camrose's heart began to beat harder against his ribs as he watched McIver weave along the dust. The rest of the miners were loudly debating the wisdom of going after McIver; they were debating Indians. Then the group turned in the other direction and at last drifted into another deadfall. McIver was a shadow down by Howison's, still traveling on.

Camrose put a hand to the gun he always carried inside the trouser band, and a dizzy feeling came upon him and coldness filled his belly. He drew shorter and quicker breaths and he turned, stepping along the building walls in McIver's direction. Then he stopped and looked closely around the street, and suddenly moved between buildings to the rear of town and rapidly made his way to his own office. Here he came upon the dark street again, and heard McIver threshing around the brush, farther on. He heard McIver say to himself: "I'm too smart."

Camrose found himself walking fast on the balls of his feet; he found himself crouching and trying to make himself smaller. He kept looking around him, he kept listening. He drew his revolver as he got nearer McIver. Then he stopped and stared at the street behind him and he was saying to himself: "A cave-in, a bullet or an Indian will get him sooner or later. What's the difference how he dies?" Far away in his brain there was a protest and a warning; but by now the wave of desperateness had pushed him too far and he resumed his stalking.

He heard McIver's boots grind along the creek gravel and he saw McIver's shadow sink into the night; then he heard McIver making sucking sounds as the miner lay belly-flat and drank the creek water. Camrose quickly slid the revolver back under his trouser band and crossed the gravel strip with a catlike quickness. He made some sound as he came upon McIver. He dropped on McIver, plunging his knees into the man's back as the latter tried to turn and lift himself from the water; he flattened himself on McIver's violently agitated body and he laid his forearm on the back of the man's neck and forced his head down into the water and against the gravel. He fought against McIver's great muscular spasms and he felt them grow smaller;

he heard the strange frothy bubbling of water come up from McIver's mouth — that sound so grisly and unnatural that it sickened and weakened him. It wasn't long. Lying on top of McIver he presently felt all motion and life go out, and when he knew he had at last killed a man he rose up and plunged back into the darkness, striking a tree in his blind fright. That stopped him and for a little while he stood still while a great shuddering tide of terror had its way with him. A little later he crept to the rear of the office, got into his own bachelor's quarters and there in the complete darkness he lay on the bed and reviewed his actions — testing them for error and the chance of discovery.

The cold feeling was in his stomach again, and now he realized it would always be there.

9

The Seeds of Doubt

John Trent and Burl McGiven left Jacksonville by early morning with thirty Stuart mules, bound for Crescent City. Stuart had not intended leaving town that day but the sound of the lead mare's bell was a stroke of restlessness through the quiet dawn, to remind him of the bright sun upon the land, the cool lanes of timber, and the motion of the horse beneath him. By noon the temptation was too great; he went at once to the barn for his horse and by six reached the Dances' and joined them at the supper table.

"Where bound?" asked Dance.

"Just riding."

"You're a movin'-around man," said Mrs. Dance.

Dance stroked his rusty beard and showed his cherry lips as he laughed. "The hound that rustles always gets the best rabbit."

Mrs. Dance considered the remark calmly. "True enough. Men that sit around the house are mostly shiftless. Still, there are hounds always thin and hungry from running too much."

Dance winked at Stuart. "Aimed at you."

The sun disappeared from a still and fragrant land; and the earth seemed to pause for a brief period before it went rolling massively down into the pit of night. Afar, Dance's ranging hounds found scent and their voices came back in bounding, musical echoes. Caroline, sweetly filled with her silence, rose and lighted the lamps of the room. Coming around the table, she refilled Stuart's coffee cup and remained near him, her hip touching his shoulder as she looked down on the black and heavy surface of his hair; her eyes grew blacker. Dance's shrewd eyes frankly looked upon that scene. "Possession," he said, and let his laugh ring out.

The boys were up and away, lean and restless, and soon out of sight. Dance went to the door and watched them disappear. He called at them: "Take a look a Goose Canyon before you come back." Caroline and Mrs. Dance were at the dishes, but presently Mrs. Dance gave her daughter a shake of the head. "Do you think Logan came up here to see you work?"

Caroline removed her apron and came over the room at Logan; she touched his arm and drew him up and went out of the house with him. Darkness had suddenly come. There was a small wind and the odor of dust and thicket and dry meadow stubble was a heavy blend in the shadows. They paced together along the trail.

"Now, Logan," she murmured, "whom

did you fight?"

"Bragg."

"He's a great bully. I hate the sight of him. I'd rather trust a Rogue." She let that subject drop, but she was more than usually talkative this night, and spoke again. "Logan, where are we to live?"

"You don't like Jacksonville, do you?"

She gave him a sober answer. "I will live where you wish to live. If it is to be Jacksonville, I'll be happy. Will it always be Jacksonville?"

"My business will always go where trade is. I do not know where that will be ten years from now."

She had, he realized, hoped for better news. She hated change and uncertainty. "It will be Jacksonville as long as possible," he added, but he realized that this was a poor offering. "You don't like me riding away so much. It would be better for you if I were farming."

"You're not the kind to farm. You like to reach out. You're happy when you're moving around." She went on, slowly parting with some of her longest-held notions. He knew it was a tremendous struggle for her and when she said, "I'll be happy, Logan," he stopped and kissed her. She came close upon him and gripped his arms and he felt the impulsive fire of her emotions. Then she stepped back and he saw that she was smiling. "Everything will be nice," she said.

"Now," he said, "when shall it be?"

"I have got nothing to wait for," she told him. "I'll wear my mother's wedding dress. If we move to your store, we won't need to build a cabin. There is nothing to delay us."

"Only one thing. I'm going to San Francisco to borrow money."

The information surprised her. "Is there trouble?"

"None at all. I'm doing very well."

"What do you need to borrow for then?"

"It's like a young boy outgrowing his pants. The business goes ahead so fast that I'm always strapped for ready cash to get mules and supplies with."

She said, "I see," gravely, and sighed — and didn't entirely see it. "When do you go and when will you be back?"

"I'll leave day after tomorrow. I should be back in two weeks."

They were a quarter mile from the house when a shadow rose from the nearby brush and the voice of one of the boys came at them. "Wouldn't go that way. Rogues around here tonight." Stuart turned Caroline about and they moved, now in silence, toward the cabin's mellowed splash of window light. The wind softly roughed up the leaves in the thicket and the smell of the land, rising with the earth's dissipating heat, whirled in streaky currents through the dark.

The main room of the cabin was empty when

164

they returned. Settling in a chair, Stuart heard the elder Dances murmuring beyond the curtain in the extra room. He stretched out his legs and lay back in the chair, watching the stove fire flicker through the iron crevices.

"The Rogues been around here much this summer?"

She had taken up her darning basket and now sat half occupied with her chore. "This is the first time since May." He watched her square and pliable hands in deft motion; she was much as her mother was — never wholly content unless busily filling in each day, and sleeping content with that day well done, and rising refreshed to take up the new day.

He lighted his pipe and he laced his hands behind his head and closed his eyes. The teakettle sang and the mild heat of the stove made him sleepy and the smells of the room — the ancient household odors of a frontier cabin — were all comforting. In this cabin a man could make a lifetime's home and never know unhappiness; and from this meadow and the hills about he might find a living and a life rich as any that could come of cruising the world over. To sleep in this warm and well-filled shelter, to cruise the timber by day with his hounds baying down the timbered reaches ahead of him, to stand in the door and watch the lean and the restless travelers go by on their perpetual search, to grow old without care and one night to drift out to space and the silence beyond the stars —

165

why wasn't this enough for any man?

He opened his eyes and saw that Caroline watched him, her face warmed by the close and pleasant world she was building for them both. He knocked out his pipe and rose.

"If people would not change," she said in a wistful tone, "if they would be content with what they had, if they would only see how good each day is and never want for another day —" She put the darning basket on the table and walked to the corner, catching up a pair of quilts. She brought them back and when he took them he saw the hunger behind her seriousness. He lifted the blankets and threw them over her head and drew her forward; he heard her laughing when he kissed her and then she whispered something he didn't quite catch. He drew back. He said, "What was that?"

She looked up to him, smiling and suddenly embarrassed. "To the barn for you. The muley cow will keep you company." She made a face at him and closed the door and stood before the stove a little while, her face settling and losing its happiness.

Early in the morning he started back toward Jacksonville. He reached the Rogue and followed its silver flashing for a matter of miles; and in this manner, moving through a fair world, he was entirely content. "Little things satisfy a man," he thought. "Great ambitions only disturb him." Little things, like the sight of the river shallowly playing on a gravel bed, like the lifting and falling of the horse beneath him. He had Caroline in his mind for a while, wondering about her and appreciating her; and then Lucy came to him quite suddenly — as she so often did — and he was no longer pleased with the day. "I ought to get the last hope of her out of my system." It would be better when she was at last married to Camrose. Then she would be entirely beyond his reach — and he would no longer struggle with those furtive small hopes concerning her. He thought, too, of George Camrose, and found that subject not entirely pleasing; and so, with one thing and another idling through his head, he came upon an area of willows and passed into it. The patch was perhaps a hundred feet in length and halfway through it he came unexpectedly upon four young Rogue men standing silent on the trail. They had heard him from a distance and they were waiting for him in this covered place.

They wore moccasins and white men's pants and from the hips upward they were bare, with stringy black hair indifferently matted on their heads. They had a certain physical symmetry, but less than some other tribes possessed. In the bony and coarse contours of their faces was some kind of story of racial intermixture or racial poverty; they had not the clean dignity of the Sioux or the handsome openness of the Crow. Like the Klamaths east of the mountains and like the tribes along the Coast, these Rogues

167

were undependable and faithless. One thing remained constant in them: a vindictiveness toward their enemies either white or red; now they were at peace according to treaty — but a treaty meant nothing. They would rise again when they saw a chance of success. Their nature was one of savage inconstancy. These four all carried guns and looked upon him with their half-veiled contempt. Since he traveled so frequently through their country he realized they recognized him, yet they gave him no sign. He reined in.

"Hello," he said.

They simply stared at him; and suddenly they looked at one another, exchanging some signal. Then, all of them giving him a hard and insolent survey, they swung deeper into the brush and presently disappeared. He listened to their departure, urged on his horse and came out to a meadow beside the river; presently reaching Evan's Ferry, he crossed over.

"Four bucks back in that willow grove," he told the ferryman. "They seem edgy."

"The chief of the Siskiyou band has been here visitin' and talkin' trouble."

"Well, fall's here. It's fall and spring when they think of trouble." He reached Jacksonville shortly after noon and from Clenchfield he heard of Mack McIver's being found dead in the creek.

"Apparently was drunk and fell in and drowned in six inches of water."

"Henry," said Stuart, "I'm leaving for San Francisco tomorrow. Ought to be back in fifteen days."

"Logan, lad, do you know you're walkin' around like a cat in a cage?"

Stuart brought himself to a standstill. He grinned at Clenchfield. "That's true. But don't I always move around?"

"You're worse. You can't stand still." The elderly man, seldom stepping beyond his own defined bounds, now did so. "Poison can be a liquid, a powder, a gas — or it can be somethin' in your head. Whatever it may be, you'd best have it out."

Stuart stared at his clerk. There sat Clenchfield, old and dry, content to sleep and eat and spend his wakefulness at a desk. Had he always been that way or had he, as a young man, possessed a young man's fevered wants? Had the air once held its wild smells to him, had a woman's face evoked for him the strains of music and visions of beauty? Had he ever felt time's cruel swiftness, or watched the stars and felt wonder? Was it that some men never felt the keen lash of wanting; or was it that all men, full of wanting, were slowly shriveled by age and disappointment until they clung only to little comforts and stray bits of security? Was there a memory in Henry Clenchfield which even now, by its recollection, burned him; or were the memories of old men gray and without heat, the lusts and beauties of life so ephemeral as to be briefly felt and then to be forgotten?

Clenchfield said: "Do not rack yourself. Do not hope for things which never are."

"Was there ever a time when you felt that there was a thing just beyond the reach of your fingers which, by the stretching out of a hand, you might seize?"

"It is never out there beyond your fingers. Do you know where it is? It is here —" and Clenchfield reached up and touched his head. "Man is a very strange creature, making images in his mind and then rushing over this world to find that image somewhere real. You had better take your beer small, for there is no beer as strong as you think."

Stuart suddenly smiled. "You had me worried for a moment. No, my friend, you have forgotten."

Clenchfield said: "Is there more than I can see? Damn you, Logan, let an old man alone."

"Gentlemen, do I hear swearing, or may I come in?"

Lucy Overmire came through the doorway, her gingham rustling as she walked. She looked at Stuart's face. "The cuts were rather deep. I'm afraid you'll have scars. Did I interfere in an argument between you two?"

"No," said Stuart. "I simply reminded Clenchfield he had forgotten something."

"I was never the one to be poking my finger through shadows," retorted Clenchfield. "It is more than I can say for you."

Clenchfield turned his glance to the girl. "He rides too much and thinks too many things. Now he goes to San Francisco in the morning."

"I had intended asking you for supper tomorrow night," said Lucy. "It is your birthday."

"You have a long memory."

"My memory is full of pleasant things I could scarcely forget — and unpleasant recollections I wish I could forget."

"One balances another."

"One leads to another."

Clenchfield, resting his hands on the high desk, observed that they had forgotten him. He noticed how quiet they were with each other, how softly their words fell, how sober they had turned. She was a handsome woman, an uncommonly striking woman.

"I am like you, Logan," she said. "I always want to see what is over the next hill. Don't get in trouble with the vigilantes down there."

"I'll bring you a pair of jade earrings for your wedding gift."

At that point the talk ceased and Lucy, after a moment of silence, turned from the store. Stuart watched the doorway a short while and then walked into the rear room. Clenchfield thought to himself: "That was a queer thing," and he sat pondering it. There was a twinge in him — a stray current of something out of the far past, a half-warm regret and a pale sentimentality.

A small crowd turned out to bury McIver, and afterwards most of that crowd moved toward the town's deadfalls. Four men remained behind — Johnny Steele, Joe Harms, Dick Horeen, and a man called Lester. It was Johnny Steele who brought up the subject of money.

"I heard Mack say he had three or four thousand in dust."

Horeen smilingly shook his head. "All miners are hell for lying. But let's just go ask Camrose if Mack has got anything in the safe."

"No," said Joe Harms. "Don't ask Camrose if Mack has anything in the safe. Ask him how much Mack's got in the safe."

"What's the difference?" Horeen wanted to know. But Steele stared at Joe Harms, recognizing what the little man suspected. The four of them turned to the express office and filed in one at a time.

Camrose stood at the far end of the room. The moment he saw them, a change came upon his face — the beginning of a sharp reaction which he at once checked. Harms and Steele, both with suspicion making their eyes inquisitive, saw that instant of shock.

"George," said Dick Horeen, "we got to talkin' about poor old Mack. How much did he leave in your safe?"

Camrose's glance ran from man to man. He moved to the counter and he drew in deeply on the cigar and expelled the smoke, thus creating a haze around his face. He grew visibly cooler.

"He left nothing, boys."

Horeen turned to his friends. "There you are. Mack was just makin' himself big."

But Lester said: "I was with him last night. He said he'd left his poke here."

"So he had," agreed Camrose. "But he picked it up."

"When?" asked Harms.

Camrose took the cigar from his mouth and stared beyond the group, evidently in careful thought. "It was ten o'clock last night." Then, turning his attention to harms, he quickly corrected himself. "No, I wasn't here at ten. Must have been eleven."

Harms said: "How much did he have?"

"I'd guess about twenty-five ounces."

"Why, by god," said Horeen, "Mack wasn't lyin'."

For quite a while the group stood silent, each man taking the story apart and putting it together again. Harms and Steele both had quicker and better minds than either Horeen or Lester; but if they reached their conclusions earlier than the other two, they failed to indicate it. Horeen was first to speak. The information had sobered him. "Well, Mack picks up his dust, walks to the creek and falls down. When we find him there's no money on him at all. That's a hell of a long jump from an accident, boys."

Harms held his magpie attention on Camrose. "George, why didn't you say something about this, instead of lettin' the camp think it was just

173

a case of a drunken prospector, with nothing in his pocket, fallin' in the creek?"

Camrose showed Harms a nettled expression. "I don't slide around the shadows watching people. Therefore I don't know how he died."

"You knew he had dust."

"Not necessarily. He may have spent it, or given it to somebody else."

"Odd you wouldn't have mentioned it anyhow," said Harms, stubbornly.

"Odd to you perhaps," answered Camrose. "But I keep my nose out of other people's business. What happened to McIver or his dust was not my affair at all."

"Seems odd," repeated Harms, unable to leave it alone.

Camrose was now in bad temper. "I guess I'll have to make it clearer, Joe. I am not your kind of man. I don't go sliding around the dark, looking through windows at people. You're a damned Peeping Tom."

Harms flushed but made no answer. Horeen said: "No use of anybody being offended," and drew the party out of the office.

Camrose moved to the rear of the room, watching through the window as the four moved toward Stutchell's, stopped at the deadfall's doorway and fell into sober conversation. Then Joe Harms broke away and recrossed the street, vanishing from Camrose's sight. He would be resuming his pulpit seat in front of Howison's stable, Camrose thought. Presently Horeen and

174

Lester went into the deadfall while Johnny Steele turned back to join Joe Harms.

Camrose dropped his half-finished cigar to the floor and stepped on it; when he brought weight down on his leg he felt his knee shaking. In his mind a phrase turned around and around, endless and bitter: "If I could only go back to before this all happened! If . . . ."

Joe Harms tipped his bench back against the wall of Howison's barn, his short legs not quite touching the ground, his pointed and ungenerous face half concealed by the forward slope of his hat. Johnny Steele crouched on the street and slowly winnowed the dry dust between his fingers.

"What do you think, Joe?"

"Not at eleven o'clock. There wasn't no light in his office then. He came down the street around ten. I was sittin' here. He went into his office. He was there fifteen minutes. There wasn't anybody with him. He went out, going to Lestrade's as usual. He came back and he went up the street. That was when McIver walked out of Hobart's deadfall."

"Where was Camrose then?"

Joe Harms raised his head so that Johnny Steele clearly saw the expression of chagrin on the man's features. "That's what I could shoot myself for. I don't know. I lost track of him while I was watchin' McIver. You got some kind of a suspicion against him, Johnny?"

"Yes," said Steele with reluctance. "I sort

of thought it queer when I went to get my dust from him. Something seemed a little out of joint."

"There was," said Joe Harms.

Steele said: "What was?" and hung his arrested glance on Harms's fox-sharp features. But he got no answer from the little man, who was reluctant to admit that he spent his time crouched against the office knothole.

Steel continued his pondering and his steady winnowing of dust. He was a fair man, not given to quick conclusions; he was also a man of firm mind and convictions. Therefore he went through the thing from beginning to end, and arrived at something new.

"When we looked through Mack's pockets," he said, "we figured it just an accident. So we weren't looking very hard. We might have missed something. I think we'd better look again."

He rose and stamped his legs. "Meet me tonight. I'll bring along a couple shovels. Better be just the two of us. It is sort of dirty business, and I'd not like to be tagged with it, if we don't find anything."

"You know Camrose has been losin' a lot of money at poker?"

"Yes," said Steele, "I know all of that. But I'm not going to start thinking what you think until I've got more to go on. Tonight."

Steele walked away while Harms straightened the chair and assumed his characteristic posture, arms across his lap, body half bent over, one leg swinging in a steady motion across the other. Thus cramped, the little man viewed the town from beneath the brim of his hat, his eyes darting about, full of slyness, full of skeptic wisdom, full of ferret-like curiosity. He saw Overmire coming down the street and his ungenerous little mouth changed shape. Overmire was an educated man and a lawyer of some importance in the Territory and it flattered Harms's vanity that he could do injury to such a man.

"Overmire," he murmured, "Lucy's engaged to Camrose, ain't she?"

"That's right," said Overmire and waited for the little man to come to the point. He knew Harms very well; for if it pleased Harms to reduce Overmire's worth to the common denominator of Jacksonville's least occupied citizen, it likewise pleased Overmire to study the queer impulses and quirks which made Joe Harms what he was.

"Well," said Harms, "he lost a couple or three thousand dollars last night in a poker game. Thackeray's got his I.O.U. for one thousand of it."

The little man, of course, wanted to shake him as well as warn him; and this was a pleasure Overmire did not propose to give him. "Joe," he said calmly, "it has often puzzled me to know how one small man could absorb so much gossip. But, then, you do work hard at the business. It is a triumph of perseverance."

He laughed at the warm resentment on Joe Harms's face, and went away; but as soon as his back was turned, he ceased to smile. Other stray bits of news and gossip had frequently come to him concerning Camrose, making the picture of a man who had a taste for the pleasant sins of life. So far there had been nothing that Overmire, himself a man of the world, could honestly carry to his daughter. But this information was serious, and something to be weighed. Abreast Stuart's store, he wheeled in and walked to the rear, finding Stuart there.

Overmire seated himself on the edge of Stuart's bunk and observed this man he greatly admired. Himself a person of considerable force and resolution, he recognized in Stuart the same qualities. In silence to himself he had often debated his daughter's choice and had often wondered at the closeness which seemed to exist between Lucy and Logan. Yet that closeness never appeared to pass a given point, a thing which puzzled him; for after all his daughter was a desirable woman in any single man's eyes and Logan Stuart, though not handsome, had action and gallantry enough to excite the average woman. In such a situation, certain attractions and compulsions should be at work, and Overmire had watched for this to happen with the eye of a realist and the sentiments of a father wishing his daughter a good match. Why had it not happened?

178

"You ought to be a traveling man by trade," observed Overmire. "Selling medicines from a wagon up and down the country. You have too much energy to be still."

"I'm going to San Francisco to set up a line of credit."

"Sensible. The want of capital strangles development in this country." He secured himself a cigar from a breast pocket, trimmed it, lighted it and placed it between his broad lips. Then he came nearer to what lay on his mind. "Do you think it a particularly good thing to be playing cards at Lestrade's?"

"I do not play there any more. Neither does Howison or Balance."

"I had not realized it was entirely that certain a thing."

"Lestrade is not the invalid he makes out." Then Stuart gave Overmire a direct glance. "You're thinking of Camrose. I told him to stay clear of the place."

"It occurs to me," said Overmire, "you are usually the first one around here to smell changes in temperatures." Afterwards he added a most casual phrase. "You're loyal to your friends, and I suppose George Camrose is the closest friend you've got."

Stuart was careful with his words. "This is a dull camp for George, and the dullness makes him restless. Whether he would be happier somewhere else or not, I don't know. There are spots of him I have not fathomed. My guess is he needs to be whipped to get the best out of him. He's not the kind of man I am, Jonas. Maybe that's why I'm fond of him. It is a fine thing to be able to laugh, to see the foolish side of life."

Overmire rose. "Better advise him to quit poker."

"I have his promise on that."

"When did he give it to you?"

"Day before yesterday afternoon."

Overmire had not intended to say more, but the information upset him; suddenly it shed a different light upon George Camrose. "That same night," he said slowly, "he lost two or three thousand dollars."

He had thought, during this talk, that Stuart's private knowledge of Camrose was greater than he was willing to disclose. Now, in observing Stuart's change of expression, he felt certain of it. The tall man before him showed anger rather than astonishment.

"He signed an I.O.U. for a thousand," added Overmire. "Therefore he lost a thousand or two in cash. Where did he get the money?"

"It didn't come out of the company safe. It was his own."

Overmire had a dry answer. "I did not know he possessed that much wealth. How can you know it?" Then he said very bluntly: "Why do you protect him?"

"He's all right. He's got too much spirit for this camp."

"Well, by God," said Overmire, "if he's going to play poker every time he gets bored during the next forty years he'll never leave the table. Come to supper tonight."

At six o'clock, Camrose locked the office door behind him and stood still momentarily to view a street along which he had traveled for a matter of two years; he saw the miners drifting in toward the deadfalls, the chimney smoke rising, the solitary riders coming down the short hill from the Applegate trail, the same dogs sprawled in the dust, the same men standing at the doorways of their shops. All this he had witnessed so many times, yet tonight he was no longer sure of the town or the people. Therefore he crossed the street, moved along the wall of McKebbin's warehouse, and took a round-about path to the Overmires'.

Dinner was on the table and Logan was here. Camrose paid his usual respects to the family and he smiled his usual smile at Logan. Then fear touched him when he thought he saw the shadow of disapproval in Stuart's eyes. He said to himself: "It is in my mind. The world is exactly the same, but I see it differently." He sat up to the table with the rest of them, he bowed his head to Overmire's brief grace, and he took his part in the idle talk that went around. He forced himself to eat heartily and he made a point of being somewhat gayer than usual. Now and then he observed Lucy's eyes

181

show a slight speculation; even behind her smile there seemed a question. That also, he thought, was his imagination. When did a man control these shadows, these fancies, these apparitions which unaccountably flung themselves across his brain? When did memory build a wall around the sound of McIver's strangling breath in the water?

In the fall of twilight Overmire and Stuart walked from the house to sit with their cigars. Camrose did not join them as formerly. He looked at Lucy and he murmured, "Let's have a look at the mountains." He took her arm, moving away along the footpath toward the southern side of town. Overmire and Stuart were talking in the yard. He listened to the tone of their voices drop away, half expecting some quick whisper between them. Lucy said: "Is something troubling you?"

"No," he said. "What would be?"

"I don't know, of course."

"Look at the shape of the mountains against the sky," he said.

"George, couldn't you be happy here?"

"No," he said, "I couldn't. I want to marry you as soon as you'll permit. Then I want us to leave here. How soon can we do it?"

The wind rose small and cool and the stars were pale pinpoints in the sky. Lucy pointed upward, her voice quite soft. "Did you ever have your thoughts stretch out until it seemed you were almost touching the top of the sky?

182

You get up there and you float against a kind of ceiling. It is soft and bumpy, like velvet cloth not quite stretched tight."

He stopped and faced her. "I'll be damned if I beg. I'm sick and I'm lonely. I've got to have you inside four walls with me, knowing you're mine. I walk this town like a beggar, owning nothing and owned by nothing. I can't bear to think you've lost faith in me. I do not know what I should do. Do you imagine I've got no feelings, no wants?" He seized her, finding no other words which would express his sudden desperation. He brought her hard against him with neither delicacy nor manners; he kissed her with this fury upon him and he knew he hurt her and could not help it. When he stepped back he was breathing quickly and the strength had gone out of his knees.

"George — George," she murmured, "why haven't you done this before? Why have you been so terribly afraid of expressing yourself? This is better."

"When shall it be?" he said, impatient and urgent.

She took his arm, turning him back. She walked in step with him, her hand warm on his arm; and again the silence lengthened. "I did not realize," she said at last, "you had feelings that deep. You've never shown them." She was again silent, walking forward with her thoughts, and then at last he heard her voice as from a far distance. "Whenever you want."

"Sunday would be a good day. This Sunday."

"Oh, no. I shall have to make a dress."

"Is a dress a marriage?" he asked. Her hand lightened on his arm and he had the impression he had hurt her. They went in silence to the cabin and found Overmire smoking out his cigar. Stuart stood in the kitchen drying dishes while Mrs. Overmire washed them.

Lucy held her hand on George's arms and said: "We have news, Father."

Mrs. Overmire, hearing it, came at once from the kitchen, folding her wet hands on her apron. She said: "When is it to be?"

"On a Sunday quite soon. Perhaps in two weeks — if I can get a dress made by then."

"Lord love us," said Mrs. Overmire, "there's no material for a dress in this camp, and nothing much in Portland."

Overmire sat with his hands over his stomach, soberly considering his daughter's expression. He found it unexcited and much too calm, too fixed. Meanwhile he kept his own feelings entirely hidden and slowly rocked back and forth. Presently it occurred to him Stuart had said nothing and he glanced toward Stuart, who was in the kitchen doorway. Overmire saw nothing there, either; then it occurred to him that his daughter had not looked at Stuart, nor spoken to him. Suddenly Overmire unlaced his hands and brought one palm vigorously down on the table top. "A long time ago I said that when my girl got married I would see it done

184

right. It has got to be the finest wedding in the Territory. I'll get the governor to come down. We'll have a holiday in the camp."

"You'll have everybody in the camp drunk," said Lucy humorously.

"You go to San Francisco with Logan," said Overmire. "Get the best to be had. There's some good French dressmakers down there. I shall give you a draft on a bank. When you return, I'll sent a wagon to Scottsburg to pick up the plunder."

He knew this was strong lure, both to Lucy and to his wife; they were surprised by the offer, but they were intrigued by it. Mrs. Overmire said slowly, "Well, I don't know. It is a long way to go for a dress, but it is dreadful to live in a land full of men and dust and horses and saloons — and no nice places to get things."

"Go along with her," said Overmire. "Make it a holiday."

"You remember what a terrible time I had on the clipper from New York? I made a vow I'd never leave land again — and I won't. But as for Lucy . . . Lucy, what do you think?"

For the first time during this scene Lucy looked directly at Stuart. "Would it trouble you too much to have me along?"

Both of them were sober and both on guard, Overmire noticed; they were more like strangers than old friends. From the beginning the relations of these two — by turns so close and laughing, so frank, so angered at each other, and now so stiffly cool — had greatly puzzled him. All he could definitely say about them was that they had seldom spared one another.

"Come along," said Stuart, considerably restrained. "We shall be in San Francisco four days. Would that be time enough for you?"

"Yes," she said, still watching him. "That would do."

George Camrose stood by and felt his isolation. He was a spectator, his own advice unsolicited. A rush of temper urged him to speak up, but he restrained the impulse for fear that he would only betray himself further. A kind of fever burned in him and a sense of catastrophe washed its steady wave of emotion all through him. He was deeply afraid.

"It is an impulsive thing," said Lucy. "I ought to think carefully of it."

Stuart walked to the door. "Come along, George. This is a family matter." He touched Camrose's arm and the two left the house.

"Now," said Lucy to her father, "is it the dress, or something else?"

"A month away from him would do you no harm."

"Do you think I am at all uncertain about it?"

"I hadn't given it a thought. Certain or uncertain, you're going to be married to this man a long time. Better make your journey to Mecca while you've got the chance."

"You weren't really thinking of the dress,"

she murmured, and studied him a longer moment, clearly showing that she wished she knew what was in his mind. Then she turned and left the cabin. Mrs. Overmire, going to the door, saw her daughter stroll on into the darkness with her head dropped thoughtfully.

Mrs. Overmire said: "You didn't want me to go with her, did you, Jonas?"

"No. Do you think she'll make the trip?"

"Yes," said Mrs. Overmire, "she made up her mind the moment you mentioned it."

"Then I don't think she is deeply bound to Camrose. Do you?"

Mrs. Overmire sighed. "I do not understand this new age. They talk different and they act different. But she has seen Logan every week for two years. This trip will not change anything. What have you got against George all of a sudden?"

He avoided that subject. "Why wasn't it Logan? I don't understand. At times I've seen them look at each other in a damned intimate manner."

"Perhaps," said Mrs. Overmire most gently, "he never asked her."

"Why not?" challenged Overmire. "She's woman enough for any man."

"Perhaps it was because she was already engaged."

"That means nothing to an aggressive man like Logan." Then he paused and shook his head. "It's true," he admitted. "George stands between them. Logan would always defend George — he always has.'' He got to thinking of it and afterwards said: "But if Lucy's fond of Stuart, why doesn't she break off with George and make everything open again, so Stuart would have a clear field?"

"It is too late now. Logan's going to marry Caroline Dance."

He stared at his wife with disbelief. "Do you intend to tell me Lucy would marry a man she didn't love just because she couldn't get Logan? I don't believe it."

She said, "I don't know how she feels toward Logan. I do know she was once in love with George. Whether she now is, or whether she's not certain, or whether —" She shook her head and added, "I don't know, Jonas."

Camrose and Stuart went down the hill in entire silence. At the store's doorway Stuart said, "Come in a moment, George," and walked through to the rear room. Camrose followed, waiting for Stuart to light the lamp, and suddenly fearful of what Logan might know. The light bloomed yellowly upward in the lamp chimney and Stuart swung about, showing to Camrose that rocky, drawn expression which always came to him when he faced a fight or a disagreeable thing.

"God damn you," he said, holding his voice down to a conversational tone. "I ought to break you up and make you crawl down the

188

street on your hands. Maybe that would make a man of you. I don't know. I don't care much."

"Here — here," said Camrose. The rough handling braced him; it stirred his temper. "Keep your tongue off me, Logan. I can't permit you to talk like that."

"You have been a sucker in this camp for any man with a deck of cards. You're a tinhorn. Any cheap sport in town can trim you. You've made a hell of a nice living for the boys, George. Thackeray ought to give you a pension. You've set him up well enough."

"Who keeps you informed — Joe Harms?" asked Camrose in a jeering voice.

"You suppose any man can drop as much as you did without the camp knowing it? You're a prime tenderfoot. How do you suppose Thackeray makes his living? Did you think you could out-play him? If God gave you any sense, you might know he could deal himself pat with one hand tied behind him. Did you expect to win?"

"I can't take that talk," said Camrose in a dogged voice. "I can't do it, Logan. I have got to warn you to quit."

"Explain to me, then, why you took the money I gave you, made a promise to quit playing, and blew it over the poker table."

"You're very pious about it, are you not? Very smug. You want the sinner to confess. Grovel and cry his weakness and his sorrow. I shan't do it. If it were in my power to raise the money and return it, I should do so. Then, clear of the obligation, I should tell you to go to hell."

Stuart stood at the corner of the room, the weight of his judgment pressing upon Camrose. The latter began to feel a change in this man he so well knew — a closing out and a drawing away — until at last the silence was worse than the unsparing speech. "Logan," he said, "how can I explain it to you? You have got your business. You are happy at it. Perhaps you will make a fortune at it. You gamble each time you send out a train. Why do you gamble? To make a million dollars. I haven't the chance of gambling that way. So I do it the only way I can. Where is the difference?"

"Damn-fool talk," said Stuart. "You know better."

"Well" said Camrose, "let it go. It happened because I'm the kind of a man I am. I am sick of this damned dull place. I never belonged here. There is your answer."

Stuart put a hand to the wall; he dropped it, and shoved both hands into his pockets. He shrugged his shoulders. "Maybe it is a good answer," he said. "I can't judge you. I'm sorry for you."

"It will all wash out," said Camrose, greatly relieved at the turn of affairs. "Let's have no more hard words. The place is dreary enough without that."

"You've tried to make it easy before, and each time it comes out worse. If you mean to make your life a thing of running and hunting, you had better think of Lucy."

"We'll pull out of here and live somewhere decent," said Camrose, full of assurance. "It will be better — it will be fine."

"Always tomorrow — always the next thing. You never face it. You'll marry her, you'll move on. You'll find nothing that pleases you. You'll play for your million and you'll get into another scrape. The hell with it, George. You stay right here and work this piece of ground. I will not think of you carrying her from pillar to post."

Camrose's temper swung up. "I'll decide that."

"Your decisions are bad. You'll play no fake games with Lucy."

For the first time in his long association with Logan, Camrose felt a suspicion. "Does she concern you that much?"

"Yes," said Stuart, "she does."

"That's too damned much. What are you covering up on your own account?"

The remark touched Stuart far deeper than Camrose imagined it would. Stuart came quickly across from the corner of the room; he flung out his arm, using the butt of his palm to jolt Camrose in the chest; and then he raised his hand and slapped Camrose across the face. Camrose recovered himself and lifted his arms, laughing in a rash way. "Now we're going to have a fight, Logan."

"You talk too much," said Stuart and struck him on the chest again. Suddenly he took two long steps backward, hearing Lucy's voice call through the store.

She came into the room somewhat excited by the decision she had made. Then she observed the bony expression on Stuart's face and she cast a quick look toward Camrose, who stood with his light hair fallen down on his forehead and his chest moved by swift breathing. She saw all this and her rapid mind grasped some of its meaning at once. But before she could comment on it, Camrose recovered himself quickly and assumed a smile.

"What is it to be, Lucy?"

"I came to tell Logan I was going with him."

"Ah," said Camrose. "You will be in good company."

"Have you two been quarreling?"

"We often quarrel," said Camrose, recovering some of his easy manner. "Then we forget it. You ought to know Stuart's positive disposition."

Whether or not she believed the explanation, she made a show of accepting it and turned to Stuart. "I shall be packed and ready in the morning."

Stuart, less changeable, still held his rough expression. He said, "All right, Lucy. We'll leave at seven."

He watched her leave, he listened to her steps go along the store; then he stared at Camrose with his hard insistence. Suddenly he turned to a corner shelf of the room and took down a whisky bottle and two glasses. He set the glasses on the table and half filled them with whisky. He sat down and he pointed to the other chair, and he continued to watch Camrose as the latter took place opposite him; he laid his heavy arms on the table and hunched his shoulders, and he took up his glass and dipped it at Camrose, and drank his whisky.

"Now," he said, "you're still shy two thousand dollars out of your safe."

"Yes," said Camrose, immensely relieved. "But that's all right."

"Nothing's right," said Stuart. "I'll cover it when I get back from San Francisco. As for Thackeray — don't pay that I.O.U. It was a crooked game. As soon as I return I am going to wring that man dry. I'll get it back from him, or I'll whip him out of camp."

Camrose relaxed in the chair. Stuart was assuming the problem, Stuart would find an answer — and this knowledge eased him and he thought: "I am safe with him behind me."

"George," said Stuart, and leveled his finger on Camrose, "you have got to stand fast. Don't shift around and don't duck. You can't run away from anything."

"All right," said Camrose. "I'll do it. I'll do it, Logan."

"We'll forget all this," said Stuart. "Drink 'er dry.'

Camrose upended his glass and put it down. He rose with easy humor restored. "I'm going to bed," he said and left the room with a casual wave of his arm.

Stuart remained at the table. He put more weight on his elbows and he dropped his shoulders nearer the table and used a forefinger to push the two empty glasses around idly. This had been bad, this night. Nothing would be the same between them again, for some good thing had died the moment he struck Camrose; and now he admitted a fact he had hitherto refused to face: Camrose was a weak man who would never stand entirely straight.

He wished he could tell Lucy that, but he realized he never could. She had made her decision in favor of Camrose long ago, and nothing would change her. There was nothing for him to do, Stuart now understood, but to make Camrose stand straight.

Leaving Stuart's Camrose discovered Lestrade at this moment walking down the street. The two fell in step and Lestrade presently said: "Little game tonight?"

"Not in the humor for it," said Camrose.

"Tomorrow night, then," said Lestrade. "I'll rustle up the boys, Stuart, too."

"He's leaving town in the morning for San Francisco."

"A long and dreary ride."

"Not that way. He's catching the boat

at Scottsburg."

They reached the foot of the street, where-upon Camrose said, "Good night," and turned to his office. Lestrade continued on to his cabin, thinking to himself: "Stuart will probably take the opportunity to carry dust. He usually does when he makes a trip. This is what Bragg wants to know." Deciding that, he saddled and rode at once to Bragg's cabin, calling the man to the door, delivered his message and immediately returned to his own place.

It was a quick and quiet trip, yet two men had witnessed his going and his returning, Howison, who had been watching Lestrade ever since the last holdup of his gold messenger, had noticed him walk down the street with Camrose — and had followed him to Bragg's. Pulled off in the timber as Lestrade cut back for town, Howison thought to himself: "I have got as much evidence as I could possibly want."

Johnny Steele, walking the night with his vivid recollections of Mrs. Lestrade, had been near the creek when Lestrade passed over it, outbound. Afterwards, Johnny strolled on until he was near the Lestrade cabin and he stood with his shoulder tipped against a tree and watched the cabin's light with his thoughts taking him into strange places. She was a beautiful woman tied to a crook, and she knew it and had her private tragedy. The memory of holding her in his arms never ceased to affect Johnny Steele; it had materially changed his life, taking some of the carelessness out of him. He had reviewed himself critically, his faults and his possibilities, and the recollection of his thousand-dollar drunk greatly humiliated him. He had not stepped into a deadfall since that memorable night at the creek; and since that night, too, he had nourished wishes concerning Mrs. Lestrade which he realized were impossible. Still he could not stop those wishes. Standing there, he observed Lestrade's return and he had a pretty good guess as to where the man had been.

10

Black Night

Traveling at no great speed, Stuart and Lucy reached Dance's near suppertime the first day out of Jacksonville. The hospitable Ben Dance made a considerable ceremony over Lucy, and Mrs. Dance was reservedly cordial. Caroline showed a mild surprise until the reason for the visit was explained. It was Lucy who took pains to explain it in considerable detail to Caroline, who said, "Why that's nice," and went about her work with no additional show of interest.

After supper the three Dance boys rose and ranged into the night while the others sat comfortably in the little room. Lucy offered to help with the dishes and was politely refused. Dance had a story to tell about a cougar — and at the end of the story he added: "That was two days ago. I found Injun tracks at the head of Goose Canyon, Stuart. You take care goin' through the mountains tomorrow."

Then, and how or why it was Stuart could not understand, the ease went away from this group. Dance felt it and his glance went shrewdly around the woman and came over to Stuart with a flicker of comprehending humor. Mrs. Dance spoke briskly of the latest news, and inquired of people in Jacksonville. Caroline worked at her darning, saying nothing; now and then she lifted her head, when Lucy spoke, and watched the girl with a narrow attention. It was the same expression, Stuart remembered, that had been on her face when Lucy had wished her well at the raising of Bartlett's cabin — somehow stiff and resisting.

He rose and stepped into the night, and stood with his pipe to watch the stars and the great black bulk of the mountains. Dance presently came out, his humor working to the surface. He murmured: "Air's sort of close in there."

"Why?" asked Stuart.

"You can't mix women, Logan. I remember a long time ago —"

Caroline stepped from the cabin and looked with suspicion at her father. "What makes you laugh?" she asked and then, not waiting for an answer, put her hand on Logan's arm and drew him down the road.

She walked fast, with her face firm and her glance pointed ahead. She was angry, and the anger came out of her like heat. Stuart kept pace with her, waiting for the tempest to break upon him; he braced himself for it and wondered how he was to meet it, and how he was to smooth it away. But it never came. Her steps began to slow down and her temper seemed to leave so that she at last stopped and looked at him through the darkness, and reached up to pull his head down. She kissed him, speaking softly. "I should not be jealous, should I? There is nothing to be jealous about is there?"

"No, Caroline."

She listened to his words and debated them in her mind. Her face was softer than it had been, but it was also touched by a reserved wonder. He could not be sure of her thoughts, he could not follow them as she stood still and went far off from him. Perhaps, he told himself, she knew more about him than he realized. Perhaps everything in him was glass-clear to her, so that she knew precisely what he offered her and what he could not offer. He was wholly uncertain about it, and once more he asked himself if he was just to her, but came no nearer the answer than he had before.

"When will you be back, Logan?"

"Two weeks."

"I'll think of you," she said and returned to the cabin with him. She stepped inside and presently reappeared with a pair of quilts. Now she was cool and self-contained and her "Good night," as she turned away, was almost impersonal.

Stuart and Lucy were on the road at sunrise, soon passing into the heavy hills. It occurred to him as they traveled along they were no longer the free-and-easy people they had been on the last trip together through this mountainous way. The fun and freedom between them was gone. Somewhere during the morning Lucy mentioned Caroline. "I should not have gone on this trip. Caroline is not pleased. I do not blame her so much."

"It will pass," he said.

"Not too easily. Logan — would you care to tell me why you and George quarreled?"

"I gave him some advice which he took poorly. But it will blow over."

"I didn't expect you'd tell me," she said.

"We've quarreled before and will again. The thing to remember is that I'll always do whatever I can for him, and for you."

"There'll be little chance of that. We're moving away."

"That's what the quarrel was about," he said.

Early in the afternoon they put up at Anslem's and on the following day passed the Umpqua at Rose's Ferry and continued to a house some fifteen miles north. The next morning, Stuart left the main trail and took a shortcut through a land of broken hills and short valleys. It made a long ride but it saved half a day. Beyond noon they camped while Stuart cooked up a meal; afterwards they rested back in the warm sunshine.

"Logan, why doesn't he like this country?"

"He's got different tastes than the rest of us. I can understand why he might get lonesome for other things. I imagine you'll like the East."

"Is he going there?"

"Haven't you talked it over with him?"

"Not much."

"Odd," he said. He rose and helped her to her saddle, her nearness troubling him, her eventual departure from the country leaving a huge gap in him. A narrow canyon brought them before the Umpqua again at a point where Stuart had remembered a suitable ford; but though the river had receded from its solid-rock bottom, the main channel still ran quick and deep and too wide for Lucy's risking. He said "Bad guess. We'll have to follow this around to Elkton. It will be a long ride and a late one."

"We've ridden late and long before."

He observed the moment's smile, the moment's break of her reserve; it took him back, it brought up all that he felt about her and made every memory uncomfortable. "I've put you through some rough times."

"You're usually rough." She was lightened by her thoughts and once more made gay. "I recall when George introduced you to me. He said, 'This is Logan Stuart, a particular friend. He has just been in a fight — look at his knuckles.' I wondered at the time what George saw in you. It took me several months to find out." She grew curious and said suddenly: "What did you think of me, that first meeting?"

"I said to myself, 'Damn George Camrose.' "

Warmth came over her face. "You have a rare moment now and then," she murmured, and looked away from him. He straightened in the saddle, with the goodness of the moment gone.

The detour took them off the trail and it became a matter of finding a passable route between river's edge and timber's edge as the afternoon wore on. They crossed several small creeks, and occasionally found clear going on a natural meadow whose wild hay stood amber and tousled. The river made great roundabout loops on its way to the sea, and occasionally the face of a cliff came down to block them, whereupon they took to the hills and slowly crossed over. At sunset Stuart halted, started a fire and cooked up bacon and coffee.

A long ride called for a long rest, and he had seen some weariness on Lucy's face. Therefore he lighted his pipe and kept the fire going while dusk came on. "I should imagine we've got ten miles ahead of us," he said. "Lucy, why did you tell me not to marry a calm woman?"

The question caught her off guard. She gave him a quick glance and shook her head. "It was just something I said. It didn't mean anything. I guess you've made a squaw out of me. I like this."

"So will you like Fifth Avenue, George in a red plush waistcoat and you in a most elegant red dress."

"I don't know," she said soberly. "I don't really know." A fish broke the river's surface, that sound carrying through the still air in a widening ripple, and somewhere a deer made a racket in the brush on its way to water, and the crickets all were singing. "I wouldn't say I'm a linsey-woolsey frontier woman, but I couldn't say I am a woman meant for elegant drawing rooms, either. I shall go where George goes and I shall no doubt be happy wherever that is. But I am quite happy here, at this moment. I am . . ."

Dusk drifted in, thinly shadowing the world; the small fire brightened against this darkness, and the light of the fire danced in her eyes as she watched him. She had spoken in a detached and unstirred voice. Yet she was not as cool as that, for somewhere within her an emotion strongly worked and left its fugitive impression upon her face. He saw it on her lips most clearly; it was her lips which always first betrayed the changes within her. He thought: "I do not know anybody as well as I know her. Nobody knows me as well as she does. A damned strange thing."

"I guess," she added in a flatter voice, "I am simply an easy woman to please."

The deer still stirred the brush, now closer. He listened to it a moment, his mind only half on it. "That's wrong," he said. "You're slow to change, slow to forget, and you don't give up what you've got or what you believe."

She said quietly: "You should know."

Then he heard the rustling progress of the deer in the brush once more, and the disinterested part of his mind began to pay attention. The sound stopped, the sound began; and it grew nearer each time he heard it. He was resting full-length, propped up on an arm, with his head turned to the flames. He moved around slightly to watch the black edge of the brush and timber fifty feet beyond him. He thought: "Not quite right for a deer." The fire was a small one, burning on its last few branches. He thought, "Time to go," and sat up; then he was flooded with warning as his mind fully woke and he swept his hand across the fire's ashes and flung wood and sparks in a scattered shower through the shadows, and he rolled against Lucy, knocking her back to the earth.

The shot came immediately after, striking close by and throwing a clot of dirt against him. He saw the flash of the gun in the thicket and he rolled again as he drew his revolver from his trouser band. He had lost his bearing on the thicket but he still heard a body moving through it, faster and more carelessly. The shadows were deepening along the meadow and the mule and two horses, all on picket, uneasily walked around.

The hidden marksman, maneuvering beyond the screen of brush and shadows, now ceased to move; and by that sign Stuart knew the second shot was due. The sound of the shot, when it broke, seemed huger than the first, but the aim was poorer. Stuart thought he heard the scuff of the bullet a good distance back of him, though he was not listening for it; he had seen the man's gun flash and he steadied his gun on that spot and tried a shot of his own.

The answer was unexpected. The marksman broke into a run, through the brush, keeping close to its edge; and thereafter he made an abrupt halt and fired three times, with a considerable delay between shots. The first shot struck one of the horses and dropped it. Stuart had risen and was rushing at the nearest brush when the second bullet broke. He skirted the edge of the brush and saw the third flash of the gun scarcely more than twenty feet from him. He fired on the flash and drew a swift answer. He thought: "That ends the loads," and rushed straight into the thicket.

The man was in full retreat before him, grunting and hardbreathing as he smashed through the brush and into the blackness of the timber; and suddenly Stuart understood the uselessness of his chase and turned about. When he got to the meadow he still heard the man somewhere in motion, apparently circling away. He passed the animals and noticed all three on the ground; he went forward to the scattered ruby glitter of the fire. "Lucy," he said.

She had drawn back toward the river. Her voice drew him forward until he found her crouched on the gravel. She said, "Here," and caught his arm and pulled him down. "Don't go back there," she said. "It was Bragg. I know. It couldn't be anybody else." She was shaking. She put her other hand on him, thus holding him with both. He saw the pale outline of her face in the night. "It was Bragg, wasn't it?"

He got up. "It was Bragg. I'm going to the horses."

"They're dead."

"I know," he said, and moved over the meadow again. He came to the animals and crouched down. He uncinched each horse and pulled out the blankets from beneath each saddle and he got his small valise with its load of gold dust. He sat still, hearing another sound, a good deal south — the brisk and padded echo of a horse in motion. He listened to it until he could hear nothing. "It was Bragg," he said, and was certain of it. The man had missed with his first charge and then he had turned sly and had retreated. But he had been obliged to kill something, and therefore had shot the animals. That was Bragg . . .

He walked back to Lucy. He pulled her up. "We'll walk away from this," he said. "I don't expect him back. He missed his try and he'll go back and wait another time. That's Bragg's habit. But if he changes his habit and waits around for daylight, we don't want to be here."

He put a hand to her and followed the river's edge, with the north star to his left. It seemed wrongly placed to him until he remembered the river was in one of its sweeping bends at this point. The gravel gave way to solid rock pitted with holes worn by eddies of the river's high water; and the rock gave way to a brushy bank forcing them inland. A mile of this put them back to the river again; another mile brought them before the silhouette of a considerable canyon, through which the river ran a great arc. Timber came close down to the water's edge and the way forward was no longer to be seen.

"Here's where we stay," he said and dropped the blankets to the ground. "Cold camp."

She knelt down, searching the ground with her hands. She lifted the blankets and moved forward with them until he lost her shadow against the timber. He heard her quietly speak and he went on until he stumbled against her. "This is a better place, Logan. A blanket underneath and a blanket on top. Come down."

He stretched beside her, beneath the top blanket; he rolled the blanket's edge beneath him. "Another rough time to remember."

"It isn't the end," she said. "I never see any end of violence for you."

He said, "I'm going back to Jacksonville. But I shall take you on to Scottsburg first and see you aboard the ship. We'll walk into Elkton before noon and I can borrow a pair of horses from Lew Waite."

"My father would disapprove of my going on alone. I'm committed to your hands, so I shall return with you. It's Bragg, I suppose. Why should he hate you so much?"

"You remember the two California miners

killed near Evans's Ferry a year ago?"

"The ones the Indians murdered?"

"I was on the road that morning. Bragg passed me, coming out of the willows, running his horse. Ten minutes later I found the two miners. I was the only witness — and a court would have hung him on what I said. I knew it, but I didn't want to hang a man on something I didn't see entirely. The ten minutes made the difference. I kept still, which was a mistake."

She was against him, turned from him. He pulled the blanket over her, feeling the damply exhaled fog of the river move over and around them.

"Logan," she murmured, "you have kept still on many things."

She lay soft in his arms, her warmth a part of him and her nearness bringing up his constant, never-lessening want. From the beginning her smile had come upon him with its personal interest, her eyes and her lips had lightened at sight of him, her anger had at times shaken him. They knew each other too well; their closeness was too much for what they had of each other, yet too little for what he wished. She was full and warm and deep. He knew this about her more than others knew it, for with him she was a different woman, not particularly caring if she hurt him or shocked him. Since he was not her man, she could be herself before him.

"You didn't answer me, Logan."

He thought to himself, "God damn George Camrose," and struggled with his intemperate wishes.

She turned in his arms and her face came close to him so that he felt the touch of her breath and had the luminous blur of her face before him. "If it gets colder than you can stand," he said, "I'll risk a fire." His urges made a turbulent eddy around them both. There was nothing he could hide from her, so that he knew she felt what was in him; her lips so near him, showed that knowledge. He felt the sudden quickening of her heart and then, rising on an elbow, he moved slightly forward and put his arm beneath her and dropped his mouth upon her lips.

The pressure of his extreme wants held him there. She was a bottomless softness, she was an acid-sweetness, she was a fire burning against him and a wind rushing through him. He was heavy on her and his arm slowly pulled her body around to him, and a kind of greed made him forget everything else. She had not resisted; her hand rested on the back of his neck and she seemed willing to give him all he could hold of her. But suddenly her lips slid aside, breaking the tension, and then he lay back bitterly angered at himself. He took his arm from her, and she rose on an elbow and brought her face quite near him. He heard her rapid, uneven murmur: "That's what you wished, wasn't it?"

"Yes."

"Then don't hate me for giving it to you."

"It's no good."

"You're lying," she said. "You'll never have another woman kiss you like that."

"It's no good. It will stick too long."

"Ah," she said, "that's different," and continued to watch him. He could not see her face clearly, but he knew she was trying to read him with that strong personal interest she always used on him. This was a moment — like other moments he remembered — when the door opened and they stood on the edge of something neither of them understood. It never remained open very long. He again asked himself the same old question: Why was it George? That closed the door.

She turned away from him and he put his arm around her and drew her close for warmth. She lay long awake, her mind apparently very active; it was an hour or better before he felt the loosening of her body and the change of her breathing. He said once more to himself: "We're too close for what we've got," and drifted off to sleep.

The sodden cold of the river woke them before daylight and put them on the road. At ten o'clock they reached the scattered cabins of Elkton Settlement and found Lew Waite, who made breakfast for them and loaned Stuart a pair of horses. "Howison's pack outfit passed by here, Jacksonville bound, about an hour ago."

"We'll catch up," said Stuart. "Do me a favor. Ride down to where I was camped and strip the dead animals for me." He helped Lucy to her saddle and set out along the wiggling course of Elk Creek; in the middle of the afternoon they overtook Howison's train and joined it for that day's march and that night's camp at Applegate's. But the pack train's progress was too slow and the following morning Stuart and Lucy moved ahead, reaching Jacksonville late in the third afternoon from Applegate's. As Stuart helped her down, he said: "I'm sorry about the wedding dress."

"Any dress will do," she answered.

11

Approach of Judgment

Stuart dropped on his bunk for a short sleep as soon as he reached camp; and woke to a heavy and angered conversation outside the back room's door — Henry violently in argument with George Camrose. He heard Camrose say: "By God, Henry, you can quit playing the part of a watch dog. I'm going in there."

Henry's voice was starched with stubbornness. "And by God back to you, sir, and you're not."

There was a scuffle, and the door came open. Rising from the bed, Stuart saw Camrose thrust Clenchfield away with a stiff swing of his forearm and stride through. Temper flushed his face and made an electric dance in his eyes. He pointed a long finger at Clenchfield, who now stood silently bitter in the doorway. "If you were a younger man, Henry, I'd knock you down. Don't ever lay your hands on me again."

Clenchfield stared at Stuart. "This man," he said with cold distaste, "is suppose to be your friend. But not enough of one to let you sleep."

"Damn you, Henry," said Camrose, "a man's not supposed to sleep in the daytime."

Stuart rose and walked over the floor and got a drink of water. He ran a hand along his jaw, feeling the length of his whiskers; he stripped off his shirt and he got out his shaving mug and razor. The sun had gone down, with twilight beginning its soft inflow from the hills. He lighted the room's lamp and set it on the table; he fixed his mirror near at hand and lathered his face. Clenchfield had gone back into the store. Camrose stood by, but Stuart was not particularly thinking of him; he was thinking back to the scenes on the trail, all of them sharp and real.

"I hear," said Camrose, "you had trouble."

"A little trouble," agreed Stuart.

"That's characteristic," said Camrose.

The shortness of his tone brought Stuart back from his other thinking. Now he paused in the lathering of his face and gave Camrose a full-on appraisal. Camrose had subdued his anger, which seemed to have been caused by Clenchfield, but he still showed his flush and his ruffled spirits. In any other condition, Stuart would have smiled the whole thing away; but awakened from insufficient sleep and empty of stomach, he was not in the best of spirits. Under such conditions he was not disposed to make too many allowances for the unpredictable ways of his friend. "What's characteristic?" he asked.

"Saying much in little," said Camrose.

"What the hell of it?"

Camrose widened his eyes at the reaction. "It was just a comment, Logan."

Stuart returned to his shaving. The razor made poor going on his beard, and the sound of it was gritty in the room's silence. Stuart set up his strop, shaved a few strokes, and stropped again. His eyes watered from the casual torture, causing him to swear.

"Wherever she goes with you," said Camrose, "she gets in trouble."

"It came out all right."

"Lucy stood it well," said Camrose. "I presume it was cold. Manage to have a fire?"

"No," said Stuart, "I didn't want to make a target." He finished one jaw and began on the other, waiting for Camrose to creep nearer the thing which was behind this questioning.

"Otherwise," said Camrose, in the lightest voice he could contrive, "you slept cold."

"Damned cold," agreed Stuart.

"Couldn't you give her any shelter at all?" asked Camrose.

"Some," said Stuart. He felt the hardening of the silence. He carried the razor down his other jaw and along his chin. Camrose walked a circle around the room and came to a stand before Logan. He pushed the subject out of his head with great effort, and turned to another.

"Are you going south again?"

"Not right off."

"I'm due to have a company agent through

214

here one of these days to check the accounts. A damned embarrassing turn of things."

"Always embarrassing," said Stuart, "to lose somebody else's money."

Camrose flushed. "I said I was a fool. Do I have to admit it every time I see you? All I want is to get out of this hole. It will be the last." Then he turned somewhat bitter. "It won't be difficult to be honest the rest of my days. Life takes the heart out of a man and leaves him a damned dry pulp. So, I can sit around this town until I die, a little fellow with no courage and no hope. I had hope once — and maybe I had courage. But it didn't work."

"Not the way you tried to work it."

"Don't tell me other men haven't done it," said Camrose sharply. "How do you suppose the millionaires of our land got rich? On borrowed money. But they were smarter than I am. They had their lawyers make everything legal. If they lost, they weren't responsible for it. If they won, they were great men."

"No doubt," said Stuart. "But they stayed away from poker."

"What's the difference between poker and manipulating railroad stocks?"

"Your rich men played with their own cards. They had 'em all marked and they couldn't lose. You played with another man's cards, and you couldn't win."

Camrose was surprised. "I have never before heard you speak cynically."

"I am only telling you where you made your mistake."

"It is going to be touch and go with me. I had counted on your help."

"You'll get it. I'm going to talk to Thackeray."

"You'll not get it all back. There were others in that game. Even so, it's not enough. It will take another two thousand, above what I lost to Thackeray."

"When your company man comes, tell him you have got your shortage — whatever amount it may be — out as a loan to me. Enter it on your books now as a loan. We can straighten it after he goes."

Relief brought a strong reaction to Camrose's face. He even managed a smile — a semblance of the old smile. It would never be the same smile as it once had been, Stuart thought, for there would never be the same faith between them. He felt the loss of it as he watched Camrose; he felt the emptiness of a place that had been filled by their friendship.

"You're a white man," said Camrose. "That takes care of it. Now I can sleep."

"And dream of making a fortune some other quick way," said Stuart. "You're getting out of this easy. You always get out easy."

"You disapprove," said Camrose. "Then why do you bother?"

Stuart lighted a cigar and took his time to answer. There had been a good deal between them, and Camrose had meant much to him; no man could cross out the fine things of his life without making a last gesture, and maybe this was his last gesture toward the good and careless days he had shared with George.

"If I thought you were a crook, I'd see you in hell. But you're not a crook. You're a man with so many things in your head that you've never been able to sort out which ones were right and which were no good. This kind of a life isn't yours. You made a mistake, but it was a mistake committed out of foolishness, not done in cold blood."

George was smiling again with amusement, with a tolerant indulgence of advice which bored him. Even now, Stuart thought, George Camrose was unrepentant. Perhaps he had learned a bitter lesson, but it was a lesson which galled him and made him feel self-pity.

"Old boy," said Camrose, "I never thought you a complicated man, yet there are times when I can't follow you. Shall I see you up at Lucy's?"

"No."

Camrose watched Stuart for a moment, the smile fading; and then he turned from the room. By the time he reached the street his face was again tight. He said to himself, "He's making these concessions for her, not for me. I've got to find out about that trip." In this mood of jealous doubt he walked up the hill to Overmire's.

Stuart moved into the lamp-stained shadows of the storeroom and was comforted by its aromatic smells. They were familiar smells with flavor to them; they reminded him of a hundred things in swiftest succession, of wet trails through the hills, and the slant of sunlight through the arched timber, of the campfire's flickering and the sound of mystery aboard in night's pit, and of warm cabins where men drowsed and drawled, and the edged air of morning before the sun came up. He stood a moment watching Clenchfield, whose dignity still was ruffled. "Never mind it, Henry."

"You had better let your friend Camrose take care of his own troubles. He's deep enough and it will do you no good to be involved."

"How's that?"

"I will let the town tell you," said Clench-field.

Stuart traveled on to Mrs. Johnson's house for his supper and afterward went into Corson's deadfall. A crowd got around him to hear about his trip and he stood awhile with his cigar and idly took care of the questions. Thackeray came in and joined the crowd. In a little while Stuart broke away, giving Thackeray a signal.

The two of them left Corson's, nothing being said until they were well down the street. Then Stuart went straight at the subject.

"How much did you take off Camrose the other night?"

"About fifteen hundred gold. Another thousand on a note. Fitz got a couple hundred and Gil Perrin took in a little, but later lost to me."

"He's damned foolish with his money," said Stuart.

"His or somebody's," said Thackeray.

"How's that?"

"I guess you can figure it out as well as I can. The suspicion's pretty general. He's come to you with his troubles, ain't he? He always does. Better quit holding him up. He'll learn to hold himself up, or he'll sink. My guess is he'd sink."

"You should have let him alone. He's got no business with cards."

"If I don't trim him somebody else will. Never pity a fool."

"You don't know him."

Thackeray shrugged his shoulders. "My business is cards. In that business you study people pretty sharp. I know Camrose. You do not. You're his friend. You don't see his rotten spots. You'll defend him since you're a pretty stubborn fellow and you wouldn't throw a man down. But for me, he's strictly a tinhorn. When I play him I always watch him. I never know what a tinhorn will do. He'd take me if he could and he would have no regrets. But when I take him he cries to you."

"No," said Stuart, patiently trying to explain it, "he's not what you think."

"Well," said Thackeray, "he ain't worth our

arguin' about."

"I want the money back," said Stuart.

"That's what I expected you wanted," said Thackeray and stopped. He turned to Stuart, his face becoming smooth. "You got a streak in you about that man. I don't understand it, and neither does the camp. It is no use, Logan. I will not do it."

"I'll expect it back inside of an hour," said Stuart.

A flurry of concern came across Thackeray's face. His business, always a dangerous one, had taught him the ways of survival and he had used these ways during his career. But he shook his head and expressed a great deal of regret with his voice. "I cannot be bluffed."

"Did you ever see me run a bluff? I mean what I say."

"Why, God damn you!" exclaimed Thackeray. "You couldn't find two men in all this camp who'd agree I ought to return the money. You know it, too. You're standing there and telling me you'll make it a fight?"

Stuart nodded. He held Thackeray's astonished and resentful glance; he was hard and he was patient and, since Thackeray always carried a gun, he was watchful. He had no grudge against Thackeray and in fact had always been on excellent terms with him, but that point had passed by. He had made up his mind and he would not recall the decision.

"Logan," said Thackeray in an almost pleading voice, "you're wrong as hell."

"It was in the books you'd clean him when he sat down. He had no chance against you."

"That," said Thackeray, "was his lookout, not mine and not yours."

"I want it back within the hour."

"You won't get it."

"All right," said Stuart, "I'll have to come after you when the hours up."

This night was cool with the quickening breeze of a fall night. Yet Thackeray lifted a hand and ran the tips of his fingers across his forehead and brought them away wet. He realized he was suddenly sweating, and the fact annoyed him. His eyes, usually half shut, were now fully open. "You'd better stay out of Camrose's affairs, Logan, before he pulls you down with him." But he realized he could not change Stuart's mind and so said wearily, "I guess it will have to be a fight," and turned away.

Stuart let the man get ten feet distant. Then he added his last remark, shrewdly withheld until now. "Maybe I better tell you one more thing. The money he lost was not his. It was mine. He had borrowed it from me for another purpose."

Thackeray came sharply about, walking back at a faster gait. He stopped before Stuart and he said in lively anger: "Why didn't you tell me? Why point a gun at a man's head and try to break him down? I'd like to swing a chair over your thick head! Since it's your money, of course I'll give it back."

Stuart put a heavy hand on Thackeray's shoulder and smiled.

"Let's have a drink on it."

"A good idea."

During this time men had gone by them, down the street and up the street, singly or in pairs; now as they turned together in the direction of Corson's deadfall, Stuart heard a man running from the lower part of town. He looked behind him and observed this man stop and touch a second man. Someone else drew in, and presently there was a group closely drawn into a circle, softly speaking.

He paid little attention to that group, for his glance had passed on to a scene which interested him far more. Mrs. Lestrade had come from Howison's store, turning off toward her cabin, and at the same time Johnny Steele walked from the shadows and lifted his hat to her. She stopped, facing Johnny Steele, and something was said between them, after which he went on with her as far as the last shed on the street. Here she stopped once more and looked up to him; a moment later, she continued on alone, with Steele standing on the walk to watch her. His first thought was: "A good man and a fine woman. But a bad thing to do. This town will see it and comment on it."

Camrose, walking up the hill with a mind made

222

fertile by jealousy, remembered how violent some of the quarrels between Stuart and Lucy had been, and he had a shrewd thought about that: "Unless they were fond of each other, why should they have quarreled?" Then he remembered how they had closed up the quarrels and had turned again to laughter, and this brought him another sharp observation: "They were too close to remain apart. I have been very stupid." As he reached the yard of the Overmire house he recalled how he had taunted Stuart into kissing Lucy. It had amused him then, but it did not now. She had been in Stuart's arms and she had felt Stuart's wants. What went on between them then?

The thought of it quickened his jealous suspicion, but even then there was a deeper fear in him which turned him sly and cautious. He was alone in this town and men were watching him closely; he had sensed their talk about him as he passed by. He could not break with Stuart, for Stuart was his only support. And Stuart would remain his friend as long as Lucy was in the scene. He had an accurate picture of Logan Stuart's position in all this; it was a love of Lucy which caused Stuart to remain fast.

The three Overmires were in the cabin's main room and they had been talking, but now stopped. He managed his smile and he made his bow and saw Lucy's smile come lightly back to him. "I have been anxious about you," he said.

"Look at her," said Overmire, with pride.

"She has got the constitution of a horse."

She was in a fresh dress and her face had no fatigue on it; she seemed as she had always been. He said: "It's chilly tonight. Don't you need a shawl, Lucy?"

"No. I'm warm and I'm content."

"You must have been miserably cold, and afraid."

"It was not that bad."

She was as reticent as Logan Stuart had been; both of them covered their memories. He looked keenly down at her, his small smile hiding his actual feelings; and her glance came back, revealing nothing to him.

Overmire said: "Well, Lucy's a good soldier. Never say a woman's weak. Also, she was in good hands."

Mrs. Overmire said: "I told the Postons we'd come over tonight for a talk, Jonas." Overmire looked up with a momentary surprise and then, reading her wishes, rose and walked into the night with her.

"Your mother," said Camrose, "is always thoughtful. I regret you didn't get your trip to San Francisco. Will you try again?"

She shook her head. "It doesn't seem that vital now." Then she saw his change of expression and amended the remark. "Any dress will do."

"Ah," he said. "You had me frightened. I thought you might —"

"Don't go back to that," she asked him.

"Don't let's try to explain things which shouldn't need explaining, or keep digging into things which are plain enough."

"Perhaps it has been a fault of mine," he agreed. He sat down in Overmire's favorite rocking chair and drew it beside her, his jealous mind still creating pictures. He kept cautioning himself, but the strain grew until at last he had to speak. "Lucy," he said, "you're fond of Logan."

"Logan and I have always been friends. The three of us have been very close. It is nothing new, is it?"

"When a man and a woman are thrown together, as you were, they are likely to discover things they had not known before."

"George," she said, "you need not be troubled about that."

He waited with his tense anxiety, expecting her to continue, to fill in his suspicions or to wipe them away. But her brevity was like Stuart's, bare and unrevealing. He said: "Naturally, I have wondered at what might have happened. You see, I have discovered something about him. I think he loves you."

The steady calm of her expression remained, though he thought it grew colder. She sat silent, with no warmth coming from her to him; she was alone and apart from him.

"You're wrong."

"I don't think I am. But I'm not so much concerned about that. What chills me to the bone is to think you may have changed toward me. I know I have distressed you at times with my ways, yet there has never been a moment when I have not thought of you insistently."

Her smile returned, small and very gentle. He had touched her; she came back to him from whatever distant place she had been and looked at him with a quiet and personal regard. "Yes, you have caused me distress, George."

"I know," he said. Then his curiosity rose and he added: "How have I?"

"Do you remember how long the days used to be when we did not see each other? How short they were when we were together? Then there came a time when you drew back and grew indifferent, as though you questioned everything between us. It left me outside of you."

"I have never changed. Only I hate to have you feel I am greedy or dominating."

"Better that than to be lukewarm."

"Ah," he said, "if you knew how desperate I have gotten, how scarlet my thoughts have sometimes been —"

"Let's have no more questions or explanations. I have got a white dress. It will do. This is Saturday. Let the ceremony be next Saturday."

He lifted her hand and put it against his cheek; he was stirred, and for one rare moment he was humble. "You will have no regrets."

"Nobody can live without mistakes and regrets," she said. "Stay close and keep me close. The rest of it does not matter."

He displayed a slight concern. "I have missed my way here. We've got to go somewhere else and start fresh. Will it hurt you so much to leave?"

"It will hurt," she admitted. "But if it must be, I'll not complain."

He rose, smiling and partially reassured; she had restored some of his confidence. "You're still tired. I'll see you tomorrow."

She looked at him with a reserved interest. "What made you say that about Logan?"

"It was something I thought I saw in him."

"If it were there, I would have seen it long before you," she said.

As soon as he left the cabin, she relaxed her guard and felt weary from the strain of holding it against him. It was difficult to keep from a man the bitter knowledge that the first great feeling of love had gone, leaving in its wake something less than love but something more than kindness. There was no precise word for that emotion or that frame of mind; but it was the thing most women had to content themselves with in marriage — the great and beautiful fire subsided to a few warm coals which furnished a kind of comfort, but no more than that.

It had never occurred to her that she would be one of those women; for in the beginning she had been so sure that George Camrose possessed all the gifts she held dear in a man.

They had been revealed by his laughter, his way of looking at her, by his moments of warmth and perception. She had been so sure, two years ago. It was this original sureness which now haunted her and made her doubt her own instincts, which made her still cling to George Camrose in the hope of seeing again what she had once seen.

It was not that she had acted in haste, or that he had been alone in her mind. She had known Logan Stuart as long as she had known George; and from the beginning she had felt the pull of Stuart's personality and the rough impact of his character. She had judged both these men and had accepted George. Stuart had never asked her; and now, looking back, she saw that he had drawn aside in George's favor. There was in Stuart that fixed affection for, and protectiveness over, George Camrose. Yet even had Stuart asked her, she would have still taken George.

How was it she had not early seen in him those things she now clearly saw? How was it he had not stirred her then, but now shook her by his nearness, by the sound of his voice and the touch of his hand? It shamed her to realize that she now so often thought of Stuart in that close and warm way she had once thought of George. It shook her faith in her own judgment and cheapened the value of her affections. Time upon time she had sought an explanation for that change. Was it George whose gradual revealment of himself had disillusioned her? Or was it Stuart whose shadow faded out the image of George within her?

She had long known Stuart's feelings for her. He had betrayed them by his silence, by his tenderness, by his quick quarreling with her. She pitied Caroline for what Stuart never could give her, and she hated Caroline for what the girl would have from him. Jealousy had its cruel and inconstant way with her. But she could not change her loyalty as she changed a dress. There was a firmness in life which had to be followed and compromises to be made, and tragedies, little and great, to be forgotten. Having taken George Camrose, she would keep him and wait for the old feeling between them to return. Logan had closed the last chance for both of them to do it differently. She tought: "If we could only start over," and thrust that inconstant and futile wish from her mind.

12

Decision of the Camp

There was still a small group on the street when Stuart, having had his drink with Thackeray, left Corson's. He identified the six men clustered together and he nodded at them, at Joe Harms and Johnny Steele in particular, and passed on to his store. In the room behind the store, he thrust a revolver beneath his trouser band, caught up his rifle and let himself into the night by the back way. He went directly to his barn, saddled a horse and soon was out of town.

He recognized a greater impatience and a shorter temper within him, and he suspected it to be caused by the breakup of the old plain and easy things of his life which he valued so much. It was grisly business to strip away the tolerance and the generosity of his friendship with Camrose and dig down into the underlying substance and at last discover that shoddy material lay there. It was a denial of all the warm impulses which sustained men and kept them sweet.

This was the man he protected, and this was the man Lucy was marrying. "He will lead her through forty years of trouble, and what will she have to show for it?" Yet there was no way of changing a woman's heart. Camrose was the man she wanted, and her wants were too firm to change. He saw the sweetness of her smile and he felt the constant pressure of her lips; and abruptly he gave the horse a sharp spurring and galloped down the road.

He saw a light glimmering through the creek willows below him, shining out of Bragg's cabin. He thought: "The man's a fool to be around here," and rough feeling spread through him. Fifty feet from the cabin he got down and led his horse into the trees; and he halted a moment to survey the area in front of the cabin as it stood vaguely revealed by the thin moonlight. A horse stood in the yard and voices came from the cabin — one voice heavy, the other a smoother and more metallic tone. That made two within the cabin.

He crossed the yard and came to the cabin's door. He had left his rifle in its saddle boot; he stood on the balls of his feet with his revolver drawn and his free hand stretched toward the door. Suddenly he lifted the door's latch and drove it open, and for a moment he had a view of the two men whose voices he had heard. Both of them — Bragg and Lestrade — sat at the table in the room's center, the lamp between them and the light of the lamp shining upon them. Their faces came up, startled by the interruption, and it was Lestrade whose quick mind first reacted. In another instant his hand swept over the table and knocked the lamp down. Bragg rose from his chair and made a diving turn as the light died out.

Stuart shot at that weaving shape and heard the bullet smash against the farther wall. Kerosene smell drifted through the door and a bullet came back at him, its echo creating a huge explosion inside the small cabin. Stuart fired again, stepped aside and heard Bragg's enormous cursing. They were both shooting at him with intemperate haste; flattened against the cabin wall, he heard their feet shuffling ceaselessly back and forth on the hard dirt floor, he heard them collide and grunt from the impact. Bragg apparently struck Lestrade out of sudden, thoughtless rage, for Lestrade's voice rose in passionate resentment. "Keep your damned brute hands off me!"

Stuart cast a glance sharply behind him, scanning the shadows for those other men always hanging to Bragg's heels. He saw nothing to warn him and he stood fast, a growing temper steadily goading him. He had them trapped but he could not flush them. He called at them: —

"Come out of there!"

"Stuart!" It was Lestrade's voice, heightened by fear. "Stuart, for God's sakes let me through! Hold your fire!"

"Both of you come out," said Stuart.

"Hold your fire."

"Make a run for it," said Stuart. "I'll let you through."

They had both stopped moving. He heard the sucking whistle of their aroused breathing; he heard them whispering. Sliding to the edge of the door, he fired a shot into the cabin and backed away. Lestrade sent up his terrible cry of protest.

"I'm not in this fight! Logan, remember Marta. Remember —" The shuffling of feet began once more and Lestrade's voice picked up a panic and a trembling. "Bragg — stop it! Let go — let go!"

Stuart backed away from the cabin, not understanding what went on in there. Bragg seemed to have lost his head, to have attacked his partner. Lestrade shouted at the top of his voice, then the cry trailed into strangled fragments. The doorway showed a heavy shadow, and on this shadow Stuart took his aim. But he held his fire, careful and puzzled. The shadow was thick enough for two men and as it moved through the door, he discovered that it was two men. Then Lestrade shouted, "I'm in front, Logan. Don't fire!" He was inside the iron hoop of Bragg's arms, calling and cursing and crying as Bragg backed away from him toward the end of the cabin. Suddenly Bragg released Lestrade and there was an obscure flurry between the two men and a hollow, woody echo clapped over the night. One shape dropped. Stuart fired on the remaining shape as it faded toward the end of the cabin. He missed his shot. He growled to himself and rushed toward the cabin's end, behind which Bragg now had taken shelter; then he wheeled and aimed at the cabin's other end. He reached it and went around it to the back side. He walked along the cabin's length and turned the corner and found Bragg retreating into the near-by timber. He fired and he saw Bragg jump as though struck. Bragg came around, issuing a great cry which had no meaning in it; he returned the fire and got into the brush and made his way through it with a careless thrashing of his body.

Stuart followed that noisy trail into the brush, suddenly to find himself facing stillness and pure blackness. Bragg, animal-sly, had frozen in his covert. He was less than twenty feet away, betrayed by his heavy, winded breathing. Stuart turned his head, seeking to orient that source; he took two steps forward and thus broke the stillness and gave away his own position. Bragg had waited for this, and at once the big one came at him with a full-charging fury. Stuart stepped softly aside. He still saw nothing, but as Bragg went by him, a yard away, he lifted his gun and let go with the last shot in the revolver.

He had missed again. Meanwhile Bragg, having failed with his surprise attack, never stopped; his momentum carried him deeper into the timber. The sound of that huge body grew fainter and after a while it faded out entirely somewhere in open country. Turning toward the cabin with disgust stinging him, Stuart crouched over the shape of Lestrade. He ran a hand across Lestrade's face; he touched Lestrade's head, and drew his hand away. This man was dead.

He got hold of Lestrade's arms and dragged the man well off from the cabin; then he went inside the cabin and lighted a match and threw it on the lamp's spilled kerosene. He watched the blue flame start up and crawl out along the floor toward the log wall; he saw it catch the wall and flicker along the kerosene splashed there. The light brightened as the fire took hold. When he was certain it would not die, he turned back to his horse and made his way toward Jacksonville.

From the slight view point of the military road he looked back and downward upon the increasing glow of the fire with a taciturn satisfaction; but his gritty anger remained, his sense of a thing incompletely done grew greater. He thought carefully of Bragg's next move, believing he knew what the big one would do: he would hole up somewhere along the river and would wait for another chance to attack. Tomorrow, Stuart decided, he would move along the river in search of Bragg.

The little group watched Stuart go into his store. Then Joe Harms said: "We've got to be careful about him. He'll go against us."

"Come down to my cabin," said Steele.

The group, now of ten men, quietly drifted to the back edge of town; when they got to Johnny Steele's cabin there were twelve of them and they made a tight fit inside Johnny's crowded walls. Johnny said: "Where's Camrose?"

"Up at the girl's."

"I been a little afraid he'd smell something and run."

"Ain't been a day I've let him get out of my sight," said Harms. "It's time now to take him in."

"We got to do it quiet," said Steele. "We'll go to his office and wait until he comes."

Harms said: "We'll have trouble with Stuart."

Dick Horeen shook his head. "Not if he knows Camrose did it."

He was the only one who believed it. "You don't know Stuart," said Johnny Steele. "Well, we'll have to be ready for it. Come on now."

They left the cabin and made a wide circle around the town, coming at last to Howison's hay barn; they drifted in behind Camrose's office building, which showed no light. Johnny Steele gently tried the door's latch. The door opened before him. He said: "Harms and Horeen — you come in here with me. Rest of you stick back in the shadows. Somebody better stay on the street and watch for him to come."

One of the crowd had already thought of that, and now returned rapidly. "He's walking this way."

"All right," said Steele and, with his two partners, stepped inside the room and closed the door. Steele said through the darkness: "Spread out along the wall."

A key grated in the front door's lock and Camrose came into the office room, locked the door in the darkness and slowly made his way across the floor. Presently a match burst the blackness and a thin shaft of lamplight slid through the partially open door which stood between the rear room and the front room. None of the miners were in a position to observe Camrose, but it appeared he was opening the company safe, for they heard the click of the tumblers and the groaning of the heavy hinges. There was a considerable silence after that; then the hinges groaned again. He picked up the lamp and came forward. The door opened before him at that instant and he saw them.

Johnny Steele said: "Stand fast, George."

Camrose looked at them and was not particularly concerned. He had, in fact, a growing air of amusement about him, as though there were a joke in all this. He held the lamp steady, betraying no nervousness, and for a moment Johnny Steele doubted his own suspicions. This man was either exceedingly cool or he had a clean conscience. In another moment Steele understood why Camrose was so calm.

"You boys," said Camrose, "are a bunch of fools. Robbery is a tough thing in this camp.

You might make the hills but you'll be followed and you'll be caught."

"Why, damn your soul," said Joe Harms indignantly, "you take us for crooks?"

"Then what are you doing here?" asked Camrose.

Johnny Steele reached forward and took the lamp from Camrose's hands, thus depriving him of a possible weapon. He placed the lamp on the room's small table. "You know what we're here for," he said.

The sound of voices brought the other nine men in from the darkness, whereupon the observant Johnny Steele saw the sharpening and thinning intensity come to Camrose's eyes. Camrose's glance searched the crowd; the normal ruddy color went from his face and the easy arrogance went from it until his cheeks were pale as ivory and a kind of numbly sickened cast showed about his heavy lips. Steele was no longer uncertain; this man was guilty. The whole thing was a miserable business, but it helped to know that they were not making a mistake.

"We'll put a guard around the place tonight," he said, "and we'll have a miners' court for you tomorrow. McIver had a lot of friends and there might be some thought of quick action. We'll see it doesn't happen. You're going to get a trial."

"Boys," said Camrose in a tone wholly unlike him, "what have you got against me?"

"You just look into yourself and find the answer to that."

"No," said Camrose. "What have you got to show against me?"

"We'll show it at the trial," said Steele. He saw a tensing of the man's body and a brisker light in the man's eyes. He stepped forward, made a swift pass with his hands beneath the skirts of Camrose's coat and stepped back with Camrose's gun. "That was in your mind, wasn't it, George?"

Camrose shrugged his shoulders. "Have a good time for yourself, Johnny."

"Listen," said Steele, "I don't like this job. I've been a friend of yours."

"My God, Johnny," said Camrose, "don't speak the word." He stared about him; his glance stopped on Harms with contempt and a distaste. "You are to be congratulated, gentlemen, in the company you keep. This man, for example. This narrow-eyed, thin-nosed specimen who hates whatever is bigger than he is — and therefore hates everybody. I should like to see his soul laid before you. It would shame you for the human race to see the littleness of it, its crooked turnings, its quavering fear, its sneaking, creeping, crawling cunning. Here is a weasel in the form of a man, using his claws to dirty the garments of his betters as they pass by. He does not belong with you. He doesn't belong in any company, and he knows it and sits aside on his box and hates the town and never ceases to use his malice on it. He could be dangerous if he had courage, but he has no courage. If you struck him he would cringe, but he would forever hate you and scheme against you. I'd greatly appreciate it if you'd not have him here guarding me."

Joe Harms kept his glance on Camrose, and when silence fell he dropped his head, a small flush on his face. It was an odd silence which seemed hard to break; and nobody came to Joe Harms's defense. Finally Steele cleared his throat. "I'll take first watch with Abrams, Cooney, Geddes and Joe Smith. The rest of you come back at midnight."

As the others filed out, Steele noticed how calm Camrose had become; it was the resigned calm of one who had given up most of his hope.

At four o'clock Stuart rose to shave and cook his breakfast and to spend his time at Clench-field's desk while the sounds of the awakening town drifted into the store's pungent stillness and the rising daylight broke the store's gray shadows. Sunlight came and men moved along the street, all talking. Clenchfield came in, cranky and taciturn. He got half across the room and, attracted by something outside, turned back to the street. Of all this Stuart was only indifferently aware as he labored with his own particular problems. Then Clenchfield came in again and silently hung up his coat and hat. Stuart said: "How much have we got in the safe, Henry?"

"One thousand gold."

"I think I'm going to The Dalles to pick up mules."

"Ah," said Clenchfield. "When will you be goin'?"

"Not today — not tomorrow. I'm going hunting first."

"A Bragg hunt," said Clenchfield.

Stuart heard talk rising at the east end of town, and Clenchfield seemed to be waiting for something. "What's on your mind, Henry?"

"You've not heard the news?" asked Clenchfield. "The world is rockin' this mornin', Logan. Your world will rock hardest. They have taken Camrose in."

Stuart said quickly: "He's all right, Henry. He's not short. His accounts will balance. Who took him in? This damned town gets excited too fast."

"Murder is hard to balance," said Clenchfield. "Mack McIver's murder."

He got from Stuart the roughest glance he had ever received from any man. The quick and intolerant anger of it troubled him. It was the way he knew Stuart would take this, believing no evil of his friend and defending his friend. If the town was against Camrose, Stuart would be against the town. There was no halfway to him. "There will be a court on it," said Clenchfield. "He will get his fair hearing."

"God damn that crowd. Who started it?"

"It was something Steele and Joe Harms have been working on."

Stuart remained still, his mind working in ways which Henry Clenchfield understood so well. There would not be any thought of suspicion in Stuart's head; there would be only a sense of the injustice placed upon Camrose. There would be no thought of letting this thing run its orderly way. He was a partisan, he was a rough-handed fighter who took care of his own injustices and would take care of Camrose's. He would be thinking of action, and action now. It was reflected in the sudden swing he made toward the door.

He stopped before he reached the door; for at this moment a dozen men were coming in, headed by Johnny Steele and Joe Harms.

"What the hell do you want here?" said Stuart.

Steele was not surprised; he had braced himself for this kind of reaction and he had carefully prepared himself. "Why, Logan, that's no way to talk to a friend."

"I don't regard you as a friend," said Stuart bluntly.

Steele shrugged his shoulders. "Sorry it's got to be this way. McIver was a friend of mine — and I'll fight for my friends the same as you fight for yours. You can see that, can't you?"

"You're a little late bringing this up."

"It took us some time to piece the thing together," said Steele. "Harms here —"

"Harms," said Stuart, "should have been shot through the head long ago for looking through keyholes."

Harms flushed and looked around him for support; but none of the other men seemed disposed to come to his help.

"Well," said Steele, "it's a disagreeable thing. But we've got to hold a court on it and we need a big room. Your store's the biggest, Logan. We'll use it."

"No," said Stuart. "I'm not having my friends tried here."

"Wait a minute," said Steele, growing quietly stubborn. "You can't buck the town. We've got the right to take over what we want for this thing."

"Who gave you that right?" demanded Stuart.

"If we've got no law in this particular matter, we'll make one on the spot. You been in mining camps long enough to know that. We'll use this place."

"You're wrong on that, Johnny."

Steele said, with his steady effort at conciliation: "You can't buck the town. It is right and you're wrong. Anyhow it is too strong for you."

"It wasn't very strong when Bragg walked through this street and kicked you boys around as he pleased. You didn't form any committees then, Johnny. You were all looking in the other direction."

More men had gathered in the doorway to view the scene; for Jacksonville, loving its drama, knew the drama of this situation very well. Steele shrugged his shoulders. "That's different."

"The difference is you figure Camrose can't hurt you, so you're brave and full of righteousness. If Bragg came along you'd run like scattered rats."

Steele flushed but held doggedly to his point. "You've always been on the right side in this camp. Hate to see you get on the wrong side."

"I am not wrong because I'm alone. The town's not right because it has got the numbers. The man who joins the pack because he's afraid to be outside of the pack is a damned poor man. The town didn't join me when Bragg came along. I don't join it now when you're all drunk with the idea of a Roman holiday."

Steele, agreeable and quiet in most things, could not back down from his position. He studied the challenge in his mind, slowly coming to some sort of decision about it; and was slowly stiffening himself to the decision's disagreeable consequences when Dick Horren swung the scene away from danger. "No use arguing," he said. "There's other places. Corson's deadfall will do. Come on."

Johnny Steele showed a degree of relief and said: "No hard feelings, Logan."

Stuart looked at him with a thin smile showing. "When we're through fighting, Johnny, I'll love you like a brother. But while we're fighting, I'll break every bone in your body, if I must."

Joe Harms, long silent, now ventured a remark. "You have got no business —"

Stuart took two steps forward, struck the man hard enough on the shoulder to whirl him half about. He seized Harms at arm and crotch and he lifted him and flung him straight into the crowded doorway. Harms fell and, in falling, carried another pair of men down with him. For a moment there was an irritable cursing among them as they got through the door. Then Harms picked himself up and shook his fist at Stuart. Stuart watched these men with his edged smile; he saw them waver between their anger and their liking for him, and his grin broadened when they moved out. He stepped through the door among them and moved past them toward the foot of the street.

He saw a circle of men around Camrose's shop, all armed, and as he came forward he noticed this circle tighten. Johnny Steele followed him and Johnny Steele's voice came at him sharply. "Keep your head, Logan. Got a gun on you?"

"No," said Stuart.

Steele said, "Let him go in," and the guards at the door stepped aside to let Stuart through. He closed the door and walked to the rear room. Camrose lay full length on his bed; he had heard Stuart's steps but he neither rose nor looked at Stuart. He stared at the ceiling as he spoke. "I thought you'd come. What do you suppose this thing will amount to?"

"The lads are hunting up a place to hold a court."

"A murder charge calls for a trial before a proper judge and jury. This thing will turn into a joke — a damned bad joke."

"The boys want it done this way. If they can make a case against you, you may be held over for a proper trial. If not, they'll let you go and forget it." He looked at Camrose and then added: "But don't plan on it. With a couple more drinks, the boys will see to it there's a case against you."

"Then," said Camrose, "I'll not be held over for a proper trial. They'll come in during the middle of the night and take me out and hang me."

"That's it," said Stuart.

Camrose lay quite still, with a hand over his eyes. He said in a soft, flat tone: "How are you going to get me out of this?"

"Take your hand off your face and look at me."

Camrose withdrew his hand and sat upright on the edge of the bed. He lifted his head to show Logan a pair of bloodshot eyes. He needed shaving and he needed fresh air; he seemed half stupid. "Looks like you've been on a hell of a drunk," said Stuart.

"I have," said Camrose. "I drank a quart of whisky between midnight and breakfast. It was hardly enough. Two quarts would have been better."

"Keep your eyes on me. Did you kill him?"

"No," said Camrose.

Stuart watched the face of this man who had been so long a friend, recalling all the shades and shifts of expression Camrose used to reveal and to cover himself. He searched that disheveled, half-pale countenance for the truth. There was a dull indifference in the man, a fatalism which cut his vitality and shadowed his spirit. It was a strange thing to see.

"Well," said Camrose, "are you convinced?"

"What have they got for evidence?" asked Stuart. "What can they show?"

"He had his money stored with me. He got it out the night he died. They think he didn't get it. They think I killed him because I needed it."

"That's not enough," said Stuart. "What have they got for proof? Think hard. Can you prove you gave him the money? Can you show where you were that night? You were with me, part of the time. You left the shop around ten. Where did you go?"

"To Lestrade's."

Stuart shook his head. "He's no help to you. He's dead."

"I heard about it," said Camrose. "You went to Bragg's last night, I hear. Well, it's rough on Marta. In a way it is. Then, in a way it isn't. He wasn't around when I was at the cabin. She was. She can testify to it. I was there about midnight."

"That's fine," said Stuart irritably. "You were alone with Marta Lestrade at midnight. How do you suppose that will sound to the camp?" He stared at Camrose with a growing suspicion. "What were you doing there? Is there anything between you and Marta?"

"I don't like you prying into my private affairs, Logan."

"Then maybe I ought to let you handle this alone," said Stuart bluntly.

"Don't be so rough about it. There's nothing between Marta and me."

"Think hard," said Stuart. "Think of everything you did that night, or before that night, or after that night. Get your mind on it. Is there anything at all they can use against you? Johnny Steele's no fool. What've you done that's made him certain?"

"They've got no proof of any kind."

"They don't need proof. All they need is two or three things that look like funny business. They'll string 'em together and vote you dead. Now how about Harms?"

"God damn Harms," said Camrose, with his first show of energy during all this talk. "I hate that little yellow dog. Somebody ought to shoot him. Somebody will." He fell silent, his eyes half closed, and at last added with sullen reluctance: "He's got nothing he can use against me."

Stuart listened to the tone, he raked the passive and numbly set face, and doubted if he had the truth. Here was a man he thought he knew well; yet here was a man he didn't know at all. There were black corners in him holding strange qualities which were better unseen. Out of friendship he had endowed George with a kind of character he wanted him to have; now he saw it was an illusion of his own making. Camrose was another kind of man, and one he liked little. Yet it made no difference; he was bound to Camrose.

"You look whipped," he said, "You act and talk whipped. What the hell's the matter with you?"

"They've ruined me, I'll have to leave the camp. Even so, it will follow me. Those things always do."

"I've heard a lot of proud talk from you," said Stuart, "but evidently it means nothing. You've never had to fight and now you don't know how. Get up and start wrestling with your troubles."

"Logan," said Camrose, "get me out of this."

Stuart shook his head, not at the request but at his final judgment of Camrose. When a man laughed at the rules of the game and dreamed of making himself big by breaking them, he had to stand the consequences when he lost; he had to be as tough when the rules broke him as when he broke the rules. But Camrose wasn't tough. He could only play the winning half of the game; he could not play the losing half.

This was the end of a man who had defied the world. It was a sorry thing to see.

"Get me out of it, Logan," said Camrose, in a quicker voice.

"I'll see what can be done," said Stuart and turned to the door.

Camrose called at him quite sharply and when Stuart turned he saw his friend upright in the room, haggard, swaying a little on his feet, with his hair fallen down over his forehead. The gallantry and the laughter were gone, leaving nothing very admirable. "I was a friend when the weather was fair," he said. "Now you'll let them tear me apart." He stared at Stuart with a growing cynicism. "I'll be out of your road. It will make things easier for you, won't it?"

Stuart shook his head and left the room. The guards were in front of the building, facing the growing crowd; and Lucy was just then coming forward. She stared at Stuart without speaking, and he gave her a short nod and went on up the street to the store. He sat down on a pile of boxes and he filled and lighted his pipe and sat forward with his hands across his knees, engrossed in a, problem that seemed to have no answer.

Men were moving back toward Corson's deadfall and a little later Lucy came into the store. He put aside his pipe and looked up to her; he had the greatest kind of curiosity as to her feelings in the matter but he made out nothing particular on her face. She said in a tone of mild surprise: "The camp doesn't like George. I never knew that before. These men mean to hang him. I can tell it. What will you do?"

"What should I do?" he said.

"You're sitting there trying to think of something. I know you so much better than I know anybody else. You'd like to break down that building and let him out. It is quite clear on your face. Your mind is going up and down and back and forth. You're hunting a way. I don't need to say it, but I will anyhow. Do what you can. I'm asking it for a particular reason."

"I know the reason well enough," he said.

"No," she said, "I think you don't." She stood a moment longer and then turned out of the store.

He called after her. "Have your father defend him."

Bragg slept in the willows a mile removed from his cabin and woke at daylight with a disposition made worse by the night's discomfort. He flattened by the creek for a drink and he stood in the morning's curt air and made debate with himself. He had no desire to go back to the ruined cabin, or to the dead Lestrade; no doubt there would be a bunch from the camp waiting for him, and ready to make short work of him. Stuart would see to that end of it.

Somewhere around the country were his two followers, but he had no interest in finding them. Having been burned out, he was footloose and did not particularly care. One camp was as good as another for his work and if Jacksonville was no longer open to him, it was a simple business to move on. It made no great difference.

But he would not go until he had reached out with his great arms and pulled Stuart down; all the tremendous hatred of which he was capable now fastened itself to Stuart, and would be satisfied with nothing less. It took him but a few moments to make a decision on that; he would stray over to the Rogue and, keeping to the river's thicket, follow toward the Oregon-California road. Sooner or later Stuart would be coming along it.

The hard ground had stiffened him, hunger worked at him, and the night's coldness had permitted him little sleep; and so he made his lumbering way through the valley's brush and across the open meadows toward the Rogue in the manner of a surly bear. At the river he flattened for another drink, and he sat in a patch of sunshine until warmth came to him. Rising again, he walked casually on. Evans's Ferry was three miles distant; at that point he promised himself a good meal. The ferryman was no friend of his, but would not dare refuse him.

Somewhere short of that point, unaccustomed to walking, he sat down and he lay back in the willows to rest himself; and so fell asleep. In his sleep he heard a voice speak and then he woke, and heard two voices near the river. He rose on his haunches and crawled forward and slowly parted the willows until he had a view of two Indian women, both young, standing neck deep in the river.

He watched them for a long while — solemn, intent, unemotional. He looked beyond them, up and down the bank, and saw no other Indians. There would be no Rogue men close by, he guessed, since these girls were swimming; they had gotten themselves away from the party to do this. He drew a long breath and, when they were about to come out of the water, he rose and gathered himself. He was foxy in his stalking; he waited until they had gotten ashore to their clothes. Then, parting the brush, he made his rush at them.

They heard his body crushing across the river's gravel and turned at once to discover this shocking and formidable figure charging forward, his blackly whiskered face all scarred and torn, his heavy chest issuing strange sounds. They saw him and broke away in full flight across the gravel in their bare feet. One of them got to the river and soon gained the middle of the stream; the other kept to the shore and presently drew away from him. Realizing he had no luck, Bragg stopped short, whipped out his gun and fired at the running girl. He dropped her and then turned his aim to the girl in the river. She understood what he was about to do, but she made no cry at all; she went beneath the surface to escape him and he saw the shadow of her body drifting with the current. He walked along the shore, keeping abreast. When she rose for air he shot at her and missed, and watched her sink again. He kept walking and he shot a second time; he broke into a run and got ahead of her, and stopped for better aim. His third shot caught her; he watched her body roll and her head drop. To make sure she was dead, he fired again and saw her body flinch slightly in the water. He squatted on the gravel and reloaded his gun and he took the time to fill his pipe and light it. The sun was rising east of the river; he looked at it, his beaten lips drawing back from his teeth. Then he rose and returned to the willows and continued his march toward Evans's.

13

At Corson's

Camrose stood against one of Corson's walls, with Overmire beside him and Johnny Steele near by. The judge — a miner popularly elected for the occasion — sat on the edge of Corson's bar with his feet hanging down. He had a snow-white beard slightly rusted around the edges of his mouth, and he took the occasion with considerable dignity, and therefore made a sat-isfactorily ornamental judge. The rest of the room was packed its length and breadth, and the windows had been taken down so that others could look in from the street. Johnny Steele was at the moment telling his story.

"One night I came into camp and asked Camrose for my poke, which was in his safe. He locked the door on me while he opened the safe, which took him a long time. Then he let me into the shop and gave me my poke. It weighed out all right, and I had nothing to be suspicious of. Nevertheless I was, so I got to talking around camp and found Camrose was losing more money at poker than he could afford."

Overmire stopped him. "That's hearsay, Johnny."

"Well, the whole camp knows it."

"The whole camp has heard stories of it, but the whole camp does not know it. You cannot convict him on what you have heard somebody else say."

"If I saw something," said Johnny, "and I told it to Bill Smith, then Bill Smith would know it as well as me."

Overmire was about fifteen feet from Steele. He reached for a coin and dropped it on the bar so that everybody could hear its echo. "Johnny, what have I got here?"

Johnny, suspecting Overmire, gave the coin a long and thorough glance. "A dollar."

"What kind of dollar?"

"A silver dollar."

"You're certain of it?"

Johnny looked again. "I'm dead certain of it."

Overmire picked up the coin between thumb and forefinger, showing it to the crowd.

He pointed to a man in the back of the room. "What does it look like to you, Moffatt?"

"Looks like a dollar to me."

Overmire pointed at another man, drawing a like answer. He solicited the answer of several miners until at last one of them said: "You're wastin' time, Jonas. It's a plain old U.S.

dollar."

"So, then," said Overmire, "you say it's a plain old U.S. dollar. Johnny has identified it and you take Johnny's testimony because you believe him to be a truthful man. He did not try to mislead you. He said it was a dollar. You jumped one step farther and made a U.S. dollar out of it, which is not true. It is Mexican. And that is the danger and unrealiability of hearsay evidence. What you do not see yourself, you cannot honestly swear to be true. As a matter of fact, you cannot always be certain that what you see is wholly true. Your eyes or your ears may betray you."

Johnny Steele studied Overmire a thoughtful while. He had a plain face made shrewd by a great amount of native intelligence and mental force. Of education he owned little and, like most men of that sort, he possessed both a respect for and a suspicion of those who were considerably schooled. Wanting wise counsel for himself, he would at once have gone to Overmire with fullest confidence; but with Overmire pitted against him he greatly feared the man's power to sway this audience and jury by words too cleverly used. The silver-dollar business was something these miners could see and appreciate; they had been influenced by it. He looked at Overmire, measuring the man; and Overmire, smiling and practical and folksy, looked back at him. Overmire and he both knew the game that was being played.

"It grew on me," went on Johnny Steele, "that Camrose was short with his accounts and was diddling with dust entrusted to him to temporarily square those accounts. He was losing a lot of money at poker —"

"Hearsay, Johnny," interposed Overmire.

"Thackeray," called Johnny Steele.

The gambler Thackeray made his way forward, his habitual coolness somewhat broken by being the center of the scene.

"Thackeray," said Steele, "did Camrose —"

"Swear him in first, Johnny," said Overmire. "You're trying a man for his life. Life is precious to you, isn't it? It is equally precious to George Camrose. Let us remember it is good to be alive, to wake to a fine morning with the sun coming up over the hill, to smell bacon frying in the pan, to drink the cold creek water when thirsty. It is good to sit in Corson's by night, the taste of whisky and a cigar on your tongue, feeling easy after a long day. A man lives a short time. He has his thoughts and his wants and his dreams and his memories, his regrets and his loves. Those things are not to be taken away by a few words lightly spoken. Swear him in, Johnny."

Overmire had spoken in a wholly conversational voice, as though making a simple observation among friends. But Johnny observed the effect of that talk and was troubled. He said: "Life was good to McIver, too. And it was taken from him."

"Was it taken from him," said Overmire, "or was it an accident? That's what we're trying to discover."

Nobody had thought of needing a Bible; but after some pause, a lean and shabby miner plucked a considerably twisted little book from his pocket. "New Testament do?"

Thackeray put his hand gingerly upon the New Testament and was sworn in.

"Now," said Steele, "did Camrose play poker with you?"

"Frequently."

"So, after beating around Robin Hood's barn," said Steele with deliberate irony, "we discover what everybody in town already knew. Did he lose money to you?"

"Considerable."

"Which everybody also knew," commented Steele. "Now it's legal ain't it, Jonas? Thackeray, how much would you say he lost to you?"

"Over a year or two, maybe five thousand dollars."

"His salary is less than that," said Steele to the crowd. Then he caught himself before Overmire could interpose. "Swear in Camrose."

Somebody gave Camrose the Testament while Overmire swore him in. "Now, George," said Steele, "what's your pay?"

"Two-fifty a month."

"Three thousand a year. But you lost two thousand more than you made. Where did it come from?"

"Some of it was Logan Stuart's. He had lent it to me for other purposes."

"For what purposes?"

"I won't say."

"You are on trial and you have got to answer the questions."

Overmire shook his head. "No accused man can be compelled to speak if he wishes to remain silent. That's the law, Johnny."

"Is it?" said Johnny, and knew he had an opening. He turned to the crowd. "If a man is innocent, why should he be afraid to speak?"

Heads began to nod before him in agreement. He had made his point, but Overmire, dueling each foot of this ground, spoke up. "I can answer that, Johnny." His glance went around the crowd and paused on Lid Shields. "Suppose Lid were walking up the street one night. Lid is going some place on an errand of his own —"

The crowd began to grin. Lid Shields's errands were well known and his destination was common knowledge, being the shack slightly beyond town which housed a woman. "So," said Overmire, "there is a killing on the street and Lid is accused and brought in. Somebody asks Lid, 'Where were you at that hour?' Lid cannot be forced to answer a question like that."

Johnny Steele pointed at Joe Harms. "Joe, come up here."

Harms shuffled forward, looking at nobody; he had his eyes pinned to a point on the wall, above and beyond the picturesque and silent judge. Steele swore him in. "Now Joe, did you ever see Camrose take gold pokes out of the office safe and shake dust from them?"

"Several times — late at night after he had locked the office door and closed the shutters. I've seen him weigh dust out of one poke, put it in another, weigh that poke, fix up the nuggets on top of the poke and put it back in the safe."

"Where were you?" asked Overmire.

"In the alley between Howison's and Camrose's."

Overmire studied Harms during a deliberately held silence — and this silence also had its effect on the crowd; it gave them time to think, and it piled weight on Harms, who shifted his position and looked around him. Then Overmire put his question softly: "How could you see all this?"

"There's a knothole, size of a robin's egg, in the boards. Lookin' through, I could just see the counter and the gold scales."

"You looked through the knothole quite often, Joe?"

"Every night," said Harms, "for some months."

"What made you start looking?"

"Never liked him. I was looking to see what I could find."

Overmire ran a hand down his beard and once more let the silence run. Harms's evidence supported what the camp suspected, and therefore it could not be wholly overthrown. Yet Overmire was well aware of the camp's general dislike of Harms and so he took a new line. "You spied on him because you didn't like him. Now, Joe, I guess I've talked with you as much as any man in camp. I have never heard you praise any human being. You dislike a great many people. Do you spy on all those people, too?"

Harms angrily met Overmire's glance. "No."

"Ever spy on anybody else?"

"No," said Harms, but it was clear to Overmire that this man lied, and it was clear as well to the crowd. Johnny Steele suddenly put in, "That's enough. I guess we've proved Camrose did monkey with the dust in those pokes."

"Maybe he was weighing out company money — which would be a legitimate part of his work," said Overmire.

Steele let that point go by. "Now, then. Mack McIver came into town. He played cards late one night. Next morning he was found dead with his face in the creek. A bunch of us went to Camrose's to get his dust and send it to his people. Camrose said Mack had already got the dust. But there was no dust on Mack when he was found."

He disliked what was to come next. It made him seem on Harms's level, and it offended his own strong sense of fitness. But he had it to say, and he said it: "I decided maybe we hadn't looked through Mack's pockets well enough.

Harms and me dug him up and took another look. We found something. It was in the little watch pocket at the top of his pants."

Everybody watched him as he drew a small bit of paper from his coat and opened it between his fingers. Overmire regarded it alertly and Harms for the first time began to look directly at the men around him, his self-respect somewhat restored. But it was Camrose whose reaction Steele wondered at. Swiftly lifting his glance, he caught the tightening expression on Camrose's face.

"This," said Johnny Steele, "is a receipt. Camrose gave it to Mack when Mack left the gold on deposit. If he had it on him when he died, he never got the gold, for it's sure Camrose would have asked for the receipt back."

Overmire shot a question at Harms. "Did you see Steele find this receipt on McIver's body?"

"Yes."

"Did you read it as soon as it was removed?"

"We turned the lantern on its first thing to see what it was."

Overmire extended his arm and took the paper and looked carefully at it. He showed it to Camrose. "This your writing?"

Camrose gave it a short glance. "Yes," he said in no particular tone.

Johnny Steele put a quick question at Camrose. "If you gave him the gold why didn't you take the receipt from him?"

The crowd waited with a strange and significant silence while Camrose formed his answer. Overmire, looking out at the miners, silently guessed they had swung against Camrose. "I seldom give out receipts," said Camrose. "You'll remember, Johnny, I never gave you a receipt for your gold. I put it in the safe for you, and I gave it back when you asked for it. That's been my common practice, as you boys know. But Mack was a suspicious man and wanted a receipt. I gave him one. When he got the gold back I never thought to ask for the receipt. I had forgotten about it, since it wasn't a customary thing with me."

"Careless, I'd say," commented Steele.

"We're all careless with gold. It's the cheapest thing in camp."

Johnny Steele stood in silence, thinking his way through and around the answer, until Overmire at last prompted him. "Is that all, Johnny? If so, it isn't enough. On the testimony of a Peeping Tom you have tried to show that Camrose shifted gold from one poke to another. On the basis of an unreturned receipt you deny Camrose gave back McIver's poke. It is not enough to deny it. It is necessary for you to prove it, which you have not done. Yet, assuming you had proved both points — you would still need to connect them to the murder and prove the murder. You have not done it. You have only said that Camrose murdered McIver and waved suspicion like a bloody flag at this crowd, hoping for passion to convict Camrose.

You brewed a witch's tale and you believed it — and now are trying to make witches of us all."

Johnny Steele said, "Come up, Pat Malloy."

Pat Malloy was a substantial ex-miner who had graduated by use of his wits and his thrift to the station of a storekeeper of small consequence; he had a brilliant red face, a stubby round nose and a set of roan eyebrows projecting over his eyes in such a manner that he seemed to be peering out from a shelter. Johnny Steele swore him in. "Tell us, Pat."

"What I was tellin' you? Well, he came into the store one night — a week ago — and he wanted a box of cigars, the kind of which I get from San Francisco —"

"Who came in?" asked Overmire.

"Wasn't we talkin' of Camrose? Him. I sold him the cigars and he gave me a nugget, and I weighed it and I gave him change. It was a fat thing of a nugget and pretty the way it was shaped. Pretty for an Irishman, that is. It was that much like a shamrock. So I made a little frame for it and set it up in the shop. The very next day Jim Hantis came in and he said: 'Where did you get McIver's lucky nugget?' Then it was three or four men who said it durin' the day and the next day."

Johnny Steele said: "Jim — and the rest of you — come up here."

Overmire gave his beard a strong pull and drew a long breath. He looked upon Camrose with a flat neutral glance. Camrose had the old, indifferent and withdrawn look to him again; he held himself straight and he seemed not to care. Hantis and the other three men, being sworn, one by one identified the nugget, and afterwards Overmire — scanning the crowd — saw there was no hope.

Johnny Steele said in a pleased and positive voice: "There is the case, Jonas. Twist it if you can."

"In all this where have you shown the connection between the nugget and the fact of murder?"

"That nugget was McIver's lucky piece," said Steele. "He found it four-five years ago and he always carried it in his left-hand pants pocket. How did Camrose get it? He could only have gotten it by taking it out of McIver's pocket. And he could have done it only at a time when Mack could not resist. In other words, when Mack was dead. I make murder out of that."

Overmire turned to Camrose. "You care to comment on that, George?"

"I took a fancy to it," said Camrose. "I offered him twenty dollars for it and he accepted."

Jim Hantis — and the other three friends of McIver's — all shook their heads in disagreement, and Hantis said positively: "McIver would never sell it. He had better offers than twenty dollars for it. He was a suspicious man and he was a superstitious man. He would have quit prospecting if he'd lost that nugget. He told me so many a time."

Johnny Steele had a closing speech in mind, and he had other witnesses. But he knew the men of this camp and as he looked around the crowd he realized he had made as good a case against Camrose as he would ever need to make. He turned to Overmire. "I am through. Your man is a guilty man, Jonas, and everybody in this room is convinced of it except you. You go ahead, Jonas, and throw your big words at us to confuse us. You talk about life being sweet. You talk about silver dollars and hearsay and all that. You try to make us cry, and make us doubt. You won't have luck. McIver is dead and his lucky nugget turned up in Camrose's hands — Camrose who has been having money trouble for a long time. We didn't take Camrose's hand and lead him to the scene of the murder and show him with a club in his hand. But we showed him with the nugget in his hand, and you can't explain that away. We all love life just as much as you, and we're all for fair play, but we want fair play for McIver as well as Camrose. There's such a thing as common sense which is a greater thing than all your rules and your warnings — common sense says he's guilty."

He stepped back to a corner of the room, fearing the speech Overmire was about to make, fearing the effect of the man's persuasiveness and umblemished reputation. He admired Overmire greatly and he knew the rest of the camp also admired the power, the force, the fairness and the resolution of Overmire. It was a thing for a camp to be proud of, the presence of such a man as a citizen.

Overmire stood beside Camrose. He was in no hurry to make a reply, since any reply called for a good deal of earnestness and conviction on his part; and the more he had listened to the testimony, the greater had become his doubt. He stood in a strange position. He was a future father-in-law to the man as well as an advocate. On both grounds he was obliged to give Camrose the best of his ability; and it distressed him to have his private feelings tell him he was defending a guilty man. He ran a hand thoughtfully down his beard; he made a gesture. The miners were of course expecting him to plead; they were looking forward to it, much as they arranged themselves to hear a Fourth of July oration.

"You're neighbors of mine," he said, "and I know you well. I understand exactly what you're thinking now. You know that this is not a legal trial. The laws of this territory are in force here, and this meeting has no sanction. It is only a popular assembly such as we had a few years ago, before law came. If you vote this man guilty, you must still hold him over to a regular court and a regular trial."

He searched them with his trenchant glance

and he saw he had their attention. "But you feel that this is a good enough trial. It was the way it was done in the old days. In your minds you have got the thing planned out. You intend to vote Camrose guilty and then, to save any possible miscarriage of your judgment, you will take him from his place of detention sometime after dark and hang him."

Looking about the crowd, he saw heads quietly nodding, and here and there a glance of admiration for his shrewdness. "What was law written for, if not to protect us all? Then let it protect Camrose as well as you. I could take the same set of facts which Johnny Steele used and I could convict any other man in this camp, guilty or innocent, if you disliked that man as much as you dislike Camrose. There is just enough logic in the facts to convince you. But there is also just enough looseness in them to kill an innocent man. In voting this man dead on that set of facts, you are setting a scene for another day when you may be voting one of yourselves dead on precisely the same set of facts. Now let us have your vote."

Johnny Steele was surprised, but also relieved, at the brevity of the plea and came forward at once. He said: "All that think he is not guilty, squat down on the floor."

Camrose gave his head a quick turn and his eyes went along the ranks of men with narrowed fascination. Two men in the fore of the crowd squatted immediately; there was some commotion in the back of the room as another man awkwardly attempted to lower himself. Otherwise the crowd stood still. It was an overwhelming vote. There had been some small play of light on Camrose's cheeks but now the watching miners — all keenly interested in seeing how he took his luck — observed dullness come to him. He turned his head away.

Throughout this affair Johnny Steele had pitted all his resources against a man he considered highly dangerous to his cause. Yet now that it was done and he had won his victory, he had a reversal of feeling. Before all the camp, Jonas Overmire stood for certain decent standards; his good opinion greatly mattered. Therefore Johnny Steele had the real fear that Overmire might feel he — as well as the rest of the camp — had acted out of baser motive than they should. "Jonas," he said earnestly, "this may not square with your idea of proper form, but it is our idea of justice nevertheless. I hope you do not think otherwise."

Overmire made a small gesture with his hand. "If I did not believe you to be sound and honest men I would not live in this camp."

Overmire left Corson's and crossed to Stuart's store, finding Stuart seated in a corner with his pipe. Stuart was anxious for the answer but he waited for it instead of asking for it.

Overmire said, "Guilty," and sat down on another box and searched himself for a cigar.

He trimmed it and he lighted it and he leaned back to an easy position. "You know," he said, "I am a strong believer in democracy. I have the greatest of faith in the ability of any group of Americans to come to a just decision. Haste and passion and prejudice and self-interest will sway us all at times. Now and then we make bad errors. Sometimes we follow bad leaders. Sometimes we descend to the animal level and are no better than the dumbest and angriest of beasts. But when you average everything out, one time upon another, one act upon another, one motive upon another, we live according to our lights — and our lights are honest and kind and colored with mercy."

"What do you mean to tell me by all that, Jonas?"

"There's always doubt," said Overmire. "But it was clear and plain enough to me. If I were a judge I should agree with the verdict and I should sentence George Camrose to be hung. Did you know about the nugget?"

"No."

Overmire settled back and made a verbal transcript of all the evidence. When he was through, Stuart gave a short nod. He was not a man, Overmire thought, to reveal himself much; he stuck by his own standards, and he was singularly independent in his actions. It was this independence which gave Overmire some concern.

"Now," said Stuart, "they've got him back

at his store under guard. They will take him out and hang him before morning."

"Maybe not."

Stuart shook his head. "If they had been willing to wait for a proper court and jury they would not have bothered with this meeting. This meeting is enough for them. They'll act on it."

"Johnny Steele started this, but Johnny's no firebrand. He won't stir them into violence."

"Johnny believes Camrose guilty," said Stuart. "According to Johnny's lights justice has got to be done, the sooner the better."

"You're a miner at heart," said Overmire. "What would you do — if Camrose were not your friend?"

"I would help hang him, Jonas. That's why I know they will."

"So would I," said Overmire, and tapped Logan Stuart's knee. "Maybe you have done all you could do, and maybe you should do no more."

"What would that be?"

"You're figuring a way to get him loose. That means you've got to go against the crowd. The camp respects you, Logan. But it respects its own decision more. If —"

Lucy came into the store. "What was it?"

"Guilty," said Overmire and did not meet his daughter's eyes. He made it blunt and swift, since he was a tenderhearted man.

She gave him a strained glance and then she was done with him, and turned her attention to

Stuart. Whatever her hope was, it seemed to lie in him. "How could they?"

Overmire said, "Listen," and quietly repeated the testimony. Then he said: "That's how." She had again turned her attention to Stuart, and Overmire, seeing and understanding it, added irritably: "Don't beg Logan for help."

"When I needed help, I've always come to Logan. Why shouldn't I now?"

"Because he'll try to do what you want, and get himself in a hell of a lot of trouble. I think there's been enough disaster caused by Camrose."

"Do you think he did all this, Dad?"

He rubbed his whiskers with the point of a finger. "I'm convinced of his guilt. He is a weak man."

This scene was interrupted by the marching in of four men, headed by Johnny Steele. It was a committee, and a self-conscious one, even Johnny Steele showing a reluctance in the matter to be discussed.

"Logan," he said, "it occurs to us you may give us some trouble. It would be like you to come down the street with the idea of getting Camrose free. It would be disagreeable. But, disagreeable or not, we'd shoot you for tryin'. Don't try."

"That's plain," said Stuart. "I'm glad you told me."

"Don't do it, Logan," repeated Johnny Steele, with all the earnestness he could command.

Then, done with an unpleasant chore, the committee left the store.

"That's it," said Overmire to Lucy. "Don't ask Logan for anything more."

It appeared that neither Logan nor Lucy had heard him. They were watching each other, Logan with his closest attention, Lucy with an expression wholly unlike her. It was neither anger nor appeal; it seemed a more primitive thing — as though she were silently delivering an unpleasant command to him. He grew uncomfortable at sight of it and glanced at Logan to observe the latter's reaction, and found nothing. These two had a way of speaking to each other in complete silence. In another moment Lucy turned and left the room. But something had been said between these two, for Stuart had nodded to Lucy as she turned away.

14

Outbreak

At three o'clock in the afternoon, Liza Bartlett left the cabin and walked diagonally across the meadow to where her husband was sawing out the winter's wood from a huge fir windfall; she carried a jug of coffee for him and the two of them sat on the log, alternately taking turns at the jug. She was the sober one of the pair, enormously determined to be a faithful and provident wife; it was young Gray who had the streak of fun in him — and it was he who spilled the coffee as he tried to seize and kiss her. "My old woman," he said and fell from the log. He was at the base of the log, laughing. She stood over him, facing the river and the river's willows, and suddenly he saw fear stretch and whiten her face, and he saw her lips form a word. Springing up he discovered a group of Indians — a swift sweep of the eye counted twenty of them — coming from the brush in a fan-shaped line, all trotting forward. One buck lifted his rifle and another buck whipped an arrow into his bow.

"Gray!" cried young Liza. "Gray!"

He reached for his own rifle propped against the log and shot the foremost Indian; then an arrow caught him in the shoulder and went deep, the shaft sticking from him. He shouted, "Run for the cabin!" Young Liza wheeled and came to him and put her arms around him. He pushed her away and got his ax and he stood with the fir log as a bulwark before him. He saw that Liza would not run and he shoved her below the log as the Rogues, still trotting, came to the log and spilled over it. A second shot killed him and the butt of another gun burst Liza Bartlett's head as she crouched by her husband and called to him. Her last gesture, as she died, was to put her arm upon him. . . .

The Rogues, rising out of the hidden creases of their reservation, followed the river's turnings, a band to one side of it and a band to the other. At McTeague's they were met by a well-determined fire, and, following two or three unsuccessful sallies, passed on to the Montgomery's cabin where they found Mrs. Montgomery and her baby alone. They caught the baby by the heels and dashed it against the cabin wall; they stabbed Mrs. Montgomery to death, pillaged the cabin and set it afire, and continued along the valley with the various household trinkets of the Montgomery family hung at their belts or knotted from their shoulders. At Partland's they found an empty cabin and burned it;

from the adjacent brush young Sam Rails saw the copper skirmish line coming over the meadow and fright gave him speed as he fled off to warn other settlers. Reaching Oldham's, the Rogues came upon a harder opposition and after an hour of intermittent firing, they continued their march to the Allen cabin. The sound of firing in the distance had warned Mrs. Allen in time. Taking her boy, she ran out to a brush pile in the meadow and buried her son and herself in it. With a hand held over the mouth of the whimpering youngster, she watched her cabin go up in flames — and lay there terrified long after the Rogues had gone.

The word of rebellions had apparently gone out to all the bands in these southern hills; for that same afternoon the miners along the Applegate were harassed and far down the river a band was seen on the Big Meadow bar. Over on the Crescent City trail, the Stuart pack train returning from the coast was caught and destroyed, beasts and men, and the supplies broken open and scattered through the timber.

Meanwhile the groups along the upper valley, passing the lower ferry without molesting it, came upon another Stuart pack train, then on its homeward trip from Scottsburg. Blazier and Murrow had some small warning and they hastily forted up in the brush to make a fight of it. Here, as elsewhere, a sense of haste impelled the Indians to make only half a try on those parties who showed resistance. They killed all the mules and mortally wounded Murrow; then, afraid to go deeper into the brush to catch Blazier, they went on toward Dance's, two miles north. Blazier made an attempt to bind up Murrow's torn side, but the older man, smiling at him regretfully, dropped back dead. Blazier, thinking of Caroline Dance, made his way toward that cabin, keeping close to the timber and the brush.

From the distance he heard a steady and stubborn fire which lasted for the best part of half an hour. Then it died away entirely and when Blazier came within view of the cabin he saw no sign of Indians or settlers. All the haycocks in the meadow were afire, and the sheds as well; but the main house stood. He weaved his way through the brush until he came within fifty yards of the place, and here he stopped and scanned the edges of the meadow and listened into the dwindling daylight for sounds. Presently he called — and heard a voice answer from the house.

He cut over the trail and went into the house. Mrs. Dance sat in a rocker with her husband dead on the floor and one son lying across the threshold of the rear doorway. He said: "Where's the other boys — where's Caroline?"

She shook her head. "I don't know. The boys are on a trip to the Applegate. Caroline — last I saw she was at the farther edge of the meadow lookin' for the no-horn cow."

"I'll stay around until help comes," he said.

"I'll go over the meadow and look."

"Caroline always could take care of herself," said Mrs. Dance in a dazed, erratic way. "She's all right. She'll be back when she finds the cow."

At noon, Stuart cooked his lunch in the back room; at one o'clock he left the store and walked down the street, past Camrose's office — the guards closely watching him — and out beyond the edge of the camp. He was not a man who could long endure sober reflection without growing stale and jaded and impatient. Action was his life, action made him run sweet and smooth; and so he tackled the rough foothills and drew sweat and felt wind pull through his lungs, and at three o'clock he returned to the store and sat down on a box with his pipe. Some kind of serenity had come to him, but the answer to his problem had not. The problem was — what now was his duty to Camrose?

He had long shut his eyes to the man's shortcomings. To those whom George Camrose liked — and therefore made the effort to please — it was an easy thing to find excuses for his moods, his easy indifference, his habit of taking so much for granted, his way of leaning on others. The man had charm when he chose to use it. But the veneer of charm had worn through the inner man showed out as a very shoddy material. Of Camrose's guilt, both in the matter of theft and in the matter of murder,

Stuart had little doubt. The judgment of the camp was sound; for after all, a man who had no scruples in the matter of stealing dust would scarcely have scruples in the matter of killing, if pressed to it by desperation.

Yet friendship had its ties which held even when friendship had gone. It was a cold-blooded man who suddenly, on the morning of bad luck, cut these ties clean and stepped away. It meant the ties were never very real; it meant a man's loyalty was a shifty thing, subject to any variation in weather. If a man could not stand fast in a few things, what kind of meaning did life have? He emptied his pipe, and refilled it. He sat wholly idle as he pushed his way through a deeper jungle than he had ever met with in the hills. The sun moved west and the shadows stretched out.

He realized Lucy now knew those things about George which he had never been able to tell her. Yet Lucy would never believe evil of Camrose; she was bound to her own principles as he, Stuart, was bound to his. So she had come to his store and she had told him — without saying a word directly about it — what he must do. It was a clear command. If he freed Camrose, the man would run, and Lucy would follow.

The foundations of the man were rotten; nothing permanent could be built upon them. What he was now he would always be; and he would ruin the girl's life. It was entirely clear.

Yet, there was nothing to do about it. Eventually she would be disillusioned and destroyed by this man. But if the camp hanged Camrose, she would still be destroyed — in another way; she would be a woman nursing a vain love for forty years and made infertile and hopeless by it. The whole thing was something written down in the Book of Judgment and no little act of theirs could erase any of it.

Clenchfield, watching with his interest, saw Stuart at last shrug his shoulders and bring a heavy hand down upon his knee. It was a decisive gesture. Then Stuart removed his pipe, gave it a displeased look and rose. "The tobacco we're getting up here is pretty foul, Henry."

"You've sucked at that thing five hours," said Clenchfield.

Stuart walked to the door and leaned a shoulder against the casing, looking both ways on the street. The guards remained in front of Camrose's place; elsewhere was the usual amount of late-afternoon traffic and activity. "They'll be in some back room figuring it out."

"Figuring what?" asked Clenchfield.

"The best way to hang Camrose without a fuss. They'll do it after dark. Henry, clean the grease out of one of those new Colts and load it for me."

"You ought not to do it. You cannot stand against this camp."

"I can stand against the camp and so can you or any man, if he's got to."

Henry Clenchfield rapped his knuckles on the counter with a rare display of anger. "Why have you got to? A man has never got to do anything which is against reason."

"Reason never won a war, or built a road, or wrote a book."

"And what makes men do those things, then?" demanded Clenchfield.

"Henry," said Stuart, and now was smiling, "do you remember when you were young and looked at a woman? Do you remember the ambitions you had?"

"I was a fool until I grew old and got sense."

"It is not reason that makes you hungry. Nor is it reason that makes you fight, or makes you scheme, or sends you into Corson's to have a drink and be comfortable. It is not reason that makes you stick to a friend, or cleave to your God or belong to your lodge. It is not reason that holds you to your friends, nor does it make you cry and laugh and sweat. You do a thing — and then you find some excuse to call it reasonable; but that is not why you do it, Henry. You do it because something a damned sight deeper pushed you to do it. Reason is a pale flicker of candlelight a man holds up to guide himself when the fire in him has burned out."

He was smiling still, released from the morbid preoccupations which had troubled him all during this afternoon. He had restored his faith in himself by falling back to those extremely simple things he believed in and which he did not have to explain.

He turned through the store and left the building by the rear door. The sun was half behind the western hills and suddenly the fall air had begun to turn cold; along the creek the smoke of supper fires began to spiral from the tin chimney tops and men were wearily walking in from their day's laboring. He skirted the back end of Camrose's office, drawing the thoughtful eye of the guard stationed there; he went on to his barn and saddled the best of his horses — a big deep-chested sorrel meant for a long run.

He loitered in the barn's doorway to watch the log building which housed Camrose, and from this point of view he saw the two guards before it and the single guard behind it. All three were now watching him across the two hundred feet. Looking beyond them, he observed one more man stationed at Meadows's store, also keeping eye upon him. The camp knew him and suspected him, and this surveillance made him smile. It was another game to be played, rougher than some others he had been engaged in, and with himself alone in the matter, opposing men who long had been his friends. They liked it little and he liked it less; yet this was the way it had to be played.

He retreated into the stable and sat down on a keg, thinking of a way which might work; and he turned it about his mind, refining it and smoothing it until the way seemed practical. A rider came along the road through the last clear light of the day at a full gallop, crossed the creek at what seemed a reckless rate and continued up the street. Stuart made out a voice shouting, but caught none of the words, since the buildings of the street were between him and the rider. The voice dropped and other voices rose.

Returning to the barn's doorway, he saw that all three guards had gone up the street; and now miners began to run from their supper fires along the creek, forward through the spaces between the buildings to the street. Excitement spread its keen incense all about.

He walked toward the back end of Camrose's office, meanwhile watching a last straggling group come from the creek; he slowed his pace until he saw that he had no eyes upon him for a moment. Then he came against Camrose's back door and tried the knob and found the lock turned. He thrust his shoulder against the door and heard the lock grind against the casing. Camrose's voice came out at him with a kind of panic. "Who's that?"

"Pull at that knob, George," said Stuart. He backed off and struck the door with the full drive of his legs and his body. The latch snapped clean and the door wheeled open. Stuart plunged through it and slammed against Camrose who violently struggled with him and tried to rush from the room. Stuart said, "Wait."

"They won't wait longer than dark. I heard them talking."

Stuart handed over his gun. "Take the sorrel in my barn. Get up in the hills and keep going. Don't come back here."

"Logan —"

"That's all the talk we'll need," said Stuart. "Your hands are red as hell. If they catch you again, don't ask me for any more help."

He backed out of the room, made a sharp survey around him and beckoned Camrose; then he ran along the back end of the street's building, slid between his own store and Howison's and came upon the growing crowd. A man stood by a sweat-black horse, both badly used. The man talked with his head hanging down, scarcely coherent. "From Evans, all the way. My wife's dead. My girl's dead —"

It was Cobb, and Cobb was on the edge of collapse. Howison stood by him, a hand on his shoulder. "How many Indians you see? Big band, little band?"

"They're all out. I tell you —"

"What's this?" asked Stuart.

The man nearest him was Johnny Steele. Johnny turned about. "He came from the lower ferry, Logan. Everything along the way is afire."

The messenger said: "If I'd been afoot they'd got me. I was comin' home and I saw 'em leave my house —"

Howison asked, "Where'd they go after they left your place?"

"They were goin' toward Dance's." His face

grew strange and alarmed and white as he felt himself losing consciousness. He managed to say: "It started on account of Bragg. Bragg killed two Indians girls this morning. A friendly Rogue told the ferryman." Then he slid through Howison's arm and fell to the ground.

"Why," said Johnny Steele, "a man ought to be tougher than that."

"A damned-fool remark, Johnny," said Stuart. "We'll have to raise a company and start tonight. Sixty men. Where's sixty men to go?"

Voices rose all around him and Steele said: "We can do better than sixty." Suddenly one of the miners — one of the guards — gave Stuart a remembering glance and rushed down the street.

Stuart said: "If it's a real break-out they might attack this camp. Somebody's got to be around for that. Sixty men is enough for traveling."

The guard came panting back from Camrose's office, crying his news before him. "He busted out. The door's open — back door. He broke the lock."

Now there were two currents of excitement to sway and disturb the crowd, and a lesser murmuring began to run around the group. Steele said: "That door opens in, don't it? If it's broke it had to be broke by a shove from outside." A righteous man's fury seized him. He yelled at the guard, "Why didn't you watch?" He swung on Stuart with his suspicions pulsing across his face. "Do you think you can buck this camp? Do you think —"

"Johnny," said Stuart, "you're making long guesses again." He looked around the crowd of miners, knowing they shared Johnny Steele's distrust. He understood them very well, their capacity for sentimental tears, for kindness, for rough justice; but he also knew their intemperate power when roused. At this minute he was in scarcely better shape than Camrose was, but he shrugged his shoulders and showed them no feeling. "Whoever is going, be here in twenty minutes. Grub for three days."

Johnny Steele shook his head. "Now we have got another chore to do, but we'll come back to this matter later. We are going to treat you rough. We are going to teach you something you need to learn. No man can stand against this camp."

Stuart turned into his store, put up his grub and moved to the barn to saddle a horse. When he reached the street again, the company had gathered, half on foot and half with horses, and already had elected its officers: Howison was captain, Steele lieutenant, and a miner by the name of Kelly was orderly sergeant. Howison explained this to Stuart in a confidential aside. "I think the boys gave me the job to demonstrate their irritation toward you." He swung to his command. "If I am to run this company I'll run it my way. If my way does not suit you, then it will be time to call an election. But while I'm running it, I want no argument over my decisions. Forward!"

Captain Howison's company swung into a loose imitation of a military line and made its serpentine way down the street, half mounted and half dismounted, with each man variously cumbered with blankets, kits and guns. The company drew an interested audience all along the street. Eli Decker had, in patriotic spirit, brought out an open-ended keg of whisky and several dippers, and for a while the marching column was neither at march nor in column. Presently, with the keg empty, the way was resumed and a last volley of remarks and casual cheers came from the bystanders.

Stuart brought up the rear of the group. As he passed along the foot of the street he observed Overmire and Lucy standing in the crowd. Overmire waved a hand at him and called, "Good luck." Lucy held his glance and spoke to him in the old and silent way he knew so well; and he spoke back to her in the same manner, and so left Jacksonville.

Five miles northeast of town, in the night's full dark, Howison took note of the growing desire for rest and halted his command. "Cook up a quick supper. I propose to march this outfit straight through to Dance's tonight."

"We'll not make it till daylight," said Kelly, the sergeant.

"If we camp until morning, we'd not make it until tomorrow night."

288

"Yet," said Kelly, "if we march all through the night and reach Dance's by daylight and then found a fresh trail to follow, we'd be too tired to follow it."

Howison stared at Kelly. "You talk like a dog chasin' its tail."

"Well, a dog's got sense enough to curl up and sleep when he's tired."

The discussion grew. Kelly made a speech in favor of rest and an early start by morning. A mounted miner by the name of Parrott suggested resting until midnight. George McFall suggested marching through the night, but with a qualification: let the horse owners go ahead a mile, tie their horses and walk on. The foot miners would come up to the tied horses, ride a mile beyond the first group and tie, continuing afoot. Ed Jensen objected, stating that this would overwork the horses. From that point the discussion went into the subject of the varying endurance of horses. "For example," Ned Gotch said, "I knew a horse on the Russian River who weighed about seven-fifty and was fourteen years old. Yet in the winter of '50 that horse carried two men fifteen miles over a mountain, on a trail three feet deep in snow."

"Not a California horse," said somebody else. "Must have been pure mustang."

Stuart tightened the cinch on his horse and stepped to the saddle. Howison called through the dark to him. "Where you going, Logan?"

"To Dance's. I didn't come out here to argue

over horses."

"Well," said Johnny Steele, "we've got to thresh this thing out."

"You elected a captain to give the orders. If you stop every house to argue with him, when do you expect to catch up with any Indians? If you mean to swap stories, go back to Corson's. If you came out to fight, quit bellyaching. You talked big back on the street, now you're getting cold feet. You won't catch any Indians at this rate, and maybe you don't want to. Maybe all you want to do is march around in easy spots for two days, and then go back to camp and make out you've been big men." Then he said with vigorous scorn: "Hell, the sight of an Indian would stampede you back to California."

Johnny Steele's outraged voice came to him. "Well, what do you want to do?"

"Those with horses should push on fast to Dance's and catch the Indian trail. The rest of you ought to swing over to the river and patrol from the Ferry to Dance's in case the Rogues double back. I'm going to Dance's. Who's going ahead with me?"

"I'm going," said Howison. "You take the boys afoot, Steele."

"No," said Steele. "Somebody lend me a horse."

The horsemen were forming in the shadows. Somewhere in this darkness a rider, urged by Steele's persuasive language, surrendered his mount and joined the foot group. Howison said: "Kelly, you're in command of the boys afoot. You cover the river."

"Which side of the river?" asked Kelly. "For how long? How far do I go and when do I turn around?"

"Never mind, Kelly," said a voice. "We'll decide that as we travel."

"Dammit," said Kelly, "if I'm to command, I can make up my own mind."

Stuart and Howison led away with twenty or more riders behind. The night sky glittered out its crusted light and a small wind carried a brisk fall coldness. Pacing along the trail as it clung to the foothills, they picked up the silver shining of the river below them, and presently came upon it and followed its turns and its straight stretches, at a walk, at a gallop, at a walk. A cabin light glinted ahead of them; and then the light died as the rumor of their horses reached forward. Then went by, with Howison shouting: "There'll be a bunch patrolling here tomorrow, Oldham." The smell of the warming horses rose rank and the sound of gear slapped and sang. They rested briefly and pushed forward; at the lower ferry they sang across the water until the ferryman came out of his cabin and brought the ferry over. "What's the last news?" asked Stuart.

"I got four families forted up here. We can make out. The Indians went toward Dance's. Perry Volk was killed, mile down the river."

The river moved northwest, the trail moved north. Stuart pushed on, through little pocketed clearings and up the face of low hills, and along flat stretches studded loosely with trees. In the dense mass of the hills ahead of them a red glow spread against the sky. This was seven or eight miles away, beyond Dance's. "They've fired the woods," said Howison. "Or it could be Jay Fitch's cabin."

They stumbled upon the litter of Stuart's destroyed pack train; mules lay all along the trail, capsized with their packs, and the smell of all this had begun to grow strong. Stuart pulled in. He got to the ground and walked along the wreckage. He was not sure of its identity until he came across one mule whose markings he knew. "Mine," he said.

Howison said: "That's bad. How big an outfit was it?"

"Thirty mules."

"Wonder if Blazier and Murrow got out of it."

Scattered bolts of cloth made ghostly patterns in the night and all the horses of the troop were shying away from the sight and smell of the disaster. They made a detour of the trail until the dead mules were well behind. The light from Dance's house sparkled in the distance and now Howison lifted his voice in a long and undulating halloo to warn the people yonder. Dance's door was open when the detachment swung into the yard — and Vane Blazier's voice called: "Who's that?"

"How is it here?" asked Stuart.

"Well now, I'm glad to see you," said Blazier. "We got jumped and Murrow was killed. Old Dance and young Bushrod Dance are dead. Mrs. Dance is all right. Caroline's gone. She was up in the brush hunting for a cow when the Rogues hit. I found her trail but I couldn't follow it. There was some Indians still roaming around and I had to back off. By God, I'm glad you're here."

15

Caroline

Stuart stepped into the house and found Mrs. Dance at the stove. She had heard them and now she proposed making some kind of meal. She looked around at Stuart, her dark face pressed into tightest composure. "Caroline's all right," she said. "We brought our youngsters up to shift for themselves. I'll have coffee in a minute."

Howison and part of the group crowded in; and others were moving around the cabin, easy-calling into the night. Stuart said: "In the morning we'd better take you down to the Ferry. It is a safer place."

"No," said Mrs. Dance, "I would not feel easy underfoot in another woman's house. Anyhow, the other boys will be back. They'll take care of it."

Blazier said, "We've got to get on Caroline's trail. It goes up there —" and he pointed to the hills eastward. He waited for Stuart to speak. When Stuart showed no immediate sign of

294

moving, young Blazier's tight-strung emotions began to break. He gave Stuart a hot and resentful glance. "Well, ain't we going?"

"What was Caroline wearing?" asked Stuart of Mrs. Dance.

"A gingham dress," said Mrs. Dance. "A blue-and-white-checked dress."

"What kind of a gun was she carrying?"

"Her pa's big pistol."

"Well," said Stuart. "That's six shots. You hear her do any firing?"

"I can't recollect," said Mrs. Dance. "There was firin' all around us while the red beasters were here. My man was killed soon. Son Bushrod was hit almost the last shot. Then they went away." She faced the stove, away from them. "It was Dance I was thinkin' about — not anybody else."

Young Blazier gave Mrs. Dance a glance of irritation, offended by what she said; it sounded callous to him. Stuart said: "Which way do you think that no-horn cow went?"

"It was a breachy animal," said Mrs. Dance. "Always knockin' down the fence. There's some kind of grass up Goose Canyon it yearned for."

"How long had she been gone," asked Stuart, "when the Rogues hit you?"

Mrs. Dance put a palm across her eyes to think. "We had the potatoes on the stove, boilin' for supper. That's five-thirty. Then she went. I was mixin' up some greens with the

295

cottage cheese. Then I turned to get the potatoes off the stove. That was mighty near six. I heard Dance shout and then he was runnin' in from the meadow. I never did get the potatoes off the stove. The water boiled out and the potatoes scorched. Well, she was gone a half hour when the beasters came."

One of the party, outside the house, said: "There's something coming up the trail." Afterwards his challenge sharply rode the night: "Who's that? Sing out."

A voice made guttural with fatigue answered. "I'm coming in."

Stuart, hearing the voice, stepped from the cabin. The miners were drifting up from the shadows; they made a group in the front yard of the house, listening to the shuffle of the approaching stranger's boots. He called again: "There's Rogues around here yet. I heard some on the trail a little while ago."

Stuart drew his gun. He said: "Stand fast. Who are you?"

Howison murmured: "Hell, Logan, it's a white man. Let him come in."

The shuffling of the stranger's boots stopped. He said in a different voice: "That you, Logan? I've been chased all day. I'm dead beat."

"Why," said Howison, "it's Bragg."

Stuart lifted his gun and fired in Bragg's general direction. The echo went out through the night in great bounding, widening waves and broke against the hills, shattering into lesser echoes. Bragg stood fast, wherever he was. He began to argue stubbornly. "You got to forget that, Stuart. Don't turn against a man with your own color of skin now. Boys, don't let him do it. Take his gun away from him."

"If you come inside my range, Bragg, I'll kill you," said Stuart.

"Listen, boys," said Bragg, "I can't run much longer. There's Rogues within sound of my voice. You know what they'll do to me, don't you? You want to see me hangin' to a tree, skinned and dressed? That's what they'll do."

Stuart stood silent and unchanged. Howison stared through the dark at him, his own feelings somewhat swayed by the grisly picture Bragg painted. The rest of the group said nothing, and Bragg spoke again with a greater note of begging. "You boys take me in. I'll go back to Jacksonville and stand a miners' court. That's fair, ain't it?"

"No," said Stuart. "You've got nothing coming to you at all."

Bragg growled, "By God, I'm coming in," and his boots began to scuff the road. He was hoping to break their nerve, Stuart thought; he was hoping to come among them, after which they would have no stomach to shoot him. Stuart brought up his pistol when he first saw the man's shape take form against the night; he fired twice and witnessed Bragg wheel and plunge out of the trail into the brush. Bragg's cursing was a winded and terrible thing in the night. His words went on and on, by turn violent and wheedling. The crowd stood fast, listening.

Stuart said: "Blazier and I are going up Goose Canyon. I don't think we'll see anything in the dark, but we've got to look." He started off with Blazier. He stopped suddenly and called back. "If you let Bragg come up here, I'll shoot him when I get back."

One of the crowd answered him. "He won't come. I'll take care of that."

Stuart turned the corner of the house and walked into the meadow, Blazier beside him. The yellow stubble gave out a faint glow and their feet made a racket on it. They waded a summer-thin creek and were at once between the jaws of the canyon, in a blackness so deep that the strip of sky above the canyon seemed bright by contrast — its stars all glittering. Stuart stopped and sank down, listening into the night. The creek made its varied and chattering racket along the stones and there was a breathing of wind along the trees; he rose and went on. He had gone only a short distance — twenty feet or so — when his foot struck an obstacle, half soft and half hard, on the trail. He put his hand to it and discovered the no-horn cow, dead.

Blazier murmured: "She must have been bringing the cow back," and hurried forward.

Stuart suppressed the notion to call him back and remained by the cow. If Caroline had gotten

298

clear, which way had she gone? Not immediately to the house, since it had been under attack. Perhaps she had circled into the timber, had settled down to wait her chance to return. Well, then, why hadn't she returned, after the Indians had left the cabin?

Maybe she had retreated deeper into the hills. If so, the likely thing to guess was that she had drifted either north or east — both directions furnishing the densest kind of shelter. There was scarcely any choice between the two routes except that by going north she kept near the Oregon-California trail and might come upon passing miners.

All this was based on the guess that she had survived. He laid a hand on the cow and felt the warmth still in that carcass; he thought of Caroline's firm and browned face, the curve of her shoulders and the smile that came rarely to her. Then, from a higher point on the trail, young Blazier loudly called her name into the night. "Caroline!"

He had scarcely spoken it when a gun's shot came dry and bitter through the dark — to be followed by a second; and afterwards Stuart heard Blazier's boots rush down the trail. Stuart rose and braced himself. He put out his hands and took the first shock of Blazier's on-springing body. He said: "Hold up," and he pulled Blazier back from the trail. He gave Blazier a shove to the ground and he himself dropped.

A voice up the trail said, "Ah-uh," and, in a

moment, Stuart made out the quick light padding of moccasined feet. Stuart crouched lower in order to catch the silhouette of the Rogue against the sky; he saw it dimly, and then saw a second — the two shapes not far apart.

The two Rogues were aware of the dead cow and slowed down as they came forward. This brought both of them together and at that moment Stuart rose forward and crashed the barrel of his gun down across the head of the foremost figure. The second Indian, warned, leaped back and fired — and missed. Blazier's bullet, aimed on the Rogue's gun flash, dropped the second Indian. The echoes rolled away, one hard upon the other.

"Come on," said Stuart, and led the way down the canyon's trail. They were out in the meadow before he spoke again. "Nothing to do until daylight."

Howison had set up a guard. The rest of the crowd had settled in the yard for rest. Standing a moment near the door, Stuart watched Blazier drop near the house, and he heard the young man breathing in a short and uneven way. Blazier was crying. Stuart thought: "That's the way he feels about her. I wonder if she knows it." There was no further sound from Bragg, but he guessed that the big man was as close as possible to the protection of this house. He went inside, finding Howison with a cup of coffee. He sat down and lay back on the chair. "The cow's dead. Two bucks jumped us."

Mrs. Dance said: "Caroline can take care of herself."

Howison gently shook his head and left the room. Stuart thought: "North is as good a bet as any," and, settling deeper in the chair, fell asleep.

Mrs. Dance, rattling the coffeepot on the stove, woke him; and he found he had during his sleep crawled from the chair and made his bed under the table. There was still no light upon the meadow when he went to the rear of the house and washed his face in the tin bowl. Miners were rousing from their brief and uncomfortable sleep, morosely silent for want of rest. A fire's pale-yellow edge cut the blackness, around which men squatted to cook up their bacon. Mrs. Dance was supplying the coffee. Stuart drank two cups black and said: "Blazier and I will scout the canyon again," and started off with the young man.

Light began to break in the eastern sky and swell in pale bands. The carcass of the dead cow was visible as they passed it, and the creek showed its streaky white edges where it foamed among the boulders. A little beyond the cow, Stuart moved into the brush and waited full light. When it came, he said to Blazier: "You go down the canyon. She should have left her prints near the creek. I'll go the other way."

Fifty feet from the cow he came upon the flat tracks of an Indian pressed deep into the creek's mud. He followed these back into the brush and watched them grow fainter on the less resilient earth; he returned to the creek again and continued upward. Other tracks were visible, but all of them were Rogue. They would be tracking her, and thus be going in the same direction she went. He turned back, finding Blazier slightly below the dead cow. Blazier pointed to the earth and made a circle with his forefinger around a small shoe print. He was greatly stirred. "She was here. She was right here."

Stuart followed these prints up the hill's slope and into the brush. She had been running — that to be observed from the deep and scuffed shape of her tracks. She had run a long distance without stopping, circling the brush where possible, otherwise breaking through it. Two hundred feet from the creek, she had stopped to rest or to hide. Her knees had made two round depressions on the forest mold.

He called to Blazier. "Go tell Howison to leave three men with Mrs. Dance, and to come along with the rest. On foot. We can't use horses."

Blazier rushed down the canyon, sounding ahead with his shout of discovery. Stuart crouched in the thicket, realizing he would have to keep an eye on Blazier during the day's march; the lad was in a frame of mind which would make him careless. He looked down at the print of Caroline's knees and he thought of the fear and the wildness which must have been in her, but when he pictured her face he saw no terror on it; she had a self-reliance great as any man's. He reached down and laid his hand on the print of her knee and suddenly he realized she was more mature than he knew. He remembered the shadow on her face when he had proposed; not even her pleasure had entirely dissolved it. She had known how much he was offering, and she had known about Lucy. Nevertheless she was a realist, taking what she could get, and showing him no tears for what he held back. It was less than she wanted, he realized; it was less than any woman wanted. But she had made up her mind to be content with it and to hide her regret.

Howison came up the canyon with the rest of the miners and the group made a loose circle in the thicket, around Stuart. "Everybody spread out," he said. "We'll drag the country best we can."

"Look behind," said Howison.

Stuart turned and stared down the canyon, to discover the unmistakable shape of Bragg coming out of the meadow into the canyon, soon ducking from sight. "He's afraid to be alone," said Stuart. "It will be a hard way to die, if the Rogues catch him." He made a signal to the group, and rose and walked into the timber, with the girl's tracks directly before him.

The sun's clear light rushed across the high sky; but once the party entered this dense stand of timber, twilight came again, broken on rare occasion by a thin shaft of sunlight slanting down through a gap in the matted ceiling of branches. These trees were old, they were huge and they stood upon the earth with their great feet building massive hummocks around them. A thousand years of destruction and decay lay upon the earth, at places making direct progress forward impossible; and fern and undergrowth luxuriantly grew in the perpetual shade. The slope rose steadily and reached a rough crest. Beyond the crest, the land pitched down at a forty-five degree angle into a canyon smothered with wild berry vines, devil's stalk and water-loving shrubs.

The print of Caroline's shoes were clear to this point; and here her trail turned with the ridge and went westward along it. Stuart thought: "She got the idea of drifting toward the Oregon-California road." He waited for the skirmish line of miners to fight up through the tangled slope. Howison appeared, drawing wind from the bottom of his lungs; some branch, whipping back, had left a welt across his forehead.

Stuart followed Caroline west. Fifty yards on he saw a pair of moccasin prints swing from the brush and march with Caroline's tracks; shortly afterward these moccasin prints were joined by others, until there was a scuffed streak along the ground, in which Caroline's marks were wholly lost. Half a dozen bucks had found her route and had followed it.

Then the trail dropped into the canyon. Stuart

moved down the slope in stiff-legged jumps and came to a narrow sluggish creek half buried in mud; all this mud had been churned by the prior travel of the Indians. A few yards away, Howison had gotten himself involved in a patch of nettles and was softly swearing. The rest of the miners arrived with considerable racket, dropping by the creek for water. Blazier, always in advance, called back. "She tore her dress."

Stuart moved up to him and saw the little strip of blue-and-white gingham clinging to the stiff crotch of a bush; he squatted and took off his hat to squeeze the sweat from its band. He had a picture of Caroline again, still stone-grave in her expression, her dress ragged and her eyes growing dark. He shook his head and continued upward. Howison called from behind. "Better rest. We're beginning to straggle."

He went on until he reached another crest. The tracks now suddenly fanned out in several directions as the Rogues had divided in their search. He said to Blazier, "Go that way. See if you can pick up her tracks."

Before him — below him — was a greater canyon and a wider one. A creek of considerable size ran along its bottom, and the sides of the canyon, worn by this creek's centuries of running, were almost vertical. The miners now slowly toiled forward to join him, to look at him, to drop on their haunches. Howison heaved himself up the last stages of the slope and opened his mouth for air. Hot as the labor was, he had turned pale.

Blazier came back. "I saw nothing that way," he said, and turned in the other direction to make his search.

Stuart drew out his pipe and filled and lighted it. The first pull of smoke freshened him, and he began to look more closely at the prints around him; he bent over one of them. So far he had assumed that this trail had been made the night before, but he now noted that the edges of the prints still were sharp and ragged. The little particles of earth had not dried and crumbled away as they would have done after eight or ten hours of time, and the dried leaves and the short fern blades which had been pressed down by the traveling weight of the Indian still were plastered flat to the bottom of the prints.

"These were made this morning," he said. "She must have hidden close by the cabin all night — the Indians also. She must have figured they were watching for her and waiting for daylight. So she moved on. They followed as soon as they could read the ground. She's not far off."

Howison shook his head. "I know how you feel, but don't be optimistic."

Blazier returned and dropped to the ground. "I wish I could read sign," he said, and was angry at his own uselessness. "I can't make out a thing."

Below them, somewhere in the canyon from which they had just emerged, brush began to rattle. Stuart rose up and counted the men around him. "We're all here, aren't we?" he said. He went to the edge of the canyon, looking into it. He heard the brush snap again, but he could see nothing through the massed timber; then the brush ceased to rattle. "Bragg," he said.

"He's afraid," said Howison.

"That will be something new for him. He was never afraid of anything before."

"He never had anything he couldn't take care of before," said Howison. "But he can't take care of this. They're going to get him, and he knows it."

It was time to move; it was time to make a guess. The steep canyon before him would prevent Caroline from continuing directly northward; by necessity, she had turned either eastward deeper into the hills, or she had swung downgrade to the west, toward the Oregon-California trail. A sound came up from the west, the sound of an animal whipping through the brush, and in another moment he saw an elk, old and heavily antlered, break through the screen. The wind was coming with the elk, out of the west, so that he had no warning until his eyes saw shapes that were not familiar to his world. Warning stopped him, but never quite stopped him. He fell to a trotting walk; he turned his head slightly aside, sucked at the air with his nostrils and then he wheeled into a run and crashed down the canyon.

Stuart said, "That's our answer. Something down that way spooked him."

He moved westward with the miners straggling beside him and behind him, wearily circling deadfalls and huge tree columns, wearily fighting the brush. The moccasin prints made zigzag designs on the ground, thickening as the Rogues came together, thinning as they wheeled away on different scents. The forest brightened and the trees gave way to an opening in this wilderness; the scars of a fire showed on nearby treetrunks and farther on the thinning timber presented him vistas of a meadow.

The group came up to the edge of the timber and paused before this open area which was a rough square of perhaps a hundred feet; sunlight brilliantly flooded this open area and fern grew waist high around charred stumps and silvered snags. Across this way the Rogues had gone, their course marked by the broken-down fern.

Howison said: "I don't relish exposing myself out there."

It became a clearer conviction to Stuart that this trail had been made not more than two hours before. Caroline was somewhere in the yonder trees, and the Rogues were also somewhere there; the sense of time's pressure got into him, the need of haste overbore his caution. He said, "Come on fast," and trotted from the trees.

The smell of the ferns rose in wild fragrance as he broke them under his feet. He hurdled dead logs matted with berry vines; quail, flushed from cover, drummed away in low flight before him. Howison and Blazier were close at his either side and he noted that Howison's face was drawn from exertion and his mouth sprung wide. The rest of the miners were scattered loosely in line across the meadow, their shapes cut off at the hips by the fern. Turning his head to scan the rear, he saw Bragg standing at the meadow's edge.

"Do I see something ahead — right straight ahead by the trees?" asked Howison.

They were half across, and faltering from the run. Stuart shouted: "Keep up — keep up," and regretted the waste of this wind. He looked at young Blazier and observed that the boy trotted with no exertion showing on his face. Seeing it, Stuart had the bitterest regret that he was no longer twenty, with the boundless stamina of twenty. He raked the line of trees ahead with his glance and, fifty feet from that shelter, he flung up his revolver at what he thought was a copper body skulking there. He checked himself, but his gesture ticked off Howison, who lifted his gun and fired point blank. Stampeded by this, the miners gathered speed and rushed forward one by one and got into the timber; there they stopped, calling to each other in short and exhausted tones.

A shout came across the meadow, full and desperate. Staring back over the field of fern, Stuart watched Bragg come forward in great haste; he cried out again, his voice going to top pitch and breaking. Stuart raised his gun and at once fired, missing. Bragg stumbled to a halt. He put both hands over his head and stood as still as his winded body would permit. He swung an arm to the rear, pointing at the woods out of which he had come, and through which Stuart and his group had just passed. He shouted: "They're in there!" Then other shots began to roll flatly in the morning, out from the miners toward Bragg. The latter ducked, turned and started back. Twenty feet from the trees he dropped out of sight in the ferns, and his own gun began to speak.

Howison shouted: "Look over there," and Stuart saw bodies weaving along the edge of the far trees. A Rogue came into the meadow, low-scurrying, and Bragg's gun sent up two swift explosions. The Rogue dropped, apparently struck, but two more Indians now rushed from the trees at Bragg; he fired again as they came at him. He rose up into view and made a final shot as the two bore down upon him.

His gun was then apparently empty, and he swept it before him as he would have swung a scythe. One Indian wheeled around him while the other came straight on. Bragg dropped his gun and jumped at the nearest Indian and locked him in his brutal arms — and the quick shout of that Rogue was a piercing signal across the meadow as Bragg crushed him. The other Indian rushed in behind Bragg and beat him over the head until he went down into the ferns; afterwards Stuart saw the two Indians bend and rise and bend as they killed Bragg.

"Good God," said Howison, and turned his head away.

The two Indians rose, each bearing some bloody trophy in his hands. Stuart took careful aim and fired, long as the range was for the revolver. He struck his target, he saw his Indian flinch and run back to shelter at an off-balance stride. Now the miners opened on the other fleeing Rogue, but did not bring him down. A long, startled yell came from the far end of the miner's line.

"Hey — over here!"

Firing began and grew lively fifty feet down the timber. Stuart murmured, "They must have crawled around," and rushed toward the source of the shots. He circled a tree and beat his way to a clump of brush; as he came out of the brush clump he faced a Rogue who, flatly inching his way forward along the earth, now sprang up with his gun. He was so close at hand that Stuart struck him in his forward plunging and smelled the savage's rank odor before he clubbed him down with his gun. Howison cried out: "Watch it!" and fired, his bullet passing quite near Stuart; wheeling half around, Stuart saw the brush tremble as Rogues rose from cover and came in. He had Howison and Blazier with him; and somewhere near at hand other miners were smashing their way forward. Bullets whipped by; a chunk of bark splintered from a fir and struck Stuart's hat.

He spoke sharply at Blazier. "Get behind a tree." He turned and shoved Blazier back, and fired at a Rogue half hidden behind a fir, fifteen feet distant. The Indian swayed as though pushed by a board; he made a grab at the rough bark of the tree and pulled himself back. A round tarnished spot showed on his chest; it bubbled and grew larger, and blood made a brighter streak down his chest. His eyes were round and bottomless and his lips drew up from his teeth — and as Stuart watched, dullness and vacancy and unknowingness came to the Indian. When he fell he was dead.

The Rogues, rushing in for the attack, had met resistance. They had seen a swift kill in prospect, or would never have charged in this manner, so uncharacteristic of their way of fighting. Now they drew away, with the miners plunging after them, the fight becoming a hand-to-hand affair, scattered all through the timber. Stuart lost contact with both Howison and Blazier as he ran forward. A bullet whipped past him, its source seeming to be beyond a dead log. He jumped aside, pulled himself over the log and saw a Rogue disappearing into a tangle of wind-fallen timber. He followed, pressing aside old branches and working his way through a kind of tunnel made by two trees lying side by side; he caught sight of the Rogue ahead of him, stooped and wheeling swiftly from sight.

When he came to the end of the tunnel he found himself facing the pit where once the roots of a tree had been. The Indian stood at the bottom of it, swiftly ramming new charges into his revolver.

When he saw Stuart he dropped his useless gun, made a quick leap, caught Stuart by the feet and dragged him off balance into the pit. He fell over Stuart, he beat at him with his fists, he slid a forearm around Stuart's throat and he rolled and locked his hands together and began to squeeze on Stuart's windpipe.

Stuart rolled with him. He had his hands free and he reached for the man's locked hands, to break the pressure. He could not reach far enough back, nor could he exert enough force to release himself. He turned his head, but the pressure increased and he drew one last thin stream of air into his lungs — and felt his heart pounding heavier against his chest. He rolled again and rose to his haunches; he reached out and caught one of the Indian's legs. He got a knee against the leg and pulled the lower part of the Indian's leg against this with a tremendous heave. The Indian turned to relieve the strain and, in turning, let his arms fall away. Stuart dragged in the sweet wind and made his grab at the Rogue now suddenly rolling clear. He pinned the man down; he laid his weight across the other's body and his forearm across the man's throat. He shoved with the weight of his shoulders until he heard the Rogue's windpipe grate. The Rogue twisted with him and unseated him, but he used his fist, stunning the Rogue with a smash against the forehead. Then he reared back and caught the revolver he had dropped. The Rogue was halfway to his feet when Stuart swung in and beat him over the head.

He stood still, with his vision blurred; his hand shook when he dragged it across his face. He could not breathe deeply enough, or fast enough. He put both arms over the edge of the pit and held himself there, at the moment doubting if he could climb from it. He heard voices shouting in the distance, and other voices answering as the firing settled to occasional reports; somewhere a voice called his name.

He opened the revolver and charged it; he pinched on the caps and gripped the gun with one hand and made a jump upward, from the pit. He fell back, and afterwards he kicked toeholds in the spongy ground and used these to pull himself into the alley made by two trees. He returned along the alley, forced a way through the branches, and discovered Howison coming forward.

Howison looked closely at him. "You get hit?"

"No."

"I think we broke 'em up. It's clear around here."

Another shot erupted deeper in the trees as Stuart and Howison moved toward the edge of the meadow. When they got to it they saw miners walking across to where Bragg had fallen. Howison stopped short and said, "I don't want to see him."

"Cry for the good ones dead," said Stuart. "Not for him. Would you want him alive, waiting around to kill somebody else?"

"I know," said Howison. "But there is a Christian mercy we have got to remember."

"There is mercy," said Stuart. "And then there is something which is not mercy, but only easy tears. The people who are dead because of this man would probably have been alive today if Bragg had been killed a month ago. I wish I had done it then." He felt stronger, but he was still shaken from the fight and he still had the grisly feeling of the Indian's arms locked around his neck. He watched the miners coming up and he said: "We won't pick up Caroline's tracks in this jungle. She was headed for the Oregon-California road. That's less than a half mile west. We'll go that way and see if we can find anything."

The miners spread out with a slow weariness and once again moved through this half-impassible forest. They walked carefully and they kept a sharp watch ahead of them, and around them, and behind them. It was not in the nature of Indians to stand fast once they had suffered a sharp defeat, yet the chance always existed that some one brave, seeking distinction, might make a lone fight. So they went on with a steady attention, jaded and winded and brush-scratched. A small break in the trees gave them a view of the trail, and somewhere short of noon they came upon it, and walked along it until they reached a creek. They dropped here and drank in greedy thirst, and wetted their faces in relief. Stuart filled his chest and sent a long halloo ringing back through all the corridors of the hills. Blazier fired one shot into the air. They stood around, listening and waiting. They had their fear but avoided speaking of it; they stared about them at the deep, dense forest and wearily thought of the drudgery of another search back through it.

Stuart said: "Two of you boys go down the road. Look for her tracks. She may have reached here and started home. Blazier and I will go in the other direction."

"Well," said Howison, "all right," and he sat down on the road and stretched himself out. Fatigue had gotten deeper into him than in the others; it had done something permanent to him, Stuart thought as he turned north along the trail with Blazier.

"Vane," he said with some sharpness, "keep your head up."

The trail ran a straight course for half a hundred yards, rose up a small grade, and curled around a long bend; the sun stood straight overhead, its light here and there turning the trail's dark dust to a sleazy gold. The surface of the trail was rough with the traffic of pack trains, so that Stuart was unable to tell whether or not Caroline had passed this way. After half a mile, he turned back.

"She wouldn't have gotten over this way."

Young Blazier followed him back along the slow bend, with nothing to say. The fight had left him in a dejected frame of mind; it had filled him with foreboding. "Vane," said Stuart, "keep your head up."

They were not quite around the bend, not quite in view of the main party ahead of them, when Stuart's glance, consistently roving back and forth along the edges of the trail, caught a motion in the deep shadows of the forest, some yards away on the left side. He was not certain of it and stopped, bringing up his gun and narrowing his eyes for a cleaner view. He lost sight of that bit of motion; then he caught it again, and in another moment he saw Caroline Dance step from the trees into the trail.

He broke into a run and he gave a shout, and for the first time he realized how black and heavy his apprehensions had been; they dropped from him, leaving him light of mind. "Why, Caroline," he said.

Blazier knocked him aside and rushed forward, calling her name over and over. Blazier came up to her and put an arm on her shoulder and suddenly the young man was crying. "My God, Caroline," he said. "My God . . ."

She was weary and she swayed when Blazier touched her. Her dress was torn, her arms scratched, and her face was welted with the slash of vines she had gone through. Her hair fell around her face, in the presence of the two men, she made a little gesture with her hand to straighten it. She had her father's revolver gripped in her fingers. Yet, tired and bruised as she was, the composure remained on her face. She had been through an ordeal, but that ordeal had not unsteadied her mind. She was now what she had been before, a reliant and practical girl who, for all the fear she may have felt and all the sudden thrusts of terror which may have gone through her, had never doubted herself.

Stuart stopped before her and put his arms around her. He held her closely and for a moment she dropped her head against his shoulder. She said: "I heard firing. I was hidden well. I guess you must have met the Rogues. I'm tired and I want to go home."

"All right," said Stuart. "We'll go home."

She stepped back from him, and looked at him with the closest of expressions; she read him carefully and thoroughly, and then she turned her glance to young Blazier. He had gotten control of himself, furtively brushing the tears from his eyes; he looked at her with the most heartfelt relief, and his own feelings were as clear as day to her. Her expression softened as she watched him, and what she saw broke the fatigued dullness of her cheeks. She turned to Stuart again and he felt that she made a comparison and came to a judgment. Whatever it was, she afterwards thought of something else. "How are my people?"

Stuart said: "Your mother's all right."

"Logan — what's wrong with my father?"

"He's dead, Caroline. And so is your brother Bushrod."

The night and day had not broken her, but now her face changed. She said: "I want to go home," and turned from them, walking on toward the main party. She stumbled as she walked, and she put a hand to her face, and was half blinded with her tears.

16

Various Farewells

As soon as they returned to Dance's the miners dismounted, cooked up a noon meal, and lay back to smoke and to rest. Presently half of them were asleep in the warm day. The door closed on the Dances' cabin as soon as Caroline entered it, and for the first time Stuart heard the sound of Mrs. Dance crying. The presence of Caroline had unlocked the older woman's tragedy. Young Blazier sat hard by the door, grown gloomy once more.

Stuart got a pair of shovels and, with half a dozen miners, went down the trail to the slaughtered pack train, and buried Murrow in the little thicket. Howison was with him and on the way back to the Dances' he spoke of Stuart's bad luck. "Thirty loaded mules is a hard loss, Logan."

"Maybe more," said Stuart. "I'm wondering about the string from Crescent City."

When they reached the cabin, the door was open, and Mrs. Dance was waiting in the yard.

"Logan," she said, "I guess you better think about Dance and Bushrod." She shaded her eyes and looked out upon the meadow to where two old oaks shaded the earth. "Make it there."

Half of Kelly's foot outfit came up the trail while the graves were being dug and Kelly said: "The rest of the boys went back home. There's nothing along the river. Those creatures don't never stay where they strike."

Dance and Bushrod were buried in the early afternoon. One of the miners seemed to have been a minister in earlier days. Unfrocked or resigned, he nevertheless stepped forward and conducted the services. It occurred to Howison to start a song. After the song, the women returned to the cabin and the men got in a circle to discuss the next thing to be done.

"The regulars from Fort Lane are scoutin' the upper Rogue," said Kelly.

"Well," said Howison, "I don't doubt the governor will call for militia companies in a few days. Meanwhile, we ought to station a few men here, and a few somewhere on the river. Six in either place should be enough. The rest of us can go home and get better organized. This will be a campaign running through fall. Who'll volunteer to stay here for three more days?"

"Where's Johnny Steele?" asked Stuart.

"He went back."

Caroline appeared in the doorway, studying the group. Young Blazier swung toward her and presently returned, briefly murmuring to Stuart. "Wants to see you."

She had changed her dress, and she had fixed her hair. As he came up he realized she had something to say to him but found it difficult; she took his arm and walked with him around the cabin and along the trail. On this trail, he remembered, he had proposed to her.

"What are you going to do, Logan?"

"Go back to Jacksonville to see what's become of my Crescent pack string. We'll have six men here for a while. You and your mother ought to come to town and put up at my place."

"No," she said. "I would not want to do that."

"You'll be doing it soon enough," he pointed out.

"No," she said, "I never will leave here. I am going to be married here and I am going to raise my children here. I could not be a town woman. I could not be a woman moving around. I could not live in the back of a store. It is a thing I even thought of last night in the hills. I would disappoint you. It came to me how much I would. We are not the same."

"Caroline —" he said.

"No," she said, "we are not the same. Maybe you think we could grow to be the same, but when we got older we'd not change." Her voice for the first time expressed her sadness. "You are not a contented man. You never will be. But I want nothing to change. It is my wish to look out from the cabin window and see my man plowing, and at night to see him in the kitchen rocker. I never want it to be different."

He said, "Who will the man be?"

She looked at him, keenly watching him. "I guess you know."

He nodded, remembering how it had been on the trail. He had not cried at the sight of her; it was Vane Blazier who had cried. She had known then where the love lay. "Blazier," he said.

She turned with him and said nothing more until they had reached the cabin. "It is a hard thing for me to think of hurting you. But I am not hurting you too much. Not nearly as much as another woman already has."

He had the answer to that question he had earlier asked himself. She had known what he lacked for her, and she was refusing him now because it was too great a lack. "And I'd be hurting you too much as time went on," he said. "That's it, I suppose?"

She gave him the smallest and briefest of smiles. "Yes," she said, and made a quick turn into the house. She stood in the kitchen, her face drawn together, and her mother saw this and spoke. "Caroline, it does no good to keep from cryin', if you've got to cry."

Caroline walked into the bedroom and stood at its open window. She was there when Logan rode by on his horse, and she stepped back so that he wouldn't see her; but she kept her eyes on him until he was far down the trail and at last turned from sight. "It is him I'll be missing — just as he has been missing Lucy. Now it's the other way around." The sense of loss was great within her, and loneliness came to her with its first unbearable shock. But even if she and Logan had lived the rest of their lives together, she would still have been lonely, knowing how much of him would never belong to her. It was better to take Vane Blazier, who brought everything to her and would be happy here.

She would not be giving Vane the kind of love she felt for Stuart; that would always be something set apart. Still, she was realist enough to know that she could hide that from Vane so that he would never know it. A man never saw the things a woman saw. Things would be good enough and time would soften much that now seemed hard.

"Caroline," said Mrs. Dance, "are you a-going to cry? Some people it helps a lot."

"No," said Caroline. "I'm not. Some people it doesn't help."

Camrose made his run to Stuart's stable unobserved, got on the horse ready for him and rode to the stable's rear door. All the miners along the creek had gone up the street, leaving the back side of town empty. With the barn's bulk shielding him from the street, he rode over the creek and into the trees; thereafter he circled the town and drifted back, until he was within a few yards of Overmire's cabin. He left the horse in the timber and walked forward. The miners were grouped along the street below him and he took somewhat of a chance when he rounded the cabin and stepped through its open door. Lucy and her mother were in the room. Overmire had gone down to join the miners.

Lucy stared at Camrose. She said, "You ought not to have risked it."

"You!" said Mrs. Overmire with considerable feeling. "You go along. Who got you out?"

"Logan," said Lucy.

"I think," said Mrs. Overmire, "Logan's done enough for you, George. And I think you've done too much." But she caught her daughters glance and rose and left the cabin.

"A very cool reception," observed Camrose. It was characteristic of him that when trouble came to him, he grew humble; when the trouble went away, his old manner returned, easy and cynical and quite forgetful. He gave her his close attention and once again he was attempting to weigh her, to discover the subtle shadings and the hesitations and qualified feelings which he always suspected to be present in her. One hour before this moment he had been a man with death closing upon him; now he was the old Camrose, digging at this girl with his dissatisfied mind.

"You'd better go," she said. "Don't you understand your danger? Even my mother might signal the miners and bring them up here."

"I have always felt the silent opposition of your people."

"You've been quite a man for feeling things," she said. "Some of those things were never true. You made them up in your mind."

"You've turned against me as all the rest have," he said. "What kind of love is it which will not stand against rumors and flimsy evidence? I see it clearly."

"You are also quite a man for seeing things," she said.

"And I have been right," he said. "There is little faith in anybody, and not too much loyalty, or great and deep feeling. I hate this camp. When the pack is for you, nothing you do is wrong. When the pack is against you, nothing you do is right."

"Do you know the risk Logan took in getting you free? Do you know what the camp might do to him? He gambled all his popularity when he helped you. If he loses it, you can say he did it because you were his friend. He never deserted you."

"Very gallant," said Camrose, with his thin amusement. "Very noble."

She looked at him with a sharp perception of his faults. They were never clearer to her than now. "You speak of feeling, and of loyalty. Yet you tear it down when you see it. You mock it. You envy it."

"No doubt Stuart is a great man," he said in

the same jeering tone.

"In your heart you know he is loyal to you. Or was."

He said: "How did you know he helped me?"

"I know him. He would never rest until he had you out of town." She rose and went to the door and looked into the falling twilight. "You've got to leave here."

"You're anxious to be rid of me," he observed.

Once she had believed in him; he had destroyed that belief by his own careless speech and behavior so that he was now a brittle man without admirable qualities. It was a hard thing to remember how she had felt about him, and how mistaken she had been. It shamed her and made her lose faith in her own honesty.

"I'll get to San Francisco," he said. "If I should send for you, would you come?"

"You already know I wouldn't, don't you?"

"Stuart," he said, "has used his friendship very well. Do you see how profitably he has used his time to ruin what was between us?"

She shook her head. "In the beginning you had everything of me. I was sure of you. I was happy. Then you began to destroy that by the way you talked, by the way you accepted and neglected everything, by the way you worked on my emotions — and stood back to see how I might squirm and twist. There came a time when I felt everything was wrong. But I couldn't admit I had been so wrong, and I hoped you were not really what I began to see you were. It is a terrible thing for a woman to fall in love, and later realize she was mistaken. It makes her doubt there is such a thing as love at all."

"All those nice words have not answered me," he said. "It is Stuart now — until you find out he's common clay, as I am. By God, I wish I could be sure you never got him. That's the only regret I carry away from here."

She turned from him and sat down. She pushed her hands together on her lap and looked down at them. "Well," she said, "you can be sure of that. I won't get him."

Voices were breaking sharply along the slopes, making Camrose suddenly aware of his danger. He had one more curosity in him. "Do you believe I killed McIver?"

"I don't know. You are capable of it."

He returned from the cabin and reached his horse, at once following a small miner's trail into the hills. It had grown dark, and the wind was considerably colder, and he got to thinking of his poor prospects. "I shall have to travel all night. I've got no blankets and no grub. I'm as destitute now as when I came here two years ago."

The trail dipped into a gulch and followed a small creek marked by the scars of miner's shafts and miner's gravel pits. He passed several deserted cabins, but about two miles from camp he saw a light winking ahead of him and he drew up to consider it. That would be Ed

Grogan's place, an old fellow who on occasion had come to town for a drunk. Grogan had food and Grogan undoubtedly had a little dust. He would not be a difficult man to tackle.

Grogan was inside cooking supper — the smell of it standing in the air. Camrose dismounted and walked quickly through the doorway and lifted his gun on Grogan as the latter, seated at his table, raised his head.

"Camrose," he said. "You broke loose?"

"I need your supper, Grogan. I need some grub wrapped up."

Grogan shrugged his shoulders. "I guess you got the best of the argument." He rose and walked to the far end of the cabin, there finding a flour sack. He looked back over his shoulder. "You'll have to travel mighty fast. The boys won't give up easy."

"While you're about it, Grogan," said Camrose, "throw your poke into the sack."

Grogan said at once: "I've got no dust."

"You're lying. You've got it in your back pocket. I see it."

Grogan stood still, his head turned on his small body. He thus watched Camrose who stood just inside the doorway; and as he watched Camrose he also watched the doorway. "You know, George," he said, "I wasn't sure you'd killed McIver. But I guess the camp was right."

"Move at it," said Camrose. "I can't wait long."

"You won't," said Grogan.

"What's that?" asked Camrose, and then remembered he had his back to the door. He swung with the fastest motion he could manage, but he swung too late. A bullet, coming out of the night, tore through him, and Grogan, now free of danger, pulled his own revolver and added a second shot. Camrose let his gun fall. He placed both hands on the cabin wall and for a moment he gave Grogan a wild, pale and bitter glance and then dropped to the floor. Grogan walked over to him, and another man stepped in from the night. Grogan said: "Good thing you came along, Ted."

Ted said: "There's a man who had a lot — an education, a woman and mighty fine prospects. He certainly panned out no color. Don't quite figure it."

"Well," said Grogan, "I guess he had notions. Those things can do a lot of harm."

Stuart came into Jacksonville after dark, and got his bad news from Clenchfield. The Crescent pack string had been destroyed over in the Applegate valley. Stuart took that news without much reaction. All he said was, "The Scottsburg string is gone, too, Henry. Blazier got clear, but I buried Murrow this afternoon." He went on to his room, and washed. He stood awhile in the room, roughly casting up his accounts. He had lost seventy animals, several horses and a good many thousands of dollars of merchandise; it required no great amount of

330

addition to arrive at his condition.

Clenchfield came to the doorway. "You know how you stand, Logan?"

"We'll owe twenty thousand. Will this store and contents cover that much?"

"Near enough," said Clenchfield.

"Then we'll be broke, but even. Not bad, Henry."

"Do you know what I did when I went broke? I had twenty pounds in my pocket. I got drunk and woke in the street with a single shilling. It was a long time ago. Maybe we both better get drunk tonight."

Stuart smiled at Clenchfield's gloomy face. "Trouble comes with fun. I've had my fun and here's the trouble. Next week I'll ride down to San Francisco and hunt up some credit. I'll have these strings moving out on the road again soon enough. Then we'll have more fun, Henry."

"All that money," said Clenchfield, and was obsessed by the tragedy of its loss.

"Never mind," said Stuart, walking through the store. "We'll get another deck and deal again. In this country, you can always get another deck. Remember that."

He stopped before he got to the doorway, seeing Johnny Steele come in. Johnny had a revolver in his hand; he reversed it and handed it over. He said: "That's what you lent Camrose, isn't it?"

"Where's Camrose?"

"He stayed a fool till the last," said Johnny. "Last night you got him clear and he would have been free if he'd kept going. Instead he stopped to rob Grogan, and Ted McGovern shot him. There's the end of the man you were willing to ruin yourself for."

Stuart moved to the store's big counter and put the gun on it. He stood there, looking down. "I'm sorry," he said. "There was good in that man."

Steele had an irritated answer. "You know better. You just got your neck bowed and you won't face the truth of the matter."

"In another kind of country he might have made the grade. Here, he lost out. It is a thin margin, Johnny, between what could be, and what actually is."

"Well," said Steele, "you ran your own luck right out to the end. Last night, I was of a mind to hang you to the same tree we had picked for him. I guess we can forget that now."

Stuart turned and looked at Steele. "You see how thin the margin is, Johnny?"

"It was thin for you, for a while," pointed out Steele.

"Thin for all of us, all the time. Where will you be tomorrow, or where will I be? Maybe lucky and alive. Maybe dead like George."

It was an unusual note of futility in Stuart which caused both Clenchfield and Steele to look at him with puzzlement; and presently Steele turned into the night without further comment. Stuart remained at the counter, his hand idly turning the gun around and around. His face, always inexpressive when in repose, now was hard and lightless as he went far down into himself. Then he pulled up. "Between the two of us, Henry, Camrose was all the camp thought he was. But I could only do what I did — and would do it again."

"It was never him you were doing it for," said Clenchfield.

Stuart gave him a quick glance and left the store. He stood a moment on the walk, watching the lamp-brightened doorway of the Overmire cabin on the hill. He thought: "She believed in him and never doubted him. Now she'll carry it in her mind the rest of her life."

He crossed the street and walked up toward the cabin.

Coming out of Stuart's, Johnny Steele paused a moment to look upon the lamp-laced shadows of the street, and then he turned with sudden decision and sudden excitement in him and walked directly to the Lestrade cabin. "She can't be grievin' much," he told himself as he knocked on her door. "He broke her heart and she knows now he was a scoundrel."

He heard her call to him and he opened the door, to find her bent before a half-filled trunk in the center of the room. She had stripped the room bare.

"You're leaving?" he said. "For where?"

"Somewhere."

"I guess you've had a bad time of it," he said. "You're free of it now. Nothing to make you cry. You've got people to go back to?"

She shook her head. "That door's shut, Johnny."

"Why go at all? You've got friends here." He paused and tried to approach what was in his mind discreetly. "There are men here who've looked at you a long while —"

"Are you one of the men, Johnny?"

"Yes," he said. "I am."

"You had your arms around me once," she said. "That made you think of something. It is very nice to think of. But I'm not free, Johnny. There will still be times when I cry — and for the same reason you saw me cry before."

"Why," he said, "the man's dead. He can't hurt you again."

"Oh yes he can, Johnny."

She realized he understood little of it. He stood before her with a feeling and a wish slowly darkening, slowly fading. She came close to tears when she saw it — the niceness and the comfort of it; but she smiled instead and came to him and gave him a kiss on his forehead. Then she turned him around, the pressure of her arm sending him toward the door. On the threshold he swung, still troubled about her.

"But if you can't go to your folks, what's to become of —"

"There are other doors open, Johnny. Good-by."

She listened to him go and she thought: "He's a fine boy," and afterwards the face of Jack Lestrade came before her, and all the memories of him, good and bad, held her still. The people of Jacksonville would judge him harshly, and they would think good of her after she had gone. In that respect they were wrong. The warmth, the color and the carelessness of Jack had drawn her because those were the things she responded to; and she would find them again in other men since she could not help it. As she had said to Johnny, other doors would be open. Still, it was nice to know she left friends behind her — people who thought her better than she was and wished her well.

Stuart came to the doorway and found Overmire sprawled before the stove. The two women were in the kitchen. Overmire said: "How was it?"

"We had a skirmish and drove the Indians west."

Lucy was behind him, listening. She said: "What about the Dances?"

"Ben and his son Bushrod were killed. The women are all right." He turned, anxious to see her face. It was calmer than he thought it would be, showing him no sorrow. The light of the lamp softened her and warmth was on her lips. The old feeling of nearness was arising again between them.

Overmire, impressed by the silence, remembered a chore to be done and rose from the chair. "Mother," he said, "I'll get that calico for you now."

Mrs. Overmire said: "You'd pick the wrong pattern, Overmire," and came instantly from the kitchen; and these two presently moved into the night.

"They are never subtle about it, Logan."

He said: "I wish I could have stayed with George and got him through."

"Do you know how he died?"

"I heard. There must have been a little mistake about that."

She said: "You would always defend him."

He shrugged his shoulders. "How could a man be really bad if a woman loved him for two years? If he was bad you would have seen it, wouldn't you?"

She meant to speak of it and explain it; but she gave him a short, sharp glance and walked on to the fireplace. "Shouldn't Caroline be coming to town? It's dangerous where she is."

"No," he said. "She'll stay. She doesn't like town."

"How will you work that, Logan?"

"There's nothing to work. She's marrying Blazier, not me."

"Logan — why?"

"I didn't bring her enough. She knew that."

She turned back to him. "What does she want?" She stared at him, her expression changing and lightening and filling. "Logan — what didn't you bring her?"

"The same sort of thing you saw in Camrose," he said.

"He came here after you got him out of the office," she said. "I wish he had not come. It's hard to look on a man and see, so openly, the things you never want to see. It didn't happen overnight, Logan. I knew it a year ago."

He said in the bluntest possible way, "Then why didn't you end it a year ago?"

"He asked me that same question — and I gave him half of the answer. How could I know if I was right in loving him, or right in not loving him? How could I change so quickly, without admitting I was foolish and irresponsible?" She looked at him keenly, anxiously. "Caroline saw that you weren't in love with her. I knew it too. Were you afraid of interfering with George and me?"

"I wanted to keep out of your way."

"Now I'll tell you what I couldn't tell George. If I had left him, what would you think of me? George grew smaller and you grew greater — but I could never explain to you how such a thing was possible."

"Why, Lucy," he said, "I held him up, because he was the one you wanted."

"I knew that too," she said. "But he ceased to be the man I wanted long ago."

He drew a great and gusty breath into his lungs and let it softly spill out of him.

"Why did you want me to help him get away?"

"If he had been hung, his ghost would always have been between us."

She grew warm and beautiful before him with the increasing fullness of these moments. She was fair and constant — and waiting eagerly for him. He spoke her name softly, as he had so often spoken it to himself. "Lucy," he said and put out his hands to her. She was smiling when she came to him and kissed him. Then she drew back and her manner changed to a terrible soberness and he saw fear in her eyes. "Logan," she said, "can you believe that this is what always should have been?"

"That time in Portland," he said. "You thought I was going out to another woman. You had hate in your eyes, Lucy. I ought to have known what it meant. You have always had something in your eyes for me."

She lifted her mouth to him and she said, "I thought we had lost each other," and her arms made a pressure around his shoulders. This was the way it never ceased to be between them, this closeness, this rough demand, this insistence. There never would be an end to it and never enough of it.

The publishers hope that this Large Print Book has brought you pleasurable reading. Each title is designed to make the text as easy to see as possible. G. K. Hall Large Print Books are available from your library and your local bookstore. Or you can receive information on upcoming and current Large Print Books by mail and order directly from the publisher. Just send your name and address to:

G. K. Hall & Co.
70 Lincoln Street
Boston, Mass. 02111

or call, toll-free:

1–800–343–2806

A note on the text
Large print edition designed by
Bernadette Montalvo
Composed in 16 pt Times Roman
on a Mergenthaler Linotron 202
by Modern Graphics, Inc.

DEMCO